179.3083
GRE

It Happened to Me

Series Editor: Arlene Hirschfelder

Books in the It Happened to Me series are designed for inquisitive teens digging for answers about certain illnesses, social issues, or lifestyle interests. Whether you are deep into your teen years or just entering them, these books are gold mines of up-to-date information, riveting teen views, and great visuals to help you figure out stuff. Besides special boxes highlighting singular facts, each book is enhanced with the latest reading lists, websites, and an index. Perfect for browsing, these books contain loads of expert information by acclaimed writers to help parents, guardians, and librarians understand teen illness, tough situations, and lifestyle choices.

1. *Epilepsy: The Ultimate Teen Guide*, by Kathlyn Gay and Sean McGarrahan, 2002.
2. *Stress Relief: The Ultimate Teen Guide*, by Mark Powell, 2002.
3. *Learning Disabilities: The Ultimate Teen Guide*, by Penny Hutchins Paquette and Cheryl Gerson Tuttle, 2003.
4. *Making Sexual Decisions: The Ultimate Teen Guide*, by L. Kris Gowen, 2003.
5. *Asthma: The Ultimate Teen Guide*, by Penny Hutchins Paquette, 2003.
6. *Cultural Diversity—Conflicts and Challenges: The Ultimate Teen Guide*, by Kathlyn Gay, 2003.
7. *Diabetes: The Ultimate Teen Guide*, by Katherine J. Moran, 2004.
8. *When Will I Stop Hurting? Teens, Loss, and Grief: The Ultimate Teen Guide to Dealing with Grief*, by Ed Myers, 2004.
9. *Volunteering: The Ultimate Teen Guide*, by Kathlyn Gay, 2004.
10. *Organ Transplants—A Survival Guide for the Entire Family: The Ultimate Teen Guide*, by Tina P. Schwartz, 2005.

11. *Medications: The Ultimate Teen Guide*, by Cheryl Gerson Tuttle, 2005.
12. *Image and Identity—Becoming the Person You Are: The Ultimate Teen Guide*, by L. Kris Gowen and Molly C. McKenna, 2005.
13. *Apprenticeship: The Ultimate Teen Guide*, by Penny Hutchins Paquette, 2005.
14. *Cystic Fibrosis: The Ultimate Teen Guide*, by Melanie Ann Apel, 2006.
15. *Religion and Spirituality in America: The Ultimate Teen Guide*, by Kathlyn Gay, 2006.
16. *Gender Identity: The Ultimate Teen Guide*, by Cynthia L. Winfield, 2007.
17. *Physical Disabilities: The Ultimate Teen Guide*, by Denise Thornton, 2007.
18. *Money—Getting It, Using It, and Avoiding the Traps: The Ultimate Teen Guide*, by Robin F. Brancato, 2007.
19. *Self-Advocacy: The Ultimate Teen Guide*, by Cheryl Gerson Tuttle and JoAnn Augeri Silva, 2007.
20. *Adopted: The Ultimate Teen Guide*, by Suzanne Buckingham Slade, 2007.
21. *The Military and Teens: The Ultimate Teen Guide*, by Kathlyn Gay, 2008.
22. *Animals and Teens: The Ultimate Teen Guide*, by Gail Green, 2009.
23. *Reaching Your Goals: The Ultimate Teen Guide*, by Anne E. Courtright, 2009.
24. *Juvenile Arthritis: The Ultimate Teen Guide*, by Kelly Rouba, 2009.
25. *Obsessive-Compulsive Disorder: The Ultimate Teen Guide*, by Natalie Rompella, 2009.

Animals and Teens

The Ultimate Teen Guide

GAIL GREEN

It Happened to Me, No. 22

The Scarecrow Press, Inc.
Lanham, Maryland • Toronto • Plymouth, UK
2009

SCARECROW PRESS, INC.

Published in the United States of America
by Scarecrow Press, Inc.
A wholly owned subsidiary of
The Rowman & Littlefield Publishing Group, Inc.
4501 Forbes Boulevard, Suite 200, Lanham, Maryland 20706
www.scarecrowpress.com

Estover Road
Plymouth PL6 7PY
United Kingdom

Copyright © 2009 by Gail Green

All rights reserved. No part of this publication may be reproduced, stored in a retrieval system, or transmitted in any form or by any means, electronic, mechanical, photocopying, recording, or otherwise, without the prior permission of the publisher.

British Library Cataloguing in Publication Information Available

Library of Congress Cataloging-in-Publication Data

Green, Gail.
  Animals and teens : the ultimate teen guide / Gail Green.
    p. cm. — (It happened to me ; no. 22)
  Includes bibliographical references and index.
  ISBN-13: 978-0-8108-5769-8 (hardcover : alk. paper)
  ISBN-13: 978-0-8108-6656-0 (ebook)
  ISBN-10: 0-8108-5769-3 (hardcover : alk. paper)
  ISBN-10: 0-8108-6656-0 (ebook)
 1. Animal welfare—Citizen participation. 2. Teenagers—Political activity. I. Title.
 HV4708.G74 2009
 179'.3083—dc22   2008037589

∞™ The paper used in this publication meets the minimum requirements of American National Standard for Information Sciences—Permanence of Paper for Printed Library Materials, ANSI/NISO Z39.48-1992.
Manufactured in the United States of America.

Contents

Introduction	vii
1 Companion Animals: What They Mean to Us	1
2 Understanding Animals; Understanding Ourselves	35
3 Friendship	63
4 Choosing Our Companion Animals	91
5 Defending the Innocent: Animal Abuse and Environmental Concerns	111
6 The Bonds of Trust: How Animals Help with Emotional and Social Issues and Interactions	139
7 Life Changes: College, Country, and Careers	165
8 Overcoming Health Problems, Pet Loss, and Other Adversities	195
9 At Your Service: Assistance Animals and Therapies	225
Appendix: Online Resources for All Things Animal	247
Bibliography	251
Index	253
About the Author	259

Introduction

Imagine yourself in a world where everyone is treated fairly and the most important thing to do is have fun. This is a place where rules are easy to understand and follow, life is uncomplicated, and love is unconditional.

Fortunately, teens who positively interact with animals *can* experience that type of world! Animals do something foreign to most human thinking, especially as we grow further away from childhood. They live in the moment, with no pocket planners or future calendar dates to remember. Animals don't cram for exams or worry about a date for the prom, nor do they need to make choices about what college to attend. That's the stuff we do. When we have a bond with companion animals and focus on them, we aren't thinking about the test we took yesterday or what we'll do on Saturday night. Instead, animals exude spontaneity, bringing us into the simplicity of their moment. Their joy becomes our own.

But animals don't only pull us away from worries and stress. They also provide us with unconditional love, even when we fall short of all those things the human world finds so important. We don't need to impress them with zit-free complexions or straight As. Instead, animals can teach us to be happy with who we are and what we have and to take pleasure in just being.

We have coexisted with animals from a time before history was recorded. Across millennia, we have walked, run, flown, or swam together as allies and as enemies. We have fed them and offered them shelter and medical assistance, while they

Introduction

have provided us with labor, protection, assistance, and food or resources from feathers and wool to hides and sinew. Prey and predator, animals and humans have hunted each other and hunted with each other. And through it all, we have shared an intertwined stake in our shared future.

We have built homes for ourselves while destroying theirs. They, in turn, damage our crops, spread disease, and ruin property and belongings we vainly think are ours. At times our choices or their instinctive responses have defined entire civilizations, such as the Native American cultures in which animals provided a basis for spirituality and identity or the Mongol barbarians and their legendary connection with their horses. The water we drink, the food we eat, and the air we breathe are our joint inheritance. It is also our common struggle as we share the planet and find ways to survive. Yet, despite our fierce competition, there is something else that draws us to them, something that reaches deep inside our very souls. In addition to physical needs, when we bond with and become emotionally involved in the welfare and social needs of animals, we gain something of extraordinary value. Animals remain mysterious in many ways, but the emotional bonds that can exist between human and animal are more than just mutually beneficial. Our ability to care for other creatures outside our own species defines who we are. Whether we are involved with the welfare of whales or enjoying a romp with our family dog, what we've gained is more than just a feeling that we've done something good. For a moment or a lifetime, we transcend who and what we are as individuals. Not only can we develop compassion for all living creatures, we also learn respect for differences and uniqueness by seeing what makes a squirrel a squirrel or a duck a duck. These lessons make us better people. They give us meaning and they give us the means to fully realize our own individual potential.

Many of the voices within these pages are teens and young adults just like you. They go to school with you, live in your communities, and have the same types of social issues and needs that you have. Let them share their love of animals with you while you learn how you too can experience that world and make a difference by connecting with animals.

Companion Animals: What They Mean to Us

OWNING A PET

What exactly makes animals so special? Is it because they look cute or are fun to play with? Or are we just fascinated with them because they are not human? The relationship between humans and animals has an incredibly complex and intertwined history that has lasted millennia and goes beyond just seeing them as pets or workers.

Exposure to animals begins when we are very young, and much of it happens without our even being aware of it. We listen to nursery rhymes about cats and fiddles and cows

"Animals don't judge you or want to talk about your problems, but at the same time they are always there to listen."

—Tina Swinkels, Australian high school student living temporarily in the United States[1]

HISTORICAL TIDBITS

In ancient Rome, people kept a variety of pets, including cats, dogs, monkeys, goats, and unusual birds like owls, magpies, and nightingales. Some animals were kept more for prestige or entertainment, or to perform specific jobs. For example, cats were kept as house pets and also to keep rodents out of grain containers. As a status symbol, some Romans even kept lions in their homes! Others decorated the pet fish in outdoor ponds by putting necklaces and gold rings around them for a little bling-bling![2]

Chapter 1

jumping over the moon, learn our ABCs with Big Bird or Barney and see animal prints on children's clothing and baby strollers. Babies born into households with existing pets may perceive them as just a natural part of their environment. Experiences like these may actually provide many of us with our first "safe" exposure to animals and pave the way for our perceptions of animals as friends and companions, and an important part of the family.

References to animals are basically *everywhere* around us—in our neighbors' backyards, in movies, in TV commercials, and on magazine covers, where dogs are often photographed with fashion models or shown lounging on furniture to "accessorize" home decor. Newspapers serving a variety of populations even have regular pet news sections and columns, while television networks produce programs or entire series that include animal actors, such as Eddy, the dog on the popular television series *Frasier* or the animals "guests" on *The Tonight Show*. Animal Planet is a television channel devoted

ANIMAL ENTERTAINMENT

Animals in the media aren't new. Movies like *Lassie Come Home*, based on the book by Eric Knight, or the popular 1957 movie *Old Yeller* are considered classics. When television was in its infancy, two of the most popular programs were *Lassie* and *Rin Tin Tin*. Horses were also popular draws, especially in the Western-themed programs of the 1950s and 1960s. Two very popular TV series where horses were an important feature were *The Roy Rogers Show* (with Trigger) and *The Lone Ranger* (with Silver). National Geographic specials and *Mutual of Omaha's Wild Kingdom* also provided Americans with glimpses into the lives of wild animals for years. But when movies such as the reality documentary *March of the Penguins*; Walt Disney's adventure *Eight Below*, in which a team of sled dogs fight for survival in the frigid Antarctic after being left behind; and full-length animated movies such as Warner Brothers' *Happy Feet*, featuring tap-dancing penguins, get star billing, it is obvious that Americans' love for animals extends beyond just their own companion animals.

entirely to programming covering companion and other animals. How many animal-loving young people regularly watch *Emergency Vet* or *Animal Rescue* on cable or network programs like *America's Funniest Home Videos* or *Pet Stars*? Plenty!

Our curiosity about and interest in animals have also expanded into a passion for the animals we invite into our homes and families. Local specialty pet shops and "big-box" retail pet supply chains sell everything from gourmet treats to fashionable outfits for pets, while pet bakeries, doggie day-care centers, spas, and dog parks thrive in communities from New York to Los Angeles. According to the American Pet Products Association (APPA), in 2007 the pet food industry was estimated to be an annual $16.1-billion business. And all the "extras"—toys, housing, collars, and so on—were estimated to total an additional $24.7 billion. Why do people spend so much money on animal-related products and services? The answer is simple: Companion animals are an important and often essential part of our lives. And we definitely *love* our pets!

According to the definition in *Encyclopedia Americana*, pets are animals usually kept in a residence for the main purpose of being played with, viewed, or studied, and are offered the status of companion because family members feel curiosity about or affection for them. Farm and other domestic animals serve more practical needs and are not usually viewed as pets. But what exactly is a "pet" in the eyes of passionate animal lovers? And how accurate is this definition in today's world?

Any and all animals we voluntarily take into our homes and lives are often referred to as pets. At the simplest level, we are expected to feed them; provide comfortable, humane living conditions; and tend to their basic physical and medical needs. In turn, they amuse us, annoy us, and surprise us. However, the animals we invite into our lives can become more than "just pets." They can also become our companions.

ANIMAL GUARDIANSHIP

When we say we "own a pet," what does that really mean? Should owning a pet be something we casually do, like taking a

Chapter 1

> "Caring for an animal teaches you how to care for something and, in turn, teaches you how to be responsible. This is a major issue when it comes to having pets because pets are like an extension of your family. To help them survive, it is imperative that you learn how to care for them."—Reshoma Banerjee, college graduate, Springfield, Illinois[3]

shower or getting gas for our car? How much thought should it take to throw some water and food into a couple bowls once a day? Or should owning a pet take more effort?

If we perceive that we actually *own* our dog or horse or gerbil, the same way we own our car or computer or designer pair of shoes, what happens when school sports, homework, friends, dating, family situations, and life in general get in the way? When we get tired of our car or it starts to fall apart, we sell it and get another one. Computer systems become obsolete; hard drives crash. We get frustrated, we get mad; we get another system, better and new. When our shoes wear out or our jeans rip or fade, we can stick them in the back of the closet, forgotten and no longer used. Or we just throw them away.

That is also how many people may feel about pets. If animals develop behavioral issues, get sick, or get in the way, people give them away, tie them up in the yard, or beat them until they stop bothering their owners for attention and other basic needs. But is that really the answer? When they grow old or no longer suit our needs, should we get rid of our pets, maybe getting newer, younger ones? Or when they no longer amuse us or we discover they are just too much work, should we then forget about them?

Changing the litter in the gerbil or rabbit cage the first few times isn't too bad, but it soon loses its appeal after doing it every week for a year—especially when you are running late for a movie with your friends or just had a fight with your dad. And being wakened at six in the morning by a dog that needs to be go out in a blizzard to relieve himself or a cat that stinks of hairball vomit is no way to start the day—especially after a late night of partying or when you need to get to class on time. If we perceive pets as objects instead of living, breathing creatures with feelings, then it is their fault if we are annoyed. But when we begin to view our pet animals as more than "just a pet," our perspective begins to change.

But what exactly changes? Is it how we treat the animals, or is it that we can actually experience something more meaningful with them that extends beyond just being their caretakers? Is it possible that we *can* have more than a casual involvement with animals that we have chosen to share our homes, our finances, and our lives with? After meeting their physical needs, can we also share an emotional bond with them—a bond that may even rival or transcend the ones we have with our human family or friends?

If you have answered yes to these last few questions, then the pets that share your life with you *are* probably more than "just a pet"! They are your *companions*, and *you* are one of the lucky ones, because you have so much more than just a possession. You have a *friend*, a companion animal with whom you can share an emotional bond and relationship—someone you can trust, who will never judge or betray you. Your pets will still be your friends even if you wake *them* up at 3 a.m. stumbling home from a party. And they won't mind if you greet them in the morning with dragon breath!

A PERSONAL GLIMPSE

Wisconsin high school student Richelle Hellpap gets up on her own at 4:30 a.m. to take care of her rabbits before leaving for school. And on weekends when she and her mom, Teresa, travel to rabbit shows, she's up before her mom. Teresa explains: "If I tell her I'm getting up by five, she'll have all those rabbits done, ready, and loaded by the time I wake up—including food and water for the trip. Most teenagers would need to be reminded or nagged to get up and take care of their pets before they leave for school! But I never have to remind her or tell her. Richelle has that alarm set for 4:30 every morning."[4]

Chapter 1

The reality is we do not "own" companions. Instead of being their "owners," we become their *guardians*, as well as their friends. Yes, we are responsible for meeting their basic physical needs, which includes responsibilities that take up our time and might not always be so pleasant. Yes, we also have to deal with doing things for them that expose our own vulnerabilities and sometimes test our trust. But in doing so, we guarantee that the bond we share is genuine on our part. And they, in turn, return our efforts in more ways than we can ever imagine. That is what this book is all about.

Of course, if you feel that a pet is no different from any other possession, then you just "own" a pet. Nothing more. Reading and exploring what other teens have experienced with their companion animals, however, might just inspire you to see animals in a different light, or even open up possibilities you never knew existed. You might even stop seeing your pet as a possession or a lot of work with little or no reward. It's your choice, and hopefully you will not miss out on one of the most wonderful experiences humans have ever known. The true reward in sharing our lives with a companion animal, no matter how small or how complex, is discovering the truth that we all possess the ability to transcend beyond ourselves—that each one of us can make a difference in the life of another.

If you have already discovered the magic of the human-animal bond, this book will further inspire you to continue your relationship with your animal companions. And the story that began centuries ago will come full circle.

THE BEGINNING OF THE HUMAN-ANIMAL BOND

Sometime in the distant past, approximately twelve thousand years ago, a revolutionary event took place that changed the world forever. On that day and over a series of days, decades, or possibly centuries, an animal that was originally born wild decided or was taught to trust and live side by side with humans. In doing so, this animal—which most scientists agree was the wolf—not only accepted another species' social order as its own, but essentially joined forces with a competitor and became a partner instead, a partner with whom it would serve as hunter, herder, and guard. In return, that choice allowed the wolf to spread over the entire face of the earth as no other animal did—except humans. And this new wolf that did not fear humans eventually developed into the domesticated animal we know today as the dog. One-fifth of all land animals on the earth today consists of a combination of humans and the animals that, by human intervention or historical accident, came to be under our protection and are referred to as domestic animals. These include animals such as horses and pigs, as well as cats and dogs.

Studies have been done at UCLA comparing the DNA sequences of sixty-seven dog breeds ranging from the Australian dingo to the Mexican hairless. The results of the study demonstrated that no matter how different the breeds may look, today's dogs are indeed all descended from a single common source, the Eurasian gray wolf. Illustration by the author.

Chapter 1

Companion animals can bring out the very best in all of us, since they tend to bring out the kindest and most generous impulses of humanity. By taming that first wild animal, a person now had an ally for protection as well as for hunting and herding. In order to keep their new animal friends, however, humans learned to treat their animals humanely.

The definition of "humane" includes being kind and compassionate to living beings, especially ones in need. Considering how valuable animals can be to our society, it is surprising how poorly some people treat them. Controversial issues involving pit bull fighting and importation and ownership of "exotic" animals such as snakes or prairie dogs, as well as stories of animal abuse and neglect reported in the media, are, to a large degree, tied up with the problem of irresponsible pet ownership and inhumane treatment. It is our responsibility, however, as animal guardians to respect them as much as they respect us and to continue to earn their trust, just as if each of them were that very first wolf.

BONDS WE HAVE WITH OUR COMPANION ANIMALS

What drives us to desire a relationship with other animal species? Does the fundamental need to have pets simply lie in the fact that they are different from us? Or does being in touch with creatures outside our own species help us see the human race in perspective? Perhaps we seek a relationship with companion animals because they give us an unparalleled opportunity to relate to another species on a level not always possible with other humans. Sincerity has always been one of the most frequently cited reasons why people love animals. And because animals do not perceive the world as humans do, their simpler view encourages us to take a simpler approach to life, to cut through all the complexities we are faced with in our human society and get back to basics. Animals also expose much of the hypocrisy in humans. They do not criticize, tease, or make us feel inadequate because our test scores are low, we've gained ten pounds, or we don't have a girlfriend or boyfriend. And they always validate our own feelings.

Nineteenth-century American senator George Graham Vest once said, "The one absolute, unselfish friend that a man can have in this selfish world, the one that never proves ungrateful or treacherous, is his dog." This sentiment was echoed by twentieth-century journalist and media personality Andy Rooney, who is reported to have said, "The average dog is a nicer person than the average person." With social trends in Western countries indicating increasing numbers of broken families and more people marrying later in life or living alone, we are becoming a society of lonely people. Add the additional stress of modern daily life and it is evident why the number of animals kept as pets grows each year. We all need a friend we can trust. It is no wonder that many people choose to have animal companions, who never disappoint and always validate.

2005–2006 STATISTICS

According to the 2005–2006 American Pet Products Manufacturers Association (now the APPA) National Pet Owners Survey, 43.4 million U.S. households own at least one dog and 37.7 million own at least one cat. Those figures compare in descending order to the 13.9 million households that own freshwater fish, 6.4 million that own a bird, 5.7 million that own a small animal, 4.4 million that own a reptile, and 4.2 million that own a horse.

Chapter 1

YOUNG PEOPLE AND ANIMALS: WHAT WE HAVE IN COMMON

> "My favorite bird at the moment is Baby, an umbrella cockatoo. Whenever they make a silent 'clicking' noise with their tongue, they are contented. When we cuddle, she twists her head around, clicks her tongue, and leans against my chest. It is rapture for both of us."—Jessica Katz, college student, University of Vermont[5]

IT HAPPENED TO ME: THE BOND IN ACTION

Butchie came into Trish Hampton's life the night before Christmas Eve. Her boyfriend had been living with her temporarily until he got his own place. But when he was almost ready to move out, Trish knew she didn't want to be alone. Her apartment allowed pets, so she decided to get a dog and searched online at Petfinders, a website that lists dogs and cats available for adoption from shelters nationwide. "When I saw Butchie's picture, I just knew I had to have her!" Although her boyfriend wasn't sold on the idea at first, he accompanied her to the shelter to see the nine-week-old puppy. As soon as he saw her he had an immediate change of heart and told Trish that he couldn't turn her away, especially at Christmas. So he got the puppy for Trish, which helped her get through him leaving.

    Trish also has a unique connection with her dog. When she first saw Butchie's picture on Petfinders, the puppy was only seven weeks old and already available for adoption. Trish suspected she was probably part of an unplanned, unwanted litter. Trish had already wanted to adopt because she knew that these animals really needed homes, but part of her connected immediately with this little black puppy because of something she had experienced in her own life. "I was adopted, so I felt this was some way I could help some other poor soul. To give this puppy a home is one of the good deeds that God has saved for me."[6]

The bond between people and their companion animals is an incredible and complex attachment that involves friendship, affection, companionship, trust, and a sense of being needed, filling the basic emotional needs all humans instinctively have and must meet in order to be truly happy. But the human-animal bond not only often transcends the relationships we have with other people, it is also an interspecies relationship.

TIDBITS: A COMMON BOND

There are many things teens and their companion animals have in common:

- **Teens and animals instinctively need to belong to a "family" or other group ranging from one companion to an entire community, pack, herd, or flock.**
- **Both teens and animals need to connect with someone on a basic emotional level.**
- **Both teens and animals need to feel safe and secure.**
- **Many teens and animals may not fit into the world around them because of sleep habits, special physical needs, and so on.**
- **Both teens and animals need to learn trust. Teens raised in loving, functional families may take trusting for granted, but teens raised in abusive or other dysfunctional environments may feel they cannot trust anyone. Animals that have been neglected, abused, or taken out of the wild may also feel the same and have to be taught to trust.**
- **Teens and animals learn to become independent as they grow up and mature. Both will challenge parents and other authority members of their group, break rules, and test to see how far they can go without consequences.**
- **Both animals and teens feel basic emotion such as loneliness, sadness, and feelings of excitement or worry, and both communicate those feelings through vocalizations or body language.**

Chapter 1

People will always let us down in some way, whether we try to love everyone or not. We also let other people down, whether they try to love us or not. Animals, however, possess the qualities each of us look for in every human being we meet, the qualities we seek in all humans but can't always find. It is the

---

A PERSONAL GLIMPSE

For many teens, acting out can escalate into problem behavior or involvement with drugs, underage drinking, risk taking, vandalism, or other things. In this respect, they are no different from the dogs, cats, birds, and other animals that wind up in shelters and refuges because of inappropriate or unacceptable behavior such as biting, screaming/barking, chewing, and other destructive behaviors. In addition to the mutual need for consistency and routine, college student Jessica Katz feels there are many similarities between teens and animals. During her internship at a bird rescue sanctuary, Jessica observed, "With a bunch of the birds, their aggression was purely lashing out because they were frustrated they weren't getting what they needed, which could have been anything from attention or a specific food item to wanting to get out of their cage. When teens lash out, a lot of times it's because they are also frustrated. I have also observed the childlike personalities of animals. I mean, when one of my favorite birds bit me over the summer, I had no idea how to tell her that was not okay. I think a lot of parents have that problem with teens that are still maturing and possibly acting out. I also think that when these teens can't work stuff out with their parents or just can't get along with them, having an animal to turn to would be very helpful."

Jessica feels high school is a big place. "You get stuck with people that you don't appreciate or people that don't appreciate or respect you. But it is always really comforting working with animals because they never act with anything other than unconditional love." For teens going through tough times, or who might feel lonely and unloved, Jessica has this advice: "Get involved! Whether it's a welfare or non-profit organization, or something else, finding something to belong to like the bird refuge where I volunteer, will help you feel like you are part of something larger than yourself. Involvement also gives teens a sense of purpose, as well as feeling like they are needed instead of just 'throw-aways' themselves."[7]

unconditional love, complete trust, nonjudgmental companionship, and the ability to accept us not only *for* ourselves but *in spite of* ourselves that makes humans of all ages fall in love with them. Essentially, companion animals are the perfect human beings.

One benefit of involvement with companion animals, especially if we are given the opportunity to spend time with them daily, is that they can teach us spontaneity as well as appreciation of the present. Family services major Katie Green observes, "My dogs have taught me to take a break, get up and away from the computer on a summer day and just go out in the yard to play ball or take a walk. If I didn't have them to whine and nag me to stop and play with them, I'd *never* get any fresh air!"[8]

REDUCING STRESS AND OTHER WAYS ANIMALS HELP

> "Dogs do the silliest things—like finding a butterfly and then trying to bite it. They find a million ways to make you laugh and feel happy!"—Nichole Freeman, Illinois high school student.[9]

Just as Shakespeare described the "harmless, necessary cat" in *The Merchant of Venice*, animals of all kinds are necessary to human well-being, both practically and emotionally. Animals have a wonderful way of relieving stress, and they possess heightened senses that often help them understand their human's emotional state of mind. The soothing effect companion animals have on people is partly due to the fact that people can talk to their pets as well as have physical contact. Interestingly, blood pressure lowers when people talk to animals as opposed to rising, which it does when people talk to each other. Studies have shown that animals being petted experience a reduction in blood pressure as well.

Chapter 1

Therapy-certified and other animals are used to help the mentally handicapped learn and help stroke victims recover their speech without feeling self-conscious. Studies done with the criminally insane demonstrate that patients relate better to the staff and to one another when animals such as fish, parakeets, gerbils, or guinea pigs are used in therapy. Previously violent men have even showed tenderness toward these animals, which become catalysts for communication and trust between patients and therapists.

Pets also satisfy our need to be needed, an emotion that runs deeply in all of us, at any age. If teen Richelle Hellpap has a bad day at school, her rabbits are always there waiting for her at home. "If I have a bad day, I come home and take care of my rabbits. It really makes me feel better to have someone that needs me. It makes me feel like, it doesn't matter what happened at school. And taking care of the rabbits doesn't take up much time. It's nice to hang around them, because it relaxes me, especially when I see some of the funny stuff they do."[10]

COEXISTING WITH ANIMALS

Domesticated animals that revert back to the wild are referred to as "feral." Animals released or abandoned into the wild or that escape from human captivity often become feral in order to survive. And once an animal becomes feral, subsequent offspring will also lose signs of domestication unless they are brought back into human contact. In other words, while the instinct to survive is genetically coded in all animals, domestication itself is much more delicate. Since it takes little time for dogs and cats to lose all domestication imprints and become totally feral, it is remarkable how adaptable animals must be to even live among humans!

When you think about it, having another species living in our home or under our care is a curious trait usually found only in humans. It is rare for other species to welcome members of another species into its lair, den, or nest. No animal would willingly choose to share its food or allow another species access to its young. We are unique in that we not only welcome

A PERSONAL GLIMPSE

High school student Nichole Freeman remembers one bleak day in her sophomore year when she failed a math test. "I had no idea what I was doing on that test. It was terrible! But when I came home from school, my dog didn't care if I had failed the test. He still loved me and was just as happy to see me. He still came up to me and cuddled. In fact, I think that because I was so upset, he cuddled with me even more."[11]

Rachel G's cat also helps her get through those really bad days at school. "Cosmo can always tell when I'm unhappy. He sits in my lap or lies with me. He makes me laugh all the time and cheers me up when I'm having a bad day. Occasionally when I'm upset about a grade I got on a test, or more often, when I just *think* I've gotten a bad grade on a test, or if I'm just bummed, he always cheers me up just by doing something silly. For instance, this one time I was looking over a test I wasn't thrilled about. Cosmo was lying on his side on the table. He stretched as though he wanted me to pet him, but he stretched too far and came crashing down to the floor. He was so embarrassed but instead pretended nothing happened. It was hilarious."[12]

cats, dogs, birds, fish, and other creatures into our homes or homesteads, we also eagerly lavish them with luxuries and comforts not often found in the wild.

And then there is the emotional bond: something we can't see or touch, but definitely feel inside. As an example, most pet owners attach importance to their animals' greeting them when they return home from work or school. For people working in stressful jobs, having difficulty in school, or who may not have much positive social interaction with family, co-workers, or others, being greeted by a happy pet that exhibits genuine joy at their return can melt stress away.

In addition to guiding us, working for us, and protecting us, animals also have special instincts and abilities that people don't have. Whether we lacked strength, speed, or the ability to survive in conditions that animals also thrived in or whether we depended on them for food, clothing, and other products,

Chapter 1

Pet antics can amuse us while also offering us a glimpse into a world where play has no rules. Illustration by the author.

animals have always been—and continue to be—an important part of people's lives. However, in today's society of synthetic fibers and inks and machines that do the work animals once did, we no longer depend on animals for as many things. Many people now question if we need to continue hunting,

TIDBIT: AN UNPLEASANT PERSPECTIVE

While dog owners in North America and Europe may think of their pets as part of the family, that is not always the case in other parts of the world. For example, in some parts of China and South Korea, dogs are viewed in the same way as farm animals: as potential food. The thought of eating a puppy may be foreign and horrifying to us, but of even more concern is that some world cultures also believe that the taste and tenderness of the meat is improved if the animals suffer a torturous death. The Animals Asia Foundation (AAF), a government-registered animal welfare charity based in Hong Kong, is working hard to end this cruelty and improve the lives of all animals throughout Asia by educating children on how to care for and respect animals. For more information on AAF programs, visit www.animalsasia.org.[13]

whaling, wearing fur, and using animals for laboratory testing. Some animal rights groups say that we need to rethink the historical view of animals as being here to serve humans, and begin thinking of animals instead as partners on the planet, deserving the same respect that we expect. Their arguments include not only animals hunted for vanity products, but also animals that are captured and used for entertainment purposes, such as cockfighting, circuses, and bullfights. Other groups have the opposite opinion and argue that hunting and relying on animal sources for basic needs are intrinsic to specific cultures or even necessary for survival in some parts of the world.

TIDBIT: WHAT WE WEAR

Where does it come from?

- **Wool sweaters, suits, pea coats, and the like all come from the fleece of sheep, goats, llamas, or alpacas.**
- **Silk fibers are wound by a special caterpillar called a silkworm.**
- **Leather goods in the United States come from cattle and calves, but worldwide sources also include horses, sheep, lambs, goats, pigs, zebras, bison, water buffalo, boars, deer, kangaroos, elephants, eels, sharks, dolphins, seals, walruses, frogs, crocodiles, lizards, snakes, and many endangered animals such as sea turtles.**
- **Down jackets, pillows, and blankets include the soft feathers from geese, ducks, and other domesticated birds.**

Chapter 1

RESPONSIBILITY: THE CORNERSTONE OF THE HUMAN-ANIMAL BOND

> "I definitely believe my experiences with animals growing up (even watching them on TV) had an impact on the person I became. My parents taught me love and compassion by example, but my pets put a new perspective on the whole idea. I felt like I was the one showing and teaching them so they would feel safe the way my parents made me feel."—Rebecca Britz, vet tech major[14]

While the rewards of having a companion animal such as a dog, cat, or hamster may be priceless, it's also crucial to understand the commitment involved and to learn as much as possible in order to become a responsible guardian. In fact, responsible companion animal guardianship begins the moment you decide to bring an animal into your life. It begins when you initially choose the right type of animal species, breed, age, and size for your individual lifestyle, as well as being certain you will also be able to provide the necessary physical needs, training, vet care, and grooming your specific pet needs to live a happy, healthy life.

Teens can learn and mature from relationships with their pets. When we give up doing something for ourselves that would cause our pet emotional or physical discomfort, we learn compassion. When we provide for and take care of a companion animal, we learn to nurture. When we want to purposefully do things just to make our pet happy, we learn to love. And when our pets accept our kind acts, we learn that through giving, we can receive as much pleasure as we give.

High school student Annalies Kocourek feels that not only caring for her service dog and taking on the responsibilities involved in training and working with him made her a better guardian, but she has benefited by knowing she can't just rely on her dog for everything; her dog also depends on her to remember things. "It has helped with my memory, having to learn things over and over again, and with the repetitiveness. Being responsible for another living thing has made me more responsible. I don't want *him* to die, so I have to remember to do things like feed him, walk him, brush him, and stuff like that."[15]

"I think having a pet is good for teaching responsibility in that it teaches you that you have to do things even if you don't really feel like doing them," explains Nichole Freeman. "Oh, at first you do things because you are so excited to get the pet, but then you kind of don't want to. But when you think 'I don't want to brush the dog today' or 'I don't need to give the dog a bath,' they just sit there looking at you like 'Come on! Do stuff with me!' And it teaches you that you can't just sit there and procrastinate—things need to get done."[16]

Teresa Hellpap feels animals can definitely help teach teens responsibility. "Animals give children and teens a sense of responsibility. But I believe strongly in every child having their *own* pet and not just sharing the family pet. With a family pet they don't really have the responsibility but when they have their own pet they then have to take responsibility for it. When it's a family pet, they can dump all the work onto someone else and they don't develop the bond with individual animals like the one I've watched my teenage daughter develop with her own animals. Her younger sister also has her own dog and she, in turn, has a bond with *her* dog and *her* rabbit."[17]

A PERSONAL GLIMPSE

Right before she started high school, Natasha McDonald's younger brother got a frog, and sibling rivalry kicked in. "Naturally I wanted one, too! And after I got a frog, I decided I also wanted a lizard! I love my frogs and lizard to death. Yes, it gets annoying that I have to feed them live crickets, but it pays off when I get to hold them and watch what they do. I still take care of them, but, because my schedule is so busy and I don't really have the time to take care of them, I have kind of given them to my brother. But it's okay because my brother has grown very attached to them and loves them as much as I do."[18]

Chapter 1

Animals need gentle care and handling. Photo used with permission, Katie Green.

Pets need the same love, care, and respect that people do. Being a responsible animal guardian is actually the cornerstone of the bond between people and their companion animals. Kyle Fetters, a suburban teen involved for years with reptiles and other animals, agrees. "The reason parents let their kids have animals in the first place is to teach responsibility. And in a way it's almost like taking care of a family member because once the animals join your family they're there and you have the responsibility to keep them healthy. They don't have the ability to get themselves something to eat, so it's all on you or they don't get it at all. It teaches a lot of responsibility in that sense. Taking care of an animal also teaches a lot about just being able to take care of someone else one day, especially because you have to reason with their body language, which is a lot different. Like with a baby, it can cry when it's hungry, but an animal like a lizard can't tell you 'I'm hungry now.' I've seen cases where people sometimes forget to feed their dogs. Those dogs will not trust them as much and often turn into scavengers. And then there can be those dogs with great trust that know 'Okay, this person will take care of me and will be around this time.' And they trust that we'll know where to go to get food and will provide them with it."[19]

RESPONSIBLE PET OWNERSHIP DAY

American Kennel Club (AKC) Responsible Dog Ownership Day is held on September 17 each year, with hundreds of celebrations scheduled across the nation. The goal of the event is to educate the public about the importance of responsible dog ownership and the rewards of a respectful human-canine relationship. Many AKC-affiliated dog clubs and other dog or pet related organizations hold celebrations in their communities, including Canine Good Citizen testing, obedience and agility demonstrations, microchip clinics, breed rescue info, and therapy dog and service dog demos.[20]

WHAT ANIMALS GAIN FROM US: THE EMOTIONAL BOND

Most relationships are based on trust and respect. And the bond our pets have with us is strongly based on trust. They learn to trust us when we show them kindness and compassion along with supplying basic needs, such as food and water. When we handle our pets with a gentle touch, they learn to trust our hands. When we speak to them in a kind tone instead of in anger, they learn to trust our voice. Break that trust, however, and the bond between human and animal can be irreparably shattered. Striking a pet in anger or screaming in frustration often makes them afraid of us and destroys the trust they have in us. But if we constantly prove by our actions, tone of voice, and gentle touch that we *can* be trusted, we wind up with a companion that chooses to be with us, will accept our touch, and is willing to please us, even it that means defending us with his or her life.

Chapter 1

Different species are capable of different levels and types of bonding. The bond we have with a dog or cat will not be the same as one we have with a fish or turtle. However, just the act of *caring* for a fish or turtle teaches us both responsibility and respect for a living creature. Animals also benefit from our nurturing. While it is more obvious when our dog wags its tail and pulls its lips back in a "smile" or when our cat sits purring in our lap, even the simpler creatures respond to positive human interaction. Kyle explains, "It's not as easy to explain when it comes to reptiles. But there are definitely times when they'll be down there hiding in a corner in their tank, and then when you come into the room, all of a sudden they start puffing themselves out, their heads will lift up and they'll start looking around. For example, snakes 'hear' through vibration. They could be under a log and then when I walk into the room and they start hearing voices, they'll respond. It will trigger them to come out and become more interested in what's going on around them as opposed to just doing their natural hiding thing, which is a self-defense mechanism. They're not going to respond with any gestures or anything, but it can change their character or colors and they definitely look healthier when I'm around. It's fascinating to see how much can really happen between humans and even some of the simplest and more prehistoric animals like reptiles with just simple human interaction."[21]

Coexisting with animals not of our species can be a rewarding experience. Or it can be an experience that has little or no value—or, even worse, a living nightmare. What causes the difference? As teens and young adults, how can we turn our "pet experience" into a rewarding relationship for both our pet *and* us? Since most humans instinctively crave companionship, animals can provide the types of companionship we might not be able to experience with another person within our families or peer groups. For example, teens who experience difficulty with relationships, move often, or come from stressful family situations might find stability and acceptance in a relationship with a pet. This honest acceptance can be a lifesaver when we feel we cannot live up to the expectations and peer pressure around us.

Vulnerability

> "I think little kids look at animals as friends. I mean, I always see little kids run up to dogs and hugging them. At first you'd just think, 'Aw, that's so cute!' but if you really stop to think about it, maybe that child really did need a hug just then. And, instead of seeing the dog as just an animal, the child saw the dog more as a friend that would give him that hug."—Janet Carhuayano, dog walker in Manhattan[22]

A common bond animals share with young people is their vulnerability. Often painful at times, our sensitivity to the ways others perceive us, and how we see ourselves, can mirror how our pets respond to us. This shared vulnerability can cement the bond we have with our pets. Knowing someone else feels what we do can make us feel less alone, less afraid, and less unsure by making us feel loved, understood, and worthy. And that bond creates incredible empathy with our companion animals as well.

Kyle has experienced this with his own companion animals. "You definitely see in some situations that they do care and it's not that they're being loyal to you because you're the one taking care of them and feeding them. It's deeper than that. Some people might not see that and only use them just for the visual loyalty they get right offhand. But when you're upset and you have an animal that's bonded with you, they have a very intuitive sense about it that's very real. We have five cats but there's one I'm particularly attached to and bonded with. When I was younger and I was upset or crying or whatever, he'd be the first one in my room. I mean, he didn't understand *why* I was upset or what I was even doing, but he just knew something was wrong. You could see it. It feels good to know I can come into my room and it is always a comfort zone, especially when I see him come walking around the corner to see what's wrong."[23]

Chapter 1

Many people may not realize it, but animals also need our protection. For example, thousands of animals across the globe are maimed or killed each year by improperly discarded garbage. A large percentage of the animals injured by rubbish are hurt by items such as broken glass, pieces of dumped plastic, metal cans with sharp edges, spoiled food, or improperly discarded medicine or chemicals. Examples of injury from improperly disposed trash include animals poisoned by eating discarded batteries or licking paint tins, and dogs swallowing plastic that embeds in stomachs, resulting in stomach cancer or life-threatening blockages.

According to an article in the February 10, 2003, issue of the *Borehamwood & Elstree Times*, a campaign in England was initiated to expose teenagers to the consequences of littering and raise their awareness of the ways animals can be injured or even killed by discarded litter. The "Keep Britain Tidy" poster campaign encouraged teens to look at the gruesome pictures of animals injured by litter and trash that is dropped on streets, sidewalks, and other public places throughout Great Britain. When questioned, the teens who regularly dropped litter responded that they did so for various reasons, including laziness; lack of bins or dirty, wasp-infested bins; or just not wanting to get their clothes dirty. The most disturbing answers, however, were those from boys dropping the litter to impress girls and girls who were too busy chatting, as well as both sexes wanting to appear "cool." These teens not only thought it was "cool" to dump trash, but were only willing to pick it up and dispose of it properly if offered something such as cash or a day off of school.[24]

In direct contrast to teens who do not seem to have any sort of bond with animals, there are dozens of other stories about teens who *do* care. As you dive further into this book, you'll read some amazing stories about some very remarkable young people who have made a difference in lives of many animals and people.

LOOKING BEYOND THE SURFACE

Animals have the incredible capacity to accept *who* they are and to live in the bodies they were given, imperfections and all.

And that attitude of acceptance is extended to us, their companion humans, as well. We don't feel too short or too tall when we're with them, nor does it matter if we're having a bad hair day or if our clothes don't look perfect. Our pets look beyond the surface, beyond all those things we are so uptight about. Instead they focus on *who* we are.

College graduate Mary Dyrhaug had an uncomfortable experience with her Shih Tzu, Mackenzie. She and Mackenzie had just come out of an upscale department store in a posh urban neighborhood when they were approached by a homeless man. "Well, he might not have been homeless but he sure looked like it. It made me kind of nervous. He started making a big fuss over her. Mackenzie was in her green bag and he was cooing all over her. I didn't mind that, but then he tried giving her 'kisses.' His teeth were rotted and falling out of his head. I didn't know what to do so I kind of said, 'Okay, thanks' . . . and walked away!"[25] While this incident would have unnerved most people, Mary explains that Mackenzie responded to this man by just wagging her tail and offering kisses back. This is because while humans base many responses on appearance, dogs and many other animals instead base their responses on actions and/or voice tone.

Always watching and studying us, companion animals learn not only about humans, but also about us as individuals. It is amazing how incredibly adaptable our pets have to be to live with us. For example, when we bring a puppy or kitten into our home, we not only introduce the young animal to humans, with all our rules and idiosyncrasies, we also remove this creature from experiences with its own species. Since dogs and cats learn about the world from other dogs and cats, just as humans learn from families and friends, bringing an animal into an environment surrounded solely by another species, scent, and behavior poses an incredible challenge, especially for a baby animal.

INTERSPECIES COMMUNICATION AND COOPERATION

Interspecies communication is not reliably based on instinct; it must be learned. Dogs, cats, and other animals communicate by

Chapter 1

Different species may use the same body language, but they don't always contain the same meanings. A dog's body posture of rear and tail up may signal "play," but a cat with an arched back and tail up may signal fear or aggression. Illustration by the author.

using voice, body language, and facial expressions, as well as leaving and reading scent markings. We, on the other hand, rely heavily on the spoken word to communicate with each other and instinctively use speech to communicate to our pets as well. Although dogs can't form words, they verbalize with crying, whining, yipping, growling, and barking, as well as variations within each category. Some dogs even develop a different whining sound when they need to go potty from the whine they use when they want a toy that is stuck under the bed. When we develop a strong bond with our dog, we also learn to differentiate between a warning bark and an attention-seeking one, as well as a cry from pain and a cry from loneliness. Dogs also learn to differentiate their owner's meanings from their different tones of voice, as well as to understand and respond to an extensive vocabulary of human words. And when we combine words with body language and facial expressions, we make our communication clearer, just as our pet does when we learn to read its body language and facial expressions.

Many companion animals, including dogs and horses, also smell things humans cannot. For example, fear has a scent, as well as some physical illnesses and diseases, such as cancer and seizures. When animals smell someone who is afraid, it often makes them nervous or afraid as well. This is because in nature, when one animal in a pack or herd is afraid, it might signal danger to the entire herd or pack. A chemical response to fear is then triggered, warning the rest of the pack or herd to be on high alert. This group warning system is essential for survival in the wild. When a dog becomes a part of our human family, he essentially becomes part of our "pack" and will respond instinctively to our sensory cues as he would in the wild.

Fortunately, not all dogs learn to fear all potentially dangerous situations. There are many stories of pets rescuing humans from danger or disaster, or seeking help when humans were injured or lost. Examples include dogs acting unusually to get attention prior to a natural disaster, waking people sleeping in burning buildings or when there is a prowler outside, or trying to prevent their humans from stepping onto a surface that is not stable or entering a structure that is unsafe.

A PERSONAL GLIMPSE

First-time pet owners often make mistakes out of ignorance and their subsequent "miscues" can result in companion animals picking up wrong informational cues—or totally misinterpreting them. Katie Green remembers one incident when her first dog, Madison, was just a puppy. "My mom was broiling something in the oven that started smoking a little and made the kitchen smoke alarm go off. Well, Madison was in his crate in the kitchen and that smoke alarm was on the wall right over him. My mom tried waving newspapers in front of it to stop it and we were all yelling at each other to open the window, turn off the oven, etc. We didn't realize, however, what our puppy was learning from our screaming, waving our arms around and running all over the place. When everything quieted down, we noticed he was trembling from head to toe and totally terrified! From that point on, if anyone cooked *any* food that made a sizzling sound, opened the oven door or took out a cooking pan, Madison would start shaking and run away to hide. And, even though we never acted that way again when the smoke alarm went off, that fear was also passed on to the next puppy, Tyler, who, observing Madison's reaction, smelled his fear and decided he needed to be scared of all sizzling culinary acts in the kitchen as well."[26]

Chapter 1

Kyle suggests that one reason we may feel such a strong bond with companion animals and view them as our closest friends is that they *would* be willing to do things for us that most of our friends would never do! That includes defending us with their lives. "There are situations where there's a dog that's never been aggressive, but in the face of danger they'll do nothing *but* protect their owner. Police dogs would take a bullet for their handler in a second—without any question—if presented with certain situations. Or they'll run right up to a burglar who might be a threat. I mean, you read a lot of stories where the dog takes the worse end of a situation and winds up getting hurt or killed itself. But the dog's always doing it in a way that's defending its owner. I don't think that aspect is shown enough in the media. I mean, the facts are reported, but not in a way that makes the dog look like as much of a true friend and companion as they really end up being."[27]

Not all companion animals have the capacity to pull us from a burning building, but that does not lessen their importance in the lives of their human companions, or their human's importance in theirs. For many teens, there is nothing quite as soothing as watching colorful fish swimming around in a tank or stroking the soft fur of a pet rabbit. Many teens away from

A PERSONAL GLIMPSE

It was difficult for Katie Green to leave her dogs when she first left for college. "I kept calling my mom and asking her how the dogs were. It felt so strange not having them with me here. But then I decided to buy a goldfish and named her Melody. I bought her a nice fishbowl with a plant and put colorful stones on the bottom, which brightened up my dorm room. I feed her 'fishy meatballs' three times a day, and when I am by myself, I watch her swim around in her bowl. I still miss my dogs but not nearly as much now that I have Melody to take care of."[28]

MEDICAL TIDBITS

Prevention is the key to keeping animals healthy. Check that your companion animals have fresh water and uncontaminated food, and that all food containers and housing (crates, cages, stalls, etc.) are cleaned regularly and bedding or litter replaced often. Make sure outside dog run areas are kept picked up, and sanitize them several times a year. Although many people are concerned with risk factors associated with vaccinations, they can prevent many of the deadly diseases that can be caught from unvaccinated domestic and wild animals. And, in some cases, such as with rabies vaccinations, it is mandated by law that you have your pet vaccinated every year.

Not all countries are as diligent or humane in preventing disease outbreaks. In 2006, approximately fifty thousand dogs were clubbed, hanged or electrocuted in southern China because of a rabies outbreak that killed three people in a six-month period. Although the government tried to control the disease by vaccinating four thousand animals, dog bites continued and the government decided to prevent rabies from spreading to people by killing all dogs not used by police and the military. According to reports, pet owners were offered a reward for killing their animals. For those trying to hide their pets, simply walking their dogs became a death sentence and some pets were grabbed and beaten to death by health officials right in front of their owners.[29]

home at college miss their families and companion animals so much that having a single goldfish in a bowl is often very comforting.

DEALING WITH STRESS

On a primitive level, when tension and stress rise, our bodies sense danger. The instinctive response to danger is to get ready to either fight or flee. We all know the feeling of the adrenaline rush as it is released into our bloodstream, coupled with heavier breathing and heart racing. That survival response works well if we're being faced with enemy fire or an attacking tyrannosaurus, but what about twenty-first-century situations that make us feel totally stressed out? Instead of staying in bed or turning to drugs or alcohol, think animals instead! They're nonaddictive and they're legal! Animals give us something to focus on outside of ourselves. They can help break the cycle of depression, isolation, and inactivity that can result from stress. Pets can reach us deep inside our depression and make us laugh. They motivate us to exercise, which lowers our blood pressure and triggers our brain to release endorphins that help elevate our moods and reduce pain. Companion animals can give people a reason to get up each day and a sense of purpose. Volunteering at an animal rescue, shelter, or vet office or working in a job that allows you to interact with animals is also a great way to help de-stress.

GROWING UP

> "I had my dog my entire life up until July 2005 when she passed away. It was great being able to grow with her, like a sister almost. Being that I am an only child I couldn't have asked for a better one."—Rebecca Britz[30]

As children, we are the recipients of care, guidance, and protection, but as children mature and enter their teenage years, they naturally become less dependent on parents and begin to achieve a sense of mastery through their own efforts. The act of nurturing requires reading nonverbal signals and reacting to them in a consistent manner. By being directly involved in a pet's care and routine, teens not only create a strong bond with their companion animal, they can also experience an increase in self-esteem, self-control, and autonomy.

Nichole thinks the transition from grade school to high school was a huge change. "Your mindset kind of switches from 'what do I *want* to do?' to 'what do I *need* to do?' when it comes to classes and extracurricular activities. And things begin to change, too, as you expand more with friendships. You become more like 'oh, how can I help you' and not so much 'how you can help me.' But having a pet helps you switch sooner into 'how can I help you' simply because your dog or cat can't take care of itself. You learn to think more like 'I'm going to give to you' instead of just taking what I can."[31]

Kyle says, "As you age you don't see things the same way. My little sister is still very creative and imaginative and she can entertain herself for hours. Things like that you kind of grow out of as you grow up. Although you miss it and may try to replicate it, it will never be the same again. But because animals are so innocent, they also bring you back to that time when you were also young and innocent. It helps you accept who you are, instead of wishing you could be younger or different."[32]

Teen years are years filled with many changes, both emotional and physical. Young people's bodies are in a constant state of rapid growth and change, creating new feelings and needs. Shaving, dealing with acne, and PMS are only a few of the changes going on inside teen bodies and brains. Caring for animals with whom teens already share a bond and with whom they feel emotionally "safe" can also serve as an anchor in their lives because the routine of caring for an animal's needs on a regular basis provides much-needed constancy while the rest of a teen's world continues to make increasingly more complex demands.

Animals can play a key role helping teens transition from loving their parents to loving other people. Caring for a pet helps develop a teen's sense of responsibility, as well as providing an outlet for the development of the nurturing instinct. Interaction with animals, as pets or in volunteer situations, can help young people better cope with their family's dynamics. Pets not only help reduce stress and ease tension, involvement with them can also raise self-esteem. Studies have shown that when companion animals are brought into families, the family members tend to argue less and cooperate more.

Chapter 1

NATURAL FAMILIES

Like humans, animals also form "families." Many of the reasons they do this are the very same reasons teens form cliques, join clubs, and insist on wearing and doing the same things everyone else their age does. A teen without any friends feels lonely, and so would most animals we consider pets or companion animals. And just like humans, animals both seek leaders and challenge authority. It's all about status. Some of us are content to just follow everyone else, while other teens are driven to lead. That leadership may not always be wise, but it can be part of the complex set of unspoken rules and rituals of growing up.

In the wild, horses live in herds consisting mainly of one stallion, a few mares, and their foals. When allowed, domesticated horses also live and graze in herds, forming small groups with individual friendships and dislikes. This group mentality is especially beneficial for mutual grooming, warmth, and protection from predators. Domesticated horses are usually kept in individual stalls, but they whinny to other members of their herd to keep in contact. This is similar to the way teens stay connected to their friends when physically separated by text messaging, IMing, or calling. Many birds instinctively form flocks that provide safety as well as socialization and physical contact. When we hear birds singing, we are actually witnessing them communicating with one another, often with birds not within their sight. According to Rich Weiner, executive director for A Refuge for Saving the Wildlife, an exotic bird rescue organization in Northbrook, Illinois, many bad behaviors exhibited by birds like cockatoos, macaws, or parrots stem from the fact that these birds *are* such social creatures. Unlike horses, dogs, or cats, these exotic birds are not really domesticated in the true sense. They retain their wild instincts, including the strong need be an active part of a flock. But they often wind up living essentially in solitary confinement as the only bird in human households where the humans are gone many hours a day.

Predator animals have similar but slightly different needs from prey animals. Dogs live and hunt in packs consisting of a hierarchy of male and female dogs of varying ages, along with a "pack leader." When brought into a human household, they must understand their place in the human social order. It is important for humans to earn their canine's respect as pack leaders without cruelty or force by being the source of all things the dog desires, including food, toys, or petting. When puppies have a clear idea of their status in the pack, they are more easily trained and adapt more readily to human rules. When they enter adolescence, however, like their human teen counterparts, even the most obedient dogs may challenge their human leaders.

Hierarchy in felines is a bit more complex to understand because it is focused more on territory than social status. When cats rub against an object (including their humans), scratch it, or urinate on it, they mark it as their territory by leaving scented pheromones. A cat's sense of smell is as important a communication tool as body language. Since humans and other animals within the household cannot detect or interpret the meaning of pheromones, there is great potential for misinterpretation.

Considering the differences between species and the many ways our companion animals are different from us, why have people chosen to care for and bond with them for centuries? Nineteenth-century psychologist and philosopher Erich Fromm once stated, "Man is the only animal for whom his own existence is a problem which he has to solve." Perhaps the only way we can find our purpose is by reaching outside of ourselves and connecting with other living creatures. Or perhaps there is something deep within us that needs to be intertwined with the rest of creation so we can become part of something much bigger than ourselves.

Interacting with animals aids us in becoming better at deciphering body language and understanding, empathizing, or "reading" other's feelings and moods. Pets also foster sensitivity and responsibility and provide companionship. But most importantly, they give us a glimpse into the best of who we can be.

Chapter 1

NOTES

1. Tina Swinkels, interview with the author, December 2006.
2. *Appleseeds* 3, no. 14 (December 2000): 20.
3. Reshoma Banerjee, e-mail to the author, December 2006.
4. Teresa Hellpap, interview with the author, September 6, 2006.
5. Jessica Katz, e-mail to the author, December 2006.
6. Trish Hampton, interview with the author, September 2006.
7. Katz, e-mail to the author, December 2006.
8. Katie Green, interview with the author, July 14, 2006.
9. Nichole Freeman, interview with the author, December 2006.
10. Richelle Hellpap, interview with the author, October 2006.
11. Freeman, interview with the author, December 2006.
12. Rachel G., interview with the author, January 2007.
13. Jennifer Schnell, "Friends . . . or Food?" *Modern Dog* (Spring 2006): 14.
14. Rebecca Britz, e-mail to the author, October 2006.
15. Annalies Kocourek, interview with the author, August 2006.
16. Freeman, interview with the author, December 2006.
17. Teresa Hellpap, interview with the author, September 6, 2006.
18. Natasha McDonald, interview with the author, December 2006.
19. Kyle Fetters, interview with the author, September 2006.
20. American Kennel Club, various articles, hwww.akc.org/news/index.cfm?article_id=2607, (accessed April 14, 2006).
21. Fetters, interview with the author, September 2006.
22. Janet Carhuayano, interview with the author, October 2006.
23. Fetters, interview with the author, September 2006.
24. Jenny Bradley, "Vets Back Litter Campaign," *Borehamwood & Elstree Times*, February 10, 2003, www.borehamwoodtimes.co.uk/archive/display.var.269936.0.vets_back_litter_campaign.php (accessed April 14, 2007).
25. Mary Dyrhaug, interview with the author, January 2007.
26. Green, interview with the author, August 2006.
27. Fetters, interview with the author, September 2006.
28. Green, interview with the author, August 2006.
29. "China Kills 50,000 Dogs in Rabies Crackdown," *Pet Product News International*, (September 2006): 38; Schnell, "Friends . . . or Food?" 14.
30. Britz, e-mail to the author, October 2006.
31. Freeman, interview with the author, December 2006.
32. Fetters, interview with the author, September 2006.

2 Understanding Animals; Understanding Ourselves

Organisms cannot live in isolation. All animals, including humans, need to connect with other forms of life, whether their own species or another one. In order to do that, animals need to communicate.

COMMUNICATING WITH HUMANS

Various forms of life communicate with each other through vocalization, body movement or posture, color, scent, and chemicals they release. The stench certain insects release when crushed by a predator signals, "Don't eat me; I stink!" while the colorful plumage of a male bird might indicate to a female bird, "Hey baby, whatcha doing tonight?" Like these animals, we also communicate with each other and with other species using vocalization and body movement that may not be understood by other species or may be misinterpreted as meaning something completely different according to another species' method of communicating.

Our human world is filled with multiple ways to communicate. We can tell by the look in someone's eye if he or she loves or hates us, and we don't trust people who avoid eye contact, walk funny, or wear clothes that look goofy. Teens in gangs develop ways to communicate through series of hand gestures or finger positioning, as well as subtle differences in how they wear their hat or pants. Radios, television, computers, and telephones are common means of communication to twenty-first-century teens that would have

"Anybody can care for an animal, or a large number of animals, but to understand them is another thing."

—Richelle Hellpap, Wisconsin high school student[1]

been foreign concepts to teens raised in the sixteenth century. Humans have developed e-mail, blogs, text messaging, newspapers, magazines, books, and the occasional handwritten note to communicate instantly with each other, with full comprehension, without sound and without nonverbal body language cues. Not only have we become used to this silent and minimally kinesthetic means of communicating, we are not even aware we have also become anomalies in the animal kingdom.

Interpreting Animal Communication Signals

As an example, when a human scolds a puppy for doing something wrong, most nondominant dogs will flip over on their backs, expose their underbelly, avoid eye contact, and possibly urinate. If Joe is upset at his puppy, Maggie, for running away and not returning to him after peeing in the house, this might appear to Joe that Maggie is continuing to disobey and the additional urinating might appear to be defiance. When she also clearly avoids eye contact, Joe thinks Maggie knows she's doing something wrong and just won't look him in the eye out of guilt. Joe responds by scolding the poor puppy again. At that point, Maggie may not know what to do, since nothing she is doing has pleased this very angry, very scary human. And if Joe also uses physical means of punishment, the puppy will lose trust and possibly be imprinted for life to be afraid of whatever body language was being exhibited by Joe (such as arms raised), or the specific way he looks (such as a man wearing a hat), sounds (angry and loud), or even smells.

However, if Joe understood how dogs communicate, he would have understood instantly what Maggie was clearly communicating through nonverbal body language. By exposing her belly, avoiding eye contact, and urinating, she very clearly said: (1) "I don't know what I did wrong but your angry tone of voice makes me know I did something you don't like"; (2) "I'm sorry! I'm sorry!"; (3) "You are the pack leader and I am a mere slug so I won't look you in the eyes out of great respect"; and

(4) "I submit to your authority and will not challenge you or attack you, so I'm bowing before you in submission by laying on my back, peeing as a gesture of my low stature and exposing my vulnerable belly, hoping you won't kill me." This is a perfect example of miscommunication between human and canine. Joe and Maggie are not using the same "language," making it difficult—if not impossible—for either of them to accurately understand one another.

It is essential to communicate our feelings to an animal in a way it can understand and not let other feelings or thoughtless actions get in the way. If our puppy runs away from us and we command it to "come" in an angry tone of voice, we only communicate that we are definitely *not* someone that puppy wants to come to! When we are angry or in a bad mood, our displeasure is what is conveyed to the animal, instead of what we are really trying to tell it. If we only communicate our own expectations to an animal without understanding what that animal is trying to communicate to us, we will fail to connect. How, then, is it possible to have a true bond with a companion animal if we have no way to communicate with each other?

Understanding Body Language

Animals communicate in a different way than humans do, but they tend to communicate with a more consistent set of actions and signals. And because animals' responses are often clearer and more predictable, they can provide a release from the very demanding and often confusing subtleties of human behavior, peer pressure, and social interactions. When we learn how to interpret their signals and become able to successfully tend to their needs, we also begin to realize that the world does not revolve around us. Companion animals can help teens not only develop empathy, but also better social skills.

We also need to pay attention to what our pets are telling us through their body language. For example, horses communicate through their head position, tail movement, ear position, muscle tension, and eyes. A nervous or excited horse will have tense neck muscles and hold its head up high. Wide eyes with the whites showing indicate a fearful horse, while soft, relaxed eyes indicate one with confidence. And, while horses will turn their ears in the direction of what they are paying attention to, ears that are pinned back may indicate imminent aggression instead.

University of Vermont student Jessica Katz agrees, based on her experience as an intern at a bird refuge: "Body language is as important with birds as it is with dogs and other companion animals. And this internship was all about body language. Reading birds is by far the most important concept anyone who interacts at the refuge needs to comprehend and an ability that I improved at superbly. When I first walked into the refuge, I had no idea that a cockatoo's tongue-clicking motion is related to happiness or that sometimes head-bobbing isn't an aggressive behavior. One might find it strange that birds have their quirks and phobias just like people . . . although I have to admit that by the end of my internship I was thinking of these birds as people in their own right. I did a lot of observing. Birds are no different than people. It's just like working with children; they have their tantrums. When I was able to build up the trust of some more of the wary ones, it was very rewarding!"

Although birds definitely communicate through nonverbal body posturing and movements, they also communicate through sounds. They are a little bit different from some other animals that people have that may not be able to make as many variations of sound. And some of them express how they feel by using learned sounds that come out as human words. Jessica explains, "African grays can speak up to a vocabulary of fifteen hundred words. And a lot of the times their vocalization will indicate *exactly* how they are feeling."[2]

As a result of her internship experience with marine mammals at SeaWorld Adventure Parks in San Diego, California, student Kaylah Dodd feels she is also better able to read body language. "I learned that instead of punishment, trainers use body language to communicate. For example, when they were training the seals for a new trick, each time the seal messed up, the trainers would look away from it and not make eye contact with it for three seconds. Then they would try again. Since then, I've noticed that when my dog makes a mess or doesn't want to do something, he doesn't look at me. For example if I call him to come inside and he doesn't want to, he'll look away and ignore me."[3]

Although humans exhibit confidence and friendliness with direct eye contact, in the animal world, direct eye contact is often perceived as dominance and/or aggression. By avoiding eye contact, dogs signal submissiveness as well as respect for the animal or human they perceive to be the pack leader. Staring directly into the eyes of an animal from the elevated stature of a human, can trigger defensive behavior since the animal can easily interpret that act as one of aggression. This is even more exacerbated when positioned in front of that creature instead of at their side or from a less threatening or more submissive position. This can be especially dangerous if a dog feels he is the "alpha" and his status is being threatened. Alpha dogs also use direct eye contact and staring as a way to show dominance over another animal or human they feel has lower status, while the "inferior" creature is expected to look away. So when two "alphas" come in contact with each other, the potential for fighting escalates quickly if neither of them looks away.

A pleasant exchange between Jessica Katz and Garth, a Congo African gray parrot waiting for adoption at A Refuge for Saving the Wildlife, an exotic bird rescue organization. Photo used with permission, Jessica Katz.

Eye contact avoidance and aggressive staring are also something humans do. For example, people who are lying to you or trying to keep something from you will not look into your eyes. Conversely, if you do not want your parents to know you snuck out with your friends instead of staying home to study, you won't look them in the eyes either. Law enforcement personnel are especially aware of this very human trait and watch for suspects who look away when asked questions they do not want to answer truthfully. Staring, however, is all about power. It is meant to make the creature being stared at feel powerless and uncomfortable. Bullies always stare directly into the eyes of their intended victims to intimidate and appear dominant and powerful.

Animals also study us. As Kyle Fetters observes, "Animals will sit and watch us a lot longer than most humans will focus their attention on an animal. They're just fascinated by us. Some may be a little hesitant at first but that's usually because

Chapter 2

A tilted head indicates recognition and interest. This dog might have just recognized a familiar word or phrase such as "ride in the car" or "cookie." Photo used with permission, Jeffrey Green, Total Recall Dog Training.

they haven't been brought up around humans. I've seen animals that are a little hesitant with new people because they've only been brought up around their own family and I've also seen other animals that live in houses where there are always new people over. These animals are usually very intuitive about it and very friendly. I've got some friends whose families just keep to themselves and when I do go over, their cats and dogs will hide. But even then, to some extent once they get more familiar with me, they kind of lighten up, too." Another example of animals learning to communicate with humans is when a dog has to go outside to do its business. Kyle explains how one of his dogs has learned to communicate that need: "He's too small to go out by himself, so he'll come and actually get us to tell us he has to go outside. Now another person will think he's just nagging us or something when he comes in the kitchen, but the truth is that he's actually trying to tell us something."

And animals can be very intuitive about us. They pick up on nuances of our body language, voice tone, or chemical scents we give off when we feel strong emotion. Kyle explains further, "Animals show recognition in different ways. Humans are based on sight first and then everything else. But animals don't necessarily rely on sight as much as humans do. They tend to depend more on things like sound and smell." A good example of this is how snakes use scent. According to Kyle, snakes actually have a very keen sense of smell. "They're so sensitive that way; they use their tongues and taste buds to smell everything. It's also the same with a lot of lizards. You'll see it when they're walking around. They'll stick their tongue out or touch the ground and check around. They'll use their noses (or muzzles or whatever) and go against things to familiarize themselves with their surroundings. Not many people would pick up on that but if you're around them enough you'll definitely notice that."[4] Vet assistant Kristy Kosinski adds, "Both my birds and dog are sensitive to our moods, but while the dog might be extra affectionate when we're down, the birds will mimic our emotions more. If our energy is too high from anger or excitement, the birds are more apt to get overexcited themselves and scream or bite."[5]

Reading nonverbal body language has also equipped many teens involved with animals to be able to "read" their peers. High school can be tough socially, so it helps when teens learn to read things like "Is this guy trying to hit on me or does he just want to be a friend?" or "Does that girl think I'm cool or is she calling me a dork to her friends behind my back"? There

Chapter 2

are also teens who may not want to express what they're really feeling. Instead, they may display actions or express themselves verbally in a way that covers up those feelings and makes them feel better or more in control, even though their words and facial expressions/body language may conflict.

Jessica feels that her ability to read body language and be more sensitive to birds has occurred because, like many people who work with animals, she was already more sensitive to body language in people. "I've always been very intuitive and observant. Because I like to write and observe people, I realize that when you look at a person or animals it is not just what you see on the outside, but there are a lot of nuances. I would actually say the way I look at strangers or friends relates to how I observe the birds."[6]

University of Oklahoma student Kelli Herbel agrees: "You do, you pick up on that stuff. I've known a lot of people who say they're intimidated by me. Whether they know it or not, I think it's because it's hard for them to lie to me. Dogs don't talk; they speak through what they do and I've pretty much learned to read that. High school was tough but it wasn't as tough on me because I was involved in the dog world and I had a whole other outside life with these dogs so school wasn't my whole world. And that really helped me get through it. I was always winning ribbons, titles, and awards through showing dogs whereas my peers didn't have this additional life so they spent all their time trying to gain acceptance and everything."[7]

Kelli and other teens involved in showing dogs, horses, cats, or other animals are often in unique positions to learn firsthand from experts in these fields, as well as to impact spectators using verbal and body language inside and outside the ring. Successfully showing dogs has given Kelli a lot of confidence, which shows in her body language. Not only does a handler have to work with a dog inside the ring with dozens to hundreds of spectators watching, she must also be able to work with the dog outside the ring, speaking knowledgeably and confidently to strangers many times her age on a range of subjects. Many people go to dog shows to learn about specific breeds and traits, and a handler's comments or ability to handle

IT HAPPENED TO ME: THE BOND IN ACTION

Teresa Hellpap remembers an experience at a 4-H event involving her teenage daughter Richelle, who has learning disabilities (LD), a girl named Katie, who had cerebral palsy (CP), and showing rabbits. "The kids involved in the rabbit events do what's called 'Showmanship' where they're judged on how well they handle the rabbits and on how much they know about them. As Youth Leader, Richelle took Katie under her wing. Because of her CP, Katie drooled all over her rabbit, so no one wanted to really touch it except Richelle. And even though Katie was nonverbal, Richelle knew how to understand her and developed a kind of informal sign language to communicate. Katie really wanted to do the Junior Showmanship event, but couldn't tell the judge anything other than point to different things on the rabbit and use her 'signals' with Richelle's help. But when Richelle wound up winning Grand Champion Showmanship, which is a *very* big deal, she took her trophy, walked right over to Katie and gave it to her instead because that girl had tried so hard."

Just like animals, it is possible Richelle understood Katie's body language in the same intuitive way she reads rabbit body language. "She just has an insight into the feelings of all animals and people. Richelle's just not wrapped up in herself, like most teenagers. Instead, she's wrapped up in everyone else." With the specific type of LD she has (expressive language), Richelle has difficulty speaking in front of people, but instead of letting her LD problems prevent her from pursuing her dreams, she continually finds ways to overcome her problems communicating. "Richelle knows tons and tons of stuff but it gets lost in her brain, so she can't extract and express it. So if she's in a stressful situation, like taking a test or during job interviews, not only does she get confused about writing it down, because it's locked in there, she also has a hard time expressing herself, so people often misunderstand what she really means." But when Richelle tackles a subject she feels comfortable about, she opens up. So not only has Richelle helped other people through rabbit showing, her rabbits have also helped her overcome some of her own problems as well. The Wisconsin high school Richelle attends requires each student to take a speech class, something Richelle would normally have great difficulty doing. Theresa explains, "She got an A+ in that class because every one of the speeches she did was about animals. She never needed note cards or anything because it came from her heart and from herself. But if she had had to speak about something she wasn't familiar with, it would have been very difficult for her. Richelle now even speaks about rabbits to other people across the country."[8]

Chapter 2

dogs can influence people's impressions about a specific breed or a breeder's line.

Body language, however, essentially becomes the dialogue between animal and human. And this heightened sensitivity to recognizing and understanding body language not only enables us to better understand the body language of our peers, it may make us more intuitive about what other people are feeling even if they don't say a word. Kyle agrees, based on his own experiences: "With animals, you definitely increase your senses when it comes to body language because they don't have any other way to communicate. You can tell to a certain point from signals, like when dogs cry or yelp, but with reptiles there is a lot of body language and characteristics in how they might act

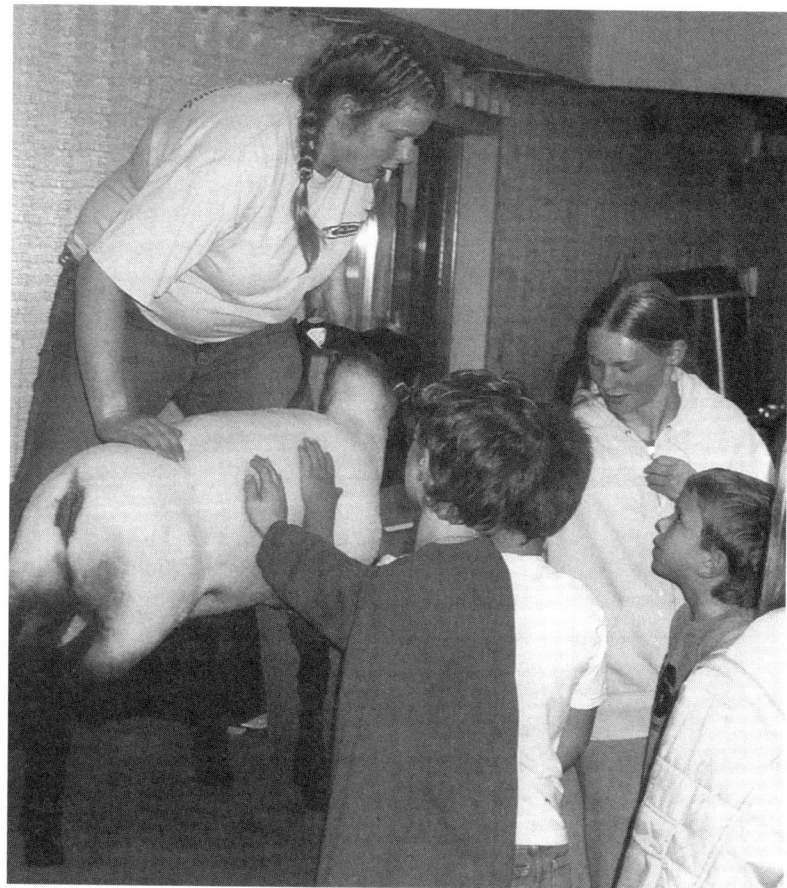

Richelle Hellpap and Charlie at a 4-H show. Photo used with permission, Richelle and Teresa Hellpap.

when you're around as opposed to when someone else is around. I mean, they get scared when someone new is holding them, but it's just like watching a new person getting introduced to someone else who may be a little shy or uncertain. They are always a little hesitant at first but they will open up to certain people, while, on the other hand, there are also some people they just don't like. I had a snake that specifically didn't like one of my friends. That was the only one. My friend didn't do anything to cause it, but it was very apparent in the snake's actions that he just didn't like him."

While people not in tune with body language may be comfortable communicating in situations where body language is not visible, many of us actually rely on it so much that when it is absent, we feel uncomfortable. Without tone of voice and/or body language, it is easy to misinterpret soundless words on a page, just as it is easy to misinterpret a voice when you can't see the body language of the person on the other end. During her internship application process, Kelli was expected to do a phone interview that made her extremely uncomfortable and nervous because she wasn't able to see the facial expressions or other body language cues of the interviewer. When asked if she felt her lifelong involvement with dogs had made her more reliant on those nonverbal body cues, she responded with a definite yes: "Not only have I had to learn to read dogs but, as a herding trainer, you also have to learn to read livestock sheep or cattle to know what they're going to do and that has taught me a lot. And, because of that, I'm also very sensitized to the nonverbal in what people are saying . . . or not saying."[9] Therefore, when visual body language cues are removed from communication, people who rely on them for communicating feel uncomfortable and insecure in the situation, just as if they had a blindfold on in an unfamiliar place.

Prey animals like horses and rabbits need to understand body language in order to avoid being killed. Because of this, horses, for example, are much more skilled at reading body language than we are. In fact, horses are one of the most perceptive of all domestic animals in reading body language in

Chapter 2

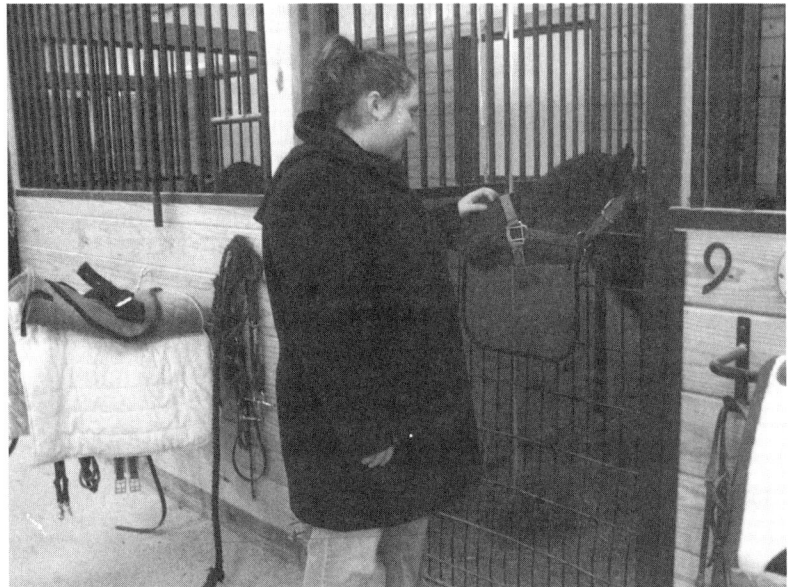

Katie Green overcomes her shyness around horses by interacting with Midnight at Equestrian Connection. Photo by the author.

non-equine species. Most teens involved with horses would agree that these animals usually know our moods as soon as we step into their world. Our posture, movement, actions, and tone of voice convey our innermost thoughts and feelings. Horses also communicate to other horses and to us using a combination of vocalizations and body language.

SPEAK TO ME

"When Tekila hears me cry she usually starts talking to me . . . but when I'm sick she usually just lays on me and licks my eyebrows."—Faye Nuddleman, Iowa pre-vet major[10]

Humans rely heavily on communicating through the meaning found in words and the way they are arranged. We can tell someone we love them in a sad, happy, or soft tone of voice, which gives nuance to our feelings—but the meaning of the words "I love you" remains the same. This is why "mixed signals" can be so confusing. For example, if a friend tells you that he or she likes you, you can interpret that in different ways, depending on the nonlanguage cues. If you hear "I like you" in a soft, upbeat tone and see your friend smiling and engaging you with friendly eye contact and body and arms relaxed, you will most likely believe that sentiment. If, however, you hear "I like you" in an angry or mocking tone of voice while your friend exhibits no facial expression, avoids eye contact, and sits slightly turned away from you, arms folded tightly, you would question his or her motive.

In animal vocalizing, however, sounds relate to meaning. For example, a broad spectrum of animals, from dogs and mice to elephants and hawks, all have one thing in common. The sounds they make and their meanings are based on something other than words, and these meanings are universally understood by species other than the one that utters the sound. Big (scary) animals make low sounds; small (innocuous) ones make high sounds. And almost universally, low-sounding growls indicate aggression, while high-pitched whines communicate fear. In some ways, humans also respond to these same rules, at least on some subconscious level. Most people instinctively use a low, rough tone to express anger or displeasure, while using a soft, high-pitched tone when talking to a baby or a loved one.

ACCEPTANCE AND SELF ESTEEM

Being needed is a basic and instinctive human desire. Whether in a job or a relationship, humans benefit from feeling necessary. It gives us purpose. And for many teens, that need is fulfilled by having a companion animal. Kelli says, "With people you're always running the risk of being dumped on. And that's a tough thing to accept whenever you've given someone so much and they barely notice. I mean, maybe it's just human nature for them to not think it's a big deal. But when you give something to a dog, they always give back. And they don't ask for much in return. I'm usually that person who gives so much to people and no one ever remembers. But that's what's so great about dogs. They *always* remember."[11]

Chapter 2

Teens with LD or other difficulties often deal with self-esteem issues along with their problems learning in school and the peer pressure that surrounds the teen years. Richelle Hellpap says, "People with LD just need a little push to get like comfortable talking to people. The rabbits have really helped me with doing

> **IT HAPPENED TO ME: THE BOND IN ACTION**
>
> Art student Andy Wick is especially in tune with subtleties of body language because of KB, a dog he rescued after a dog-fighting sting in a Chicago neighborhood. "What's crazy about this guy is how I've trained him to communicate to me. He'll express what he's thinking and feeling at that time with his facial features. His ears will do something weird if he doesn't understand you. His tail says a lot, too. Even the direction he puts his paws in will mean something different." What Andy realizes is that not only has he encouraged KB's nonverbal communication through positive reinforcement, he has actually learned to read his dog's body language to the point where he can understand even the most subtle expression. And KB also understands Andy's body language, including the nuances and meaning of voice tone and specific words.
>
> Andy also feels this ability has made him better able to read human body language. "I mean, like, you can't really communicate with a dog and here you're basically trying to teach them English but yet they can't talk or speak it. So you've got to learn what they're saying in a different manner. And this is the best way I've come up with to understand him. Through body language." Like Richelle, Andy has also developed the ability and sensitivity to "read" other people, to the point that he can understand what people are saying even if they also cannot speak. Through body language and other subtleties we learn from close contact with animals, is it possible that interactions with them not only make people more sensitive to them and them to us, but also give us a whole level of communication that most people just don't have? Andy says, "It definitely did help me quite a bit to understand people and all animals. Like all dogs I come up to just to say hi to and pet on the street. You find out all about who they are right off the bat. You let them smell your hand real quick and then you know just from looking at their eyes if they accept you or not. KB's taught me so much about that."[12]

stuff and meeting new people. They even got me able to talk in front of a group! I am comfortable around the rabbits and animals in general, so when I talk about them it's like I am a whole different person than I would be if I didn't have the animals. So if I didn't have animals, I know I wouldn't be able to tolerate the feelings of talking in front of a group of people, or meeting new people. But the rabbits help me to basically relax. I don't have to impress anybody. I can just be myself around them." Richelle feels that one reason teens get such positive feelings from animals is that animals don't judge. "A lot of the high school 'drama' that goes on is because humans do judge and they can do it in a cruel and unfair way. I think animals feel *who* you really are, while your friends think you are so much like them. So if I am with a whole bunch of friends, or even when I am with a few of my friends, I am kind of different. I am not myself. They all think I am this one person and I have to live up to these expectations. But with the rabbits, I am *me*."[13]

HOW ANIMALS AND HUMANS LEARN

> "Whenever I do homework, [my cat, Cosmo] always comes onto my desk and sits on my work or behind my computer. He loves the company and probably also the heat of the computer. He's my companion when I work. Sometimes, when I need to study for a test, I'll pretend I'm teaching him because it helps me learn."—Rachel G., New York high school student[14]

One of the most universally recognized tools for imparting knowledge is learning by example. Since humans are such social and visual animals, we have always had the advantage of taking in surprisingly great amounts of knowledge just by watching and imitating others. This is referred to as "learning through observation." For example, we are able to learn the specific movements to a new dance just by watching our friends

Chapter 2

perform the different steps. This is how many teens learn skills such as fixing cars, playing sports, or keeping up with the latest fashions or hair and makeup. And it is also how children growing up in environments that include gangs, drug users, or criminal activity learn to mimic those types of behavior.

But humans aren't the only ones who learn this way. Learning through observation also helps baby animals learn important life skills such as how to catch food, what dangers to avoid, and how to communicate within packs, herds, flocks, and other groups. And it is one of the ways companion animals, such as dogs and cats, learn about us. When we touch a kitten or puppy very gently, we teach it that humans can be gentle and trusted not to hurt it. Conversely, when an animal is treated roughly or even abusively, it learns not to trust our species.

There are also more abstract forms of learning through observation. While the expression "Imitation is the best form of flattery" doesn't condone copying someone else's poem and passing it off as our own, it does reinforce our awareness of the benefits of learning through observation. This is partly because as humans, we all have the ability to shape what we learn by a process called modeling. This occurs when one person imparts knowledge to another through examples of behavior. We say we are "modeling a behavior" when we do something in a certain way and whoever observes then imitates or adapts that behavior to what he or she has already learned. The familiar term "role modeling" means exactly that: We are modeling something specific and assuming the role of example behavior. Through modeling, parents teach their children, teachers teach students, and friends and peers teach and learn from each other. And like human children, a puppy raised with other dogs that act aggressive or are fearful of other people, animals, or physical characteristics (such as people wearing hats) will often learn these same aggressive or fearful responses, since that is the only behavior being modeled and taught by the other canines in the pack. Animals may also become role models for humans. For example, teens who have never experienced

> **TEENS AND GRADES:
> HOW PETS CAN IMPROVE LEARNING**
>
> A survey mentioned in an issue of the trade magazine *Pet Products News* and discussed in Deborah Straw's book *Why Is Cancer Killing Our Pets?* seems to suggest that animal companions can also help students achieve higher test scores and grades. The study included two hundred people between the ages of seventeen and twenty-five, and found a remarkable correlation between owning a pet and achieving high SAT scores and grade point averages. On average, pet owners achieved scores that were higher than those of non–pet owners. And it seems that the more time the student spent with the animal, the higher the scores or grades.[15]

positive physical interaction and do not know how to touch others in a nonaggressive manner may learn to be gentle through therapeutic interaction with animals that interact in a nonthreatening, gentle manner.

Humans also have the capacity to deceive or offer contradictory visual signals that can be inconsistent or confusing when coupled with verbal or other sensory signals. As an example, a "poker face" hides all thoughts and emotions to prevent someone from "reading" you. But the subtleties of our body language, chemical scents, and nuances of our posture or voice tone are readily observed, learned, and understood by our companion animals. And repetitive behavior modeling can reinforce their knowledge. Of course, not all repetitive behavior modeling results in positive behavior. Dogs placed in environments that encourage gentle play will learn to interact

Chapter 2

> **A PERSONAL GLIMPSE FROM THE AUTHOR**
>
> "I never had a dog growing up because my mother was afraid of dogs and didn't want the responsibility that accompanied owning one. Her reaction to approaching dogs was that of apprehension and avoidance, which I also modeled when I was young. Each time a neighbor's dog got loose and started racing around, I would run into the house, modeling the fear behavior my mother had taught me.
>
> However, my girlfriend Andrea, who lived a few houses away, had a dog: a well-mannered, gentle collie named Toy. Although we didn't realize it at the time, through years of observation and role modeling Andrea, I not only learned I didn't have to be afraid of dogs, I also learned, by observation, how to interact properly with a dog by the time I was a teen. It was not only Andrea but also Toy who taught me. Observing the dog's responses and actions, I learned about dogs and their behavior. And as I became more comfortable and confident around the collie, I subsequently took that knowledge and adapted it, molding it into my own personality and using it with other friends' dogs that were not always as gentle and well-behaved. Those wilder, often untrained dogs also taught me, as well, as I observed their behaviors and discovered how to get them to respond. Eventually, I stopped running into our house when a neighbor's dog got loose and instead learned how to get the dog to come to me and settle down so I could simply clip on a leash and bring it back to its home.
>
> Had I continued to model my mother's fear, however, and never had the opportunity for the positive interaction and role modeling from Andrea and her collie, I might have remained unsure around dogs and, as a parent, would have modeled the same behavior to my children as my mother had modeled to me."

without harming another. Dogs placed in environments that encourage fighting, however, learn to fight. And because of its fear, an animal that is afraid will not necessarily learn what a human is trying to model, and may learn to associate human actions as something fearful instead.

THE REAL "BITE" ON BITING

All of us have bad days. We miss the school bus or our car won't start. Then we get a bad grade on a paper, flunk a test, or

SCIENTIFIC TIDBITS: WHO'S LAUGHING NOW?

Animal behaviorist Patricia Simonet's discovery of a panting sound with a louder and higher frequency than a dog's regular panting suggests dogs may actually express a form of laughter. Caught on tape, this discovery may possibly help dogs cope in stressful situations. According to the research paper "Dog Laughter: Recorded Playback Reduces Stress Related Behavior of Shelter Dogs," published in the proceedings of the 2005 International Conference on Environmental Enrichment, dogs vocalize during play encounters using barks, growls, whines, and a "breathy, pronounced forced exhalation" often referred to as a play pant. Canines typically exhibit a play face (mouth open, lips pulled back, similar to a human smile), play bow (front down, rear up), and/or chase movement to initiate play when they hear the play pant sound.

The Spokane County Regional Animal Protection Service (SCRAPS) in Washington State operates a shelter where a tape of this sound is being used to study the effects on stress-related behavior in shelter dogs. When the canine laughter recording was played in half of the kennel but not in the other half, the therapeutic results were astounding. According to the research paper, typical stress-related behaviors such as lunging, cowering, pacing, and cage biting greatly decreased in the dogs who heard the tape. These same dogs also exhibited improvement in social behavior, while the animals not hearing the recording exhibited no behavioral changes at all. The long-term effects could potentially help make shelter dogs more adoptable by reducing stress-related behaviors. Playing the tape in other stress-inducing environments such as boarding kennels, grooming salons, and veterinary offices could also help reduce dogs' stress and change their association to anticipated pleasure instead of fear.[16]

have a fight with our best friend. We've all been there. The instinctive "fight or flight" response, coupled with the hormone swings of adolescence, can sometimes swing us out of control and evoke anger, rage, or other emotional extremes. But those feelings can get us into trouble if we decide to take on the school system, other drivers on the road, or our girlfriend instead of the saber-toothed tiger we were meant to fight when we were hard-wired with that instinct. There is a difference between having a bad day and having a bad day where we also express or act out our feelings inappropriately through

Chapter 2

aggressive acts that hurt ourselves or others, or damage property. Prisons and juvenile detention facilities are filled with teens and young adults who didn't quite understand that difference.

Animals in the wild can also act in ways viewed as dangerous and unacceptable in human society—especially when they feel threatened or unsafe. It is part of nature and survival. Sadly, many pets wind up in animal shelters for displaying "aggressive behavior," which usually means an animal has bitten a person or another animal. While there are many domestic animals and pets that have learned inappropriate behavior responses—as well as animals that are truly aggressive—many of these biting incidents may be caused by approaching and handling an animal incorrectly: It was simply the animal's instinctive reaction to that unintentional threat.

The good news is that much of what makes a pet feel threatened and respond aggressively can be reduced by simply learning how to think like that animal. For example, staring into a dog's eyes, especially when approaching from the front, would be interpreted by many dogs as a threatening, aggressive act. In the wild, frontal approach and staring is equivalent to saying "Oh *yeah*? Just *try me*! I'm in charge here, not you!" Staring is used similarly by humans with other humans as a means to intimidate. Watch any sports event to see the referee or the umpire getting right into someone's face, eyes wide and staring in an angry expression, and yelling as loudly as possible to get his or her point across. Like animals that fluff up feathers or raise hackles so their fur stands up, we also try to make ourselves appear larger so we can dominate the other person in a confrontation. When animals displaying all these signs begin to close the space between themselves and the creature they are trying to impress, a fight is imminent.

When done properly, however, humans also indicate *interest* by staring, such as staring at performers on a stage or into the eyes of someone we love. These complex combinations of body language illustrate how easy it can be to misunderstand cross-species behavior and why animals can easily misinterpret our body language and respond inappropriately to other signals.

Understanding Animals; Understanding Ourselves

In obedience training and competition, a dog needs to pay strict attention to its human handler and not be distracted by other dogs and people nearby. The dog must also perceive its own status beneath that of the handler to perform the exercises required and not challenge the handler's authority. When coupled with positive reinforcement such as a treat, a clicker sound, or verbal praise, most dogs can be taught the "obedience watch," which basically enables the dog to maintain eye contact for extended periods of time with its human handler. In this activity, dog and human are positioned side by side (a nonthreatening position) and the dog stares right into the handler's eyes, performing various obedience exercises, while the handler returns the dog's gaze. The positioning difference is subtle but important, and any threat is removed by conditioning the dog to receive something pleasant while the staring occurs.

With ears alert, mouth open, and lips pulled back in a smile, this dog's body language signals intent, nonaggressive interest in his handler. Illustration by the author.

Animals can also misread humans because of specific instincts. Herding instinct in dogs, for example, is actually a redirected prey drive, shaped and molded by centuries of careful breeding. Instead of finding prey and killing it, these dogs have been bred to control the animal's movement without harming it. While some herding dogs use their herding instinct to independently protect the flock and others wait for their human owner to give them commands to move stock, they all have the one thing in common: a strong redirected prey drive that can be aroused in a totally human environment where small children are running around, waving their arms, riding bicycles, laughing, and doing all the normal things human children do. Dogs like shelties or corgis that herd by nipping at the heels of livestock will instinctively nip children if not taught otherwise, while dogs like the German shepherd dog may also perceive children or others who approach *their* children as intruders and respond with protective aggression. Children wearing shorts and sandals can easily wind up with bite wounds from a single nip. These dogs are then sent to shelters and labeled as aggressive.

Kyle Fetters feels this can also happen with any dog from any breed that isn't familiar with or comfortable around children. "My neighbor had a purebred golden retriever that attacked kids. It even wound up biting me when I was younger! The owners were teens when they got him and maybe because of my size the dog didn't view me in a positive way. We have a golden ourselves, which is probably the gentlest dog I've ever met. Our little min pin [miniature pinscher] will bite onto [our golden's] leg and the golden will just walk around with him hanging from him. He's just very understanding and tolerant. But that's his individual personality."[17]

Cats may also display territorial aggression toward non-family-member animals. Not usually territorial toward people, cats tend to bite humans for different reasons than dogs might, often responding aggressively with what appears to us to be little or no provocation. Many cats have a threshold for being touched or petted. For some cats, it can take longer than most people engage in touching them to reach their threshold, but for others, the threshold is met within minutes. When that happens, the cat's body will change from relaxed and loose to tense; its tail will begin switching, its ears may flick, its head may quickly turn to look at the hand that is petting it, and its pupil size may become reduced. The moment any of these body signals begins, it is time to stop touching the cat. If these nonverbal body cues are ignored, that person is likely to get bitten or clawed.

Birds, horses, hamsters, and other prey animals will also bite if provoked and warning signs are not recognized. For example, birds use their beaks as protection in the wild against predators such as snakes and birds of prey, but rarely against members of their own flock. Instead, they vocalize (scream) or use body language that includes posturing or fluffing their feathers to make them appear larger to resolve conflict. Large-billed birds in captivity, however, will bite human members of their "flock" when they feel threatened, fearful, or injured—or just for control. Learning to read a bird's body language is essential to prevent getting bitten and to learn not to "reward" inappropriate behavior.

COMPETITION AND CONFIDENCE

In the movie *Babe*, a little pig learns to herd sheep as successfully as a dog with generations of genetic sheep herding programmed into it. The basic lesson of the movie is that success isn't about what you're born with or what others think of you; it's about perseverance and having confidence that you can accomplish your goal. Sometimes that goal may be one that involves animals. Teens can participate in a variety of competitive sports and activities that concentrate on how their animal looks or sports that involve intense training and physical activity. Involvement in sports such as the various animal breed shows; dog agility, obedience, freestyle, or flyball; or in equestrian barrel racing, jumping, or dressage is not only fun, these activities can definitely increase the bond between a teen and their animals through spending time together and intensifying communication. They can also help teens gain confidence, poise, and the willingness to not give up—traits that will later benefit them in interpersonal relationships, schooling, and careers.

Chapter 2

Smooth-coated collie racing through an agility competition course. Photo used with permission, Jeffrey Green, Total Recall Dog Training.

It may seem like a lot of work to train an animal to the level needed for competition or performance, but what really happens during the hours spent is that the teen and the animal are spending quality time together doing something positive and creating a strong bond. Initially, handler and animal build confidence and trust by learning the skills needed for competition as well as learning about each other as individual creatures. For the animal, the time spent positively reinforcing behavior also reinforces the idea in the animal's mind that these activities are pleasurable and that this person can be trusted completely. Training also provides an opportunity for the animal to learn how to better interpret human body language and vocalization. And young people who learn and understand how to communicate with another species also learn to respect other living creatures. Working and accepting an animal as an equal member of a team changes the playing field of "man and beast" into a human-animal bond.

A beautiful example of that human animal bond is visible between canine obedience handler and dog or between equestrian and horse. Watching a deeply bonded obedience or riding team in action is like watching a carefully choreographed pas de deux in which each movement is skillfully matched, step by step, with both members of the team perfectly in tune with each other. Additional examples of this poetry-in-motion bond are the dog-handler agility, flyball, and freestyle dance teams or the various horse-handler jumping, harness, or barrel-racing teams. Training a dog or horse for these activities takes many hours of work, beginning with basic obedience and simple skills and gradually working into more precise and complex movements until the animal and handler are working in complete unity, focused only on each other and not on the distractions around them. And, in addition to the trust and the bond they develop, the main reason they *can* work in unity is that both the animal and the human handler have learned how to clearly communicate with each other.

Animals can also teach a deeper discernment to teens involved with them. Because animals do not communicate with language as we do, we must learn to read their body language and vocalizations. Two of Brigitte Mason's horses exhibit totally different responses to being called to come. "We think my Arab mare was abused before we got her. If she's in the pasture and she doesn't have her halter on, she won't go anywhere near a man if they try to get her. Of course, I just go, 'Cookie, come,' and she comes right over, but my dad has to stand there for ten minutes trying to coax her to let him put a halter on her. She's just not trusting. The quarter horse, however, is completely trusting and will come to anyone. If you ask him to come, he'll go, 'Sure, I'm coming!' whereas you have to really earn the mare's trust."[18]

BONDING THROUGH COMMUNICATION

The bond between our pets and us can be so intense it sometimes rivals the closest of human friendships and adds to or even takes the place of other types of social expression. Animals study us and even adapt to our often strange human expectations in ways that totally contradict their own instincts. Those of us who are closely bonded with a companion animal often feel our pets are so incredibly intuitive to our moods and needs, they seem to read us better than we can even know ourselves. Kyle has had some friends who don't understand his connection with animals or share his empathy with them. "Certain guys tend to think of animals as nothing more than 'just an animal.' They don't see things the same way as I do. But the innocence that animals portray is why I'm so attached to animals and why I will empathize with them, even sometimes over a human." This sentiment also relates to movies where animals appear to get hurt. While Kyle knows the animals aren't really being hurt, it just looks too real! "The animals being portrayed didn't want to get hurt or be there in a battlefield, but they are so loyal to their humans that they wind up in the middle of a battle. It's like the loyalty between a police dog and a police officer or just a dog and his owner, where they'll defend you with their lives without any question. I think that shows true character in a way that few humans can match. And you can't beat that, having someone who's going to be there for you no matter what."[19]

Many young people feel their human friends, peers, or family members do not always understand them nearly as well as their companion animals do. Is that because we also struggle with our own emotions and social situations? Or perhaps, because of our own unique complexities, it is much more difficult for us to fully understand ourselves, much less other humans who are equally unique and complexly different. On the other hand, in addition to their own complex behaviors, animals have the built-in ability to observe and understand. These may be instinctive survival skills for hunting, mating, and safety, but that ability to learn, understand, and *adapt* is also how they survive in our world of complex human behavior.

NOTES

1. Richelle Hellpap, interview with the author, October 2006.
2. Jessica Katz, interview with the author, December 2006.
3. Kaylah Dodd, interview with the author, September 2006.
4. Kyle Fetters, interview with the author, September 2006.
5. Kristy Kosinski, interview with the author, January 2007.
6. Katz, interview with the author, December 2006.
7. Kelli Herbel, e-mail to the author, September 2006.
8. Teresa Hellpap, interview with the author, September 2006.
9. Herbel, e-mail to the author, September 2006.
10. Faye Nuddleman, interview with the author, April 2007.
11. Herbel, e-mail to the author, September 2006.

12. Andy Wick, interview with the author, September 16, 2006.
13. Richelle Hellpap, interview with the author, October 2006.
14. Rachel G., interview with the author, January 2007.
15. Deborah Straw, *Why Is Cancer Killing Our Pets?* (Rochester, VT: Healing Arts Press, 2000), 5.
16. Kirsten Vance, "Is Rover Rolling Over with Laughter?" *Modern Dog* (Spring 2006): 12; plus information from articles found at www.petalk.org/research.html (accessed April 14, 2007).
17. Fetters, interview with the author, September 2006.
18. Brigitte Mason, interview with the author, August 23, 2006.
19. Fetters, interview with the author, September 2006.

Friendship

Human association with other living creatures is an essential part of who and what we are. This need, in fact, is a basic biological imperative similar to that of hunger. We function better when we have regular and satisfying social contacts, both physically and emotionally. Studies show that people connected to other people live longer—not because social interaction makes problems go away, but because friendship helps us cope better with adversity.[2]

But what exactly is a "friend"? According to Merriam-Webster's Online Dictionary, a friend is "one attached to another by affection or esteem," as well as "a favored companion." That's the meaning most of us would recognize. However, another definition of friendship also includes "one that is of the same nation, party, or group."[3] Most teens and young adults would consider that definition to be as important as the first!

Friendship is very important for humans; without friends we become isolated and feel lonely. Developing and maintaining active, healthy relationships gives more meaning to our lives. Whether friendships are made through attending church youth programs, being part of neighborhood organizations and clubs, or hanging in the mall with a couple friends, belonging to a group can afford teens a sense of security and belonging to something larger than one's self.

FRIENDSHIP AND BELONGING

Once humans and dogs became allies, we were no longer alone in the world. We not only had a friend to stand by us for

> "Animals always tell the truth; they never lie. I mean, it's not like your cat will rub up against you, settle into your lap, start purring and all the while be trying to figure out a way of escaping and finding a different family to live with! You can always depend on your pet."
>
> —Christina Aviza, former Kentucky State University student[1]

Chapter 3

hunting and farming, we also had a companion to cheer us on! Instead of treating animals as merely a commodity for food, clothing, or other resources, we learned to trust them and taught them to trust us. By taming animals, we became a little tamer ourselves, because in order to maintain trust with our new friends, we also had to become gentler and less savage.

One fundamental reason we need positive interaction with animals is simply that they *are* different from us. By being in touch with creatures outside our own species, we are reminded that humans occupy only a small place in the grand scheme of existence. It helps us see the human race in perspective—that we are *part* of the natural order, not the dictators of it. In allowing us a glimpse into peaceful coexistence between humans and animals, companion animals remind us that we and the material things we surround ourselves with are not as important as how we treat others, that we show compassion and accept others because of who they are instead of how they look or what their financial or social status might be. A dog will treat both a wealthy celebrity and a physically disabled veteran equally. Cats do not distinguish between designer clothing and clothes off the discount sale rack, nor do horses, ferrets, rabbits, and other kinds of companion animals. In fact, celebrities and other people with wealth and power, as well as those with physical disabilities or disfigurement often bond closely with pets simply because animals love them for themselves and not for their social, financial, or physical positions or limitations.

HUMAN-ANIMAL INTERACTION: THE MUTUAL BOND

> "I don't think a dog or cat could actually ever really lie to you, but lots of people are quite willing to lie to you to just benefit themselves. You can't beat the trueness that an animal gives."—Kyle Fetters, suburban Illinois teen[4]

How, then, does the human-animal interaction help in mutually satisfying ways? While we all need some sort of social contact, in animals (such as birds that hang in flocks or horses that live in herds) this need seems to parallel that of young people seeking peer group membership. Chase Herndon, a college student at Indiana University, believes humans and animals have mutual needs. "All animals—including human—require some kind of sociality, whether it is with their own species or another. Interaction is an important part of life. By working with animals, I am able to provide that interaction to both the animals and myself. With animals, socializing is required in order to survive at all. This is especially true with prey animals that need a group for safety. Humans can easily survive on their own. Henry David Thoreau did fine, as an example, but people may be less happy being alone than if they were part of some tangible community." Chase feels that being part of a community also gives animals and humans greater opportunity to learn skills they would not have been able to learn alone. "For example, there's no way birds could migrate as far as they do without drafting behind their group nor could wolves hunt as successfully without their packs. I mean, emulation is crucial to survival as instincts can only take animals so far."[5]

It is possible humans could *survive* alone, but humans would not *thrive* alone. Because healthy touch is crucial to humans, depriving a baby of love and touch, for example, can have devastating results. Young people in conflict with their families or who are not in social peer relationships might find stroking a cat's fur or holding a snuggling guinea pig in their arms to be very pleasurable. Additionally, the technical age in which we live is often devoid of sensory experiences. We spend most of our time touching plastic or other nonliving surfaces when we hold cell phones and iPods, load MP3 players, or IM our friends. Touching and being touched by an animal connects us emotionally and physically with another living creature.

High school junior Dana Bouchard agrees: "I definitely think owning and caring for an animal can help teens from feeling lonely or unloved, especially having a pet you love and that loves you back. They are always there for you. I have one

Chapter 3

KITTY, BY CHRISTINA AVIZA

**Since 8 yrs old,
lucky number birthday,
my baby
named kitty
sleeps with me,
comes when I call her,
greets me at the door.**[6]

cat Angel, who we adopted a couple years ago. I'm the only person in the house he trusts; he only goes in my room if he's not hiding away in the basement. It's like he's guarding me. All he wants to do is lay next to me. Whenever he does, he's the happiest cat in the world."[7]

Cuddling with a puppy can be very soothing as well as initiating the bonding process. Photo used with permission, Jeffrey Green, Total Recall Dog Training.

BRINGING THE FAMILY TOGETHER

> "My mom has been an animal lover since she was a little girl and she has had a huge influence on me. That's why we have three dogs, two cats, and a horse!"—Dana Bouchard, suburban high school student[8]

Mutual love for animals can also build bridges between teens and their parents during rough years when conflicts test even the best of relationships. When parents and teens are involved in a mutually pleasurable activity that allows them to spend time together, such as training and showing animals in competition sports, they can develop more respect for and trust in each other in addition to achieving their goals and developing close bonds with their companion animals. Brigitte Mason has lived with animals as long as she can remember. It was Brigitte's mom, however, who influenced her respect for animals and brought her into this circle of animal involvement. "My mom wanted me to have horses and be able to have the kind of experiences she had had when she was younger. And because she had really, really loved her horses, she wanted me to experience the same thing. And my dad was okay with that."[9]

Christina Aviza's grandmother was quite influential in her appreciation for animals. "My grandmother and I have always been close. She's only owned a dog as a pet herself, but even as a kid, she said I had a lot of patience. My grandmother always thought I should go into teaching or vet services."[10]

MEETING OTHER PEOPLE

Having a pet can open new doors to making friends. It's hard to say why people seem more comfortable speaking with a

Chapter 3

> "If I am walking alone, no one talks to me. But, having my dog's a real conversation opener. People have something to start talking about."—Kelli Herbel, college student from rural Oklahoma[11]

stranger who has a dog than they do with one who is walking alone; perhaps a person with a dog appears more nurturing or caring, or more trustworthy because the dog trusts that person. Kelli Herbel feels that people with dogs just tend to interact more. "For guys, it's easy to approach and talk to me when I'm by myself, but it will either be about me or about him. But if I have a dog with me, he can approach me and make it about the dog. And I think that eases things up for some people. Maybe it eases tension cause then it's not a boy-girl thing. It kind of neutralizes everything."[12]

Kyle Fetters agrees. "I think that has a lot to do with it. I think that, for a girl, if I was walking down the street with a dog, she'd probably feel a lot more comfortable saying, 'Oh hey, I really like your dog, dude,' or whatever. I think animals have a lot to do with a comfort level of like, *Hey, he's got that animal so he must be a good guy* or vice versa—like if he had a scary looking animal to be wary of him. However, I think people read into that a lot without even knowing it. I mean, walking a dog you are *always* bumping into people. It's a topic of conversation if nothing else and it always seems to be on the lighter side as opposed to walking up to someone with a sad or unfortunate situation or story. It seems to be that people always associate better things with animals than with anything else."[13]

Art student Andy Wick lived in an apartment in Chicago with his dog, KB. When asked if KB ever helped him make friends or meet girls, he responded, "Definitely! The dude's gorgeous. Every time I take him walking, without a doubt I get at least ten to fifteen girls stop to pet him and say, like, 'Hey, what's going on?' or 'He's so beautiful,' or something like that! Definite socializer; helped me out in those terms. And he just loves meeting other people as well. It's actually been a beautiful thing."[14]

Tracy Glickauf is a college grad who grew up in the suburbs and attended a small college in Wisconsin but now lives in an upscale trendy area in a large midwestern city. She jokes about a friend's response to her dog, Risky: "I had a friend who hated animals. However, when she saw how many people talked to me simply because I had Risky, she wanted me to rent Risky to her to pick up men."[15]

Because animals pick up on nonverbal cues humans often miss, they can be good judges of character. Veterinary X-ray technician Karen McCoy rescued a dog that came from a real abusive situation and was afraid of men. "She was terrified of or would hide from every guy I dated. Then one night, Brian came over. I went into the basement to get him a can of soda and told him my dog was afraid so she'd just leave him alone. But by the time I came back upstairs with the drink, she was sitting in his lap. So much for my dog who was afraid of men! She picked 'the one'! We've been together now for eleven years."[16]

Jessica Katz says, "I think my dog is a really good judge of character. When it comes to some of my friends, my dog has been a better judge of character then I was. I dated someone in high school for a month but Hobbs didn't like him at all! And after a month he just dumped me. Hobbs was happy and so was I."[17] Christina also feels her cat is a good judge of character. "She doesn't like a few of my friends. The one friend she dislikes the most smokes. Every time he comes into the house she gets angry and the hair on her back stands up. But with my current boyfriend, she liked him instantly. I'm not sure if it's because every time I'd come home I'd smell like him or if she just really liked him. Sometimes she even trades my lap for his but will keep her eyes on me, unless she's sleeping."[18]

Bonding with an animal that understands them and doesn't expect them to talk helps teens who are shy, and having that animal at their side during social situations deflects attention away from them and onto the animal. And when the other person's attention is focused on the animals, shy teens don't have to talk about things that might be bothering them or things they don't want to reveal about themselves. Andy says, "I am a little shy; it's just my style. I can definitely talk someone's ear off but I've got to be comfortable around them first."[19] Kelli agrees strongly that her dogs have helped her meet people and feels her involvement with animals has made her more approachable—especially to her peers—since it gives them something else to focus on. "I walk my dogs all around town and it seems like if I see someone, they are much more willing to talk to me when I'm with my dogs. It's really a[n] . . . ice breaker, if you have a dog!"[20]

PEER ACCEPTANCE AND UNDERSTANDING

Teens who are closely bonded with pets or involved in activities involving animals may discover that other people don't always understand. It may even be difficult to find friends through the "mainstream" outlets of school. Kelli's family has been involved in showing dogs for many years. She states, "Growing up in a household with so many dogs, you're always watching and observing different interactions, different relationships between the dogs. That's something that's made me more sensitive to how people react to one another. When I went to dog shows I made a lot of friends, but that was mostly because they understood me. People in my high school did not understand why I spent so much time with my dogs. Instead of partying or going to the mall when my friends wanted to, I'd be like, 'Guys, I have dogs!' They just didn't understand that. They'd say, 'Well, I have a dog, too, and it's out in the backyard.' I'd be like, 'No, there's a difference.'"[21]

Other teens are fortunate enough to have friends who do understand. Jessica says, "My friends are all really wonderful about things like that. Whenever I am home over breaks Hobbs goes everywhere I can take her. My friends completely understand. They don't mind going for a walk around the block with her because they all adore her."[22]

Our love for animals can also create a bond between ourselves and other people with similar interests. Activities and organizations with animal interaction often become catalysts in developing friendships with others who share the same passion for animals or a specific animal or related activity or sport. These are often people a teen would not have met any other way, since they may come from a different area or go to another school. And the bond that can develop between people with a passion for animals transcends age, race, or background. For example, Janet Carhuayano visits several urban dog parks during her dog-walking client runs in Manhattan and has met many other dog walkers that way. Although most are much older than she is, Janet knows she could completely rely on any one of them if she ever needed help. Richelle Hellpap also has made an entirely separate group of friends of various ages and backgrounds through her involvement with rabbit shows and 4-H. And because Richelle is involved with educating the general public about rabbits, she also meets hundreds of people at the various county and state fair competitions.

Dana Bouchard relaxing with her dog, Chase. Photo used with permission, Jane and Dana Bouchard.

IT HAPPENED TO ME: THE BOND IN ACTION

High school student and rabbit expert Richelle Hellpap lives in a small town in rural Wisconsin and has been actively involved in 4-H programs since she was a child. When one of her hamsters died, she decided to change to rabbits for practical reasons. Richelle explains: "Hamsters don't live as long as rabbits; they only live about two years whereas rabbits live seven to eleven years. I wanted to have something that would live longer, be more social than a cat but not as big as a dog." After reading and researching about rabbits, Richelle and her mom obtained a mini lop-eared rabbit, a breed that is very gentle and laid back. Then a friend invited Richelle to come to a rabbit show with her and show her bunny. He was actually the worst bunny at the show according to the judge. Even though her rabbit didn't win, Richelle soon got another bunny because she liked the competition. She also started meeting people at the shows, and, according to her mom, even though Richelle was always the kind of kid who'd speak to anyone, she just bloomed throughout the years of showing her rabbits.[23]

Chapter 3

A teen can accomplish amazing things when the motivation comes from within. Richelle Hellpap wanted a portrait of herself with her favorite rabbit. She decided to teach herself to paint and signed up for an evening adult open painting class. Although a self-portrait can be difficult for even an accomplished artist, she saw it through with lots of encouragement from the teacher and her adult classmates, who all enjoyed her enthusiasm and determination. Photo used with permission, Richelle and Teresa Hellpap.

WORKING ANIMALS

While most of us think of teens as having a bond with the family dog or cat, some teens can develop friendships with animals that would be not be considered household "pets" and do not live in their homes. They may have parents who are reluctant to take on the responsibilities involved in caring for a dog or cat, so they have no family pets. There are many different avenues young people can explore with both domestic and nondomestic animals that do not actually live with them or live outside a human household. Entertainment venues such as SeaWorld's marine mammal shows or Renaissance Faire

---

IT HAPPENED TO ME: THE BOND IN ACTION

Brigitte Mason is an Illinois high school student who loves horses, competes in horse shows, and is planning to pursue a career in equine genetics. Like many teens involved with animals from a young age, Brigitte started riding lessons when she was young. "We always had pets at home. Once we got our barn completely built and we got Cookie (my horse), my dad said we could have animals as long as there was a place to have them live. We've had horses since I was eight and have since added four goats, a dog, and two cats. So animals have just always been here."

Because of the variety of animals Brigitte lives with, she has developed different relationships with the different species. "The goats are just kind of there; those are my mom's. I'm quite attached to the two cats just because I like their personalities. I wouldn't consider them as companions, but more like a pet. They come up to me when they want to be petted and then they leave when they want to be left alone. And that's how I like it. So I pet them when they want it and when they don't, I don't. But it's different with the horses, especially now with my quarter horse, because he's a *companion*. He's someone I like to go and spend time with and talk to. I'm usually out there doing something with him every chance I get. The first mare I got, my Arab, she's also a companion. Just because she was my first horse, there's that special bond of 'first horse' and being an animal that's all yours."

Like people, animals have different personalities. And sometimes their personalities do not mesh with ours. While Brigitte feels close to her two horses, she does not feel that way about all horses, even with other horses her family owns. For example, she doesn't consider her mom's horse to be a companion to her. "It's because she doesn't get along with *me*. So we have, like, some personality issues there. And then we have the older horse. He's really just more of a pet. He's just someone who's there, someone who is fun to do stuff with sometimes because he's safe and easygoing."[24]

Chapter 3

jousting and hawk demonstrations also offer chances to become part of the entertainment as well as participation as a spectator. Teens interested in nondomesticated animals or who want to pursue careers in related fields can also find internships and employment opportunities in places such as zoos, aquariums, amusements, and wildlife parks or refuges. Here they not only develop bonds with the animals, they also can develop friendships with other people involved in these places.

4-H is a huge nationwide organization with clubs and chapters in nearly every state. Originally developed at the beginning of the twentieth century to introduce new agricultural technology into farming communities, it gradually expanded to focus on teaching "leadership, citizenship and life skills" to young people living in both urban and nonurban areas. Its membership currently consists of youth from all types of backgrounds and walks of life. This national community has been instrumental for decades in encouraging youth and teens in positive involvement with animals.[25] Through local 4-H clubs, teens can raise animals classified as "livestock" and become involved in various county and state fair exhibitions and competitions. Many of these teens then go on to study for

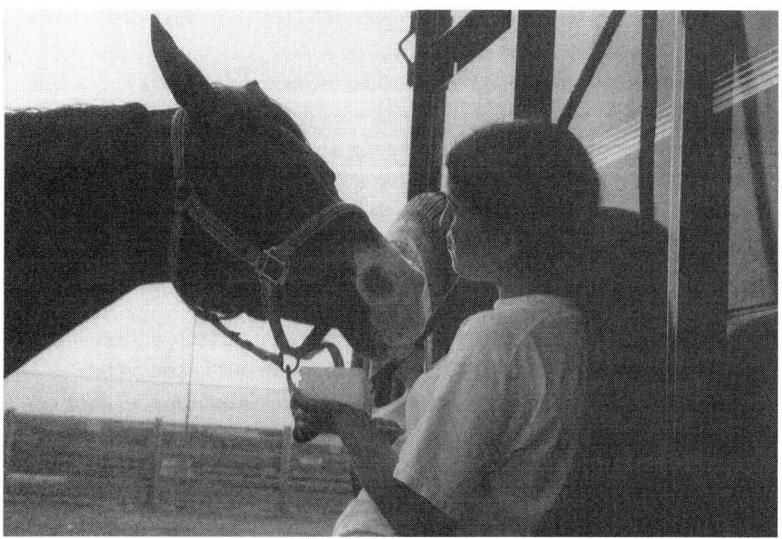

Brigitte Mason offers a salt lick to her horse Cookie, after a horse show. Photo used with permission, Brigitte and Robert Mason.

agricultural or other animal-related careers. Teens involved in 4-H activities often come from farming communities or families where raising livestock means that the animals are primarily being raised not as pets or companions, but for food and an income for the family. Kelli was involved in 4-H in high school, but she did not show livestock. "I think the mentality for that type of involvement with animals is that if you do well showing your animal, then they're gone; they're auctioned off if you win. I think some of that mentality does come from the area because you really couldn't be bonded with an animal knowing the end result. I could never do something like that. I've always thought of all my animals as friends."[26]

When animals are raised with lots of contact with humans and in human environments, they become used to things we take for granted. For example, a working dog kept in an outdoor kennel in the country, with no contact with people outside the owner's own family, is unlikely to be interested in meeting and greeting people it doesn't know, whereas a dog that is raised and kept inside a busy suburban family house where doorbells ring, people (including strangers) come and go, and the high-pitched shrieks of children are a daily occurrence will be more outgoing. While some working dogs can adjust if brought into a new environment with people who understood how to properly help the animal make the transition, much of the dog's personality will still be shaped by that initial imprint as a working dog. Brigitte's dad, Bob Mason, explains: "How a horse acts has something to do with how the horses were raised. Were they raised like horses or were they raised like dogs? If you have a horse that's a working animal and is raised like that, then that's how it will behave. They may become pets, but they start off as a working animal and, as such, you expect certain things of them. All our horses are working animals. Some people think they can change the animal into something else if they've been raised as working animals but they can't. But if you raise horses as pets, you get a different personality out of them."[27] Brigitte adds, "And we treat them in different ways. Like, my horse is more my performance companion than my pet, but I'll always expect stuff out of him that people who just look at their horses as pets or companions would not expect. Like, when I'm riding my horse, I expect him to behave the whole time I'm sitting on him."[28]

In addition to working with domestic animals normally associated with agriculture, teens may also become involved with working animals through participation in various sports that include anything from tracking or hunting with dogs to riding in rodeo competitions. Some teens also own or live with service dogs or miniature horses that work as therapy horses or guide horses. These animals are considered working animals, although they may also be treated as pets when not working. The difference between working animals and animals that are considered "just a pet" is that the working animal's primary function is to perform a task or series of tasks in addition to

> **IT HAPPENED TO ME: THE BOND IN ACTION**
>
> In addition to her rabbits, Richelle Hellpap also raised a lamb one year as a 4-H project. She knew going into it that whether she raised Charlie or someone else raised him, he was still going to be butchered, so she decided to make sure he had a good life for as long as he was alive. Because the Hellpaps could not take care of the lamb with Richelle in school and her parents were at work, Charlie stayed on the sheep farm during the week and came home with the Hellpaps on the weekends. At the Hellpaps' home, Charlie hung out on the deck with the family's golden retriever. Richelle feels strongly that Charlie had a better life than he would have if he had just been at the sheep farm all the time. "And we also had a better life bringing him home with us because we enjoyed him and he enjoyed us, although he mostly enjoyed being with our dog!"[29]

providing companionship, whereas a pet's primary purpose is to provide companionship. The bond between teens and these types of working animals, however, can still be very strong.

Kyle Fetters says, "It's amazing how selfless these animals can be. You know, like guard dogs that will give everything they have. Or working dogs that bring livestock wherever their owner tells them to, without any question, without them asking for anything in return. It really shows how strong a bond with an animal can be. In a human situation, there would be immediate questions and doubts, like 'Why am I wasting my time?' or 'Why am I even doing this for this person?' But that's never there when it comes to these animals."[30]

NURTURING AND COMPASSION: IT'S NOT ALL ABOUT ME

> "My dog has taught me to take a break, get up and away from the computer on a summer day and just go out in the yard to play ball or take a walk. If I didn't have a friend like him to whine and nag me to stop and play, I'd *never* get any fresh air!"—Katie Green, college student, Northern Illinois University[31]

Friendship is based on more than just accepting another creature's friendship and offering yours in return. Trust is an important part of the equation in both human-human and human-animal friendships. We trust our friends not to harm us, and they expect the same from us. But beyond basic trust that we will not harm them, what other ways do we demonstrate that they can trust us? While we may benefit greatly from our bond with animals, friendship should be mutually beneficial. Our companion animals are always there for us. But are we always there for them?

Chapter 3

Taking care of animals and bonding with them teaches young people many valuable life skills, including communication, responsibility, and compassion. People who interact positively with animals may actually become better nurturers. Teens who develop a strong bond with the animals they live with sometimes start thinking more like their animals and like adult humans than like people their own age. Because animals are dependent on us for so many things, teens actually need to think differently if they want the animal to survive and thrive. High school sophomore Jenn Papa agrees. "Our family recently got a new puppy and he is a handful! Someone has to be there all the time. You have to take him outside to go to the bathroom, walk him, run him, and basically do everything! Taking care of this puppy is kind of like being in training for having kids one day. If you have an animal, it's the same thing as having a kid in that you have to care about them in the same way."[32]

In developing a friendship with another living creature, we begin thinking outside ourselves. Once that transition occurs, we may also talk more about our animals than we talk about ourselves and choose their needs, feelings, and happiness above our own. This behavior is extremely atypical for most teens, who are normally in the "It's all about *me*" mode for years before they develop serious long-term relationships, have children, and turn to the "It's all about my child" mode instead. When teens become closely bonded to an animal, do they stop being self-centered and instead feel, "This is *my* responsibility; this is *my* baby"?

Brigitte believes the answer to this question is complex. "The nurturing part is definitely something my horse taught me, because although I may have cared because I knew it was the right thing to do, that's as far as it would have gone. But once I got my own horse and realized I had to start taking care of the horse and it isn't all about me, I became much more caring in general. I also became much more aware of other people's feelings and how different situations sometimes necessitated different feelings and responses. So, if I asked someone, 'Are you okay?' it actually meant that. I really *did* care if they were okay. If someone got hurt and needed something, I would actually go and get it, not just because I had to but also because I really did care."[33]

Mary Dyrhaug feels the same way about her dog, Mackenzie. "I almost know what she wants and needs by the looks she gives me. Our bond is very strong. There have always been babies in my family, so I'm used to taking care of others. But having her always around, always needing something, has taught me a lot—especially patience!"[34]

To have a life worth living, we need more than just our health and having our basic physical needs met. We also need to connect with those around us and to contribute to their lives. Many teens find it difficult to connect with family or social peers in a positive way. Interacting with a companion animal, however, can offer important moments of love, friendship, responsibility, and dependence we all crave. A dog's wagging tail or a cat's purring against our legs can instantly transform us from feeling isolated and alone to feeling needed. And because animals also look beyond our clothing, hair, and piercings and instead see the subtleties of our facial expressions and body language, they may understand us more intimately than most people are capable of doing.

Caring for an animal also introduces teens to respect, self-control, and responsibility. Although animals will not "cure" them of their problems, animals often reach them in ways other people and traditional treatments cannot, especially because an animal friend can offer unconditional love that is nonjudgmental. And as a result of positive interactions with animals, many troubled young people can become more responsible, more caring, and more able to improve their outlook on their situations or conditions. Teens who care for animals may also learn to take better care of themselves through taking care of others. Instead of sitting around for hours playing video games, chatting online, or just vegging in front of the television, teens can take their dog for a walk, play a game of cat-and-mouse with their cat, or make sure that their hamsters' bedding is clean. In doing so, they interact with another living creature instead of communicating solely through inanimate technology and also get some exercise at the same time. Making sure an animal is kept clean and comfortable can help reinforce the benefits of good hygiene in themselves.

Chapter 3

FRIENDS AND ACCEPTANCE

Much of what teens do and how they act is for the sole purpose of being acceptable to their peers. It takes courage to act out of the ordinary, especially in front of your peers. In human society, where girls are expected to be gentle and the guys are expected to be tough, showing compassion or nurturing in front of peers can often elicit varying responses.

For example, when it comes to empathy, Kyle has always had an appreciation for the simpler creatures that runs much deeper than just curiosity. "I think that there are times growing up when kids get the 'boys being boys' tough-guy attitude when they're trying to be tough and be hunters, like chasing after squirrels or whatever they might be doing. But I was always the one that was, like, 'Why are you doing that? *Save* a life!'"[35] Brigitte explains further: "If people know *how* I became caring they might think, 'Oh that's really weird,' but since I kind of started off teen-wise in [high school] with a new group of friends, they just kind of expect it. This is because at our school you don't push, you don't shove, you don't say mean things about anyone, and you are expected to be kind, caring, and a leader. You aren't expected to be a teen; you're expected to be a nice person. So the kids at my school wouldn't think that a caring aspect is weird at all although some other kids outside my school might."[36]

Pets can help teens feel less lonely just by wagging their tails or initiating play. Illustration by the author.

> "For me, animals have always been the perfect definition of innocence. That's where my appreciation comes in, because I think that what humans seem to lack, animals still can provide. When it comes down to it, all they really do is just *care* when they're attached to you. That's all. They're just like kids in a way."—Kyle Fetters, suburban teen[37]

Developing this mature attitude is especially important when owning a companion animal. Many typical college lifestyles put animals at risk by either exposing them to non-pet-proofed dwelling places with secondhand smoke, exposed electrical cords, and extermination chemical residue, where there is sometimes access to alcohol, drugs, and spoiled food.

Trish Hampton notes that owning her dog has completely changed how she thinks: "I was *the* typical college student before I owned my dog, Butchie. I used to go out drinking or partying with my friends three or four nights a week. I didn't care what time I got home and wasn't really even paying attention if I got to work or class on time. I just figured if I got there, I got there; if I didn't I'd just call in sick." Once Trish adopted her dog, however, all that changed. Trish now chooses to spend money on her dog's safety and well-being instead of on her own pleasure. Butchie has totally changed her life, but it is a change Trish willingly sought. "Not only have I cut down on how many nights I go out, I won't leave until I know she's settled in her kennel. I'll leave the music on so she doesn't feel she's alone in the dark or I'll get a sitter or board her for short periods of time. I am so concerned about making sure everything will be okay for her, that I've actually stopped calling up friends and saying, 'Let's go out.' Now technically I can still go out, but after paying a boarding fee, I don't have the money to party!"[38]

While taking care of animals and being responsible for their physical and emotional needs increases young people's levels of independence and responsibility, it also requires commitment and time. Teens are so busy with school, activities, and social life that spending time with their pets might not always be convenient. When teens have daily responsibilities taking care of multiple animals—or, in the case of teens like Brigitte or Richelle, who also have responsibilities getting ready for a show—what happens when their human friends want to do something like go to the beach or shop at the mall? How do teens respond when the voice on the other end of the phone is a classmate saying, "Hey, come to a party"? How understanding will friends be when you have to tell them you can't hang with them because you need to do something with your horse, dog, cat, or rabbit instead?

Brigitte responds: "Most of my friends understand because they also have extra activities that are as important to them as my horses are to me. The first words out of my friends' mouths will be, 'I know you have something to do with your horse, but . . .' They will actually ask me things like, 'I'm having a party from this time to this time, so tell me when you could be available to come just so I can see you for a little bit.' Overall my friends are all pretty understanding, and if they're not, it's kind of like I've chosen my horse and that's what I'm going to do. I can't tell my horse, 'Sorry, I can't feed you tonight because I decided I'm going to a party!' Now, my best friend does get tired of it a little bit, but that's because we've have known each other since second grade. She'll just roll her eyes and say, 'You're *always* doing something with your horse!' The one thing, however, is that the parties start later now. So if a party starts at eight o'clock instead of in the afternoon like they did when I was younger, I usually have most of my chores done by then, anyway. Otherwise I do my chores and then go."[39]

Not all of Trish's friends, however, accept the limitations that come with the responsibility of owning an animal. "A lot of my friends are *very* ticked off I have a dog! One of them actually told me he misses hanging out with me, but every time he calls me to see if I want to go out for a drink or hang out somewhere, I tell him, 'I have to find a sitter for the dog' or 'I need to do this for her' or 'I can't leave until she's asleep.' I can understand why he is upset with me though because he just had to put his two dogs down."[40] So while her friend truly misses the spontaneity of doing things with Trish, he may not lack understanding. It might be easier for him act annoyed and dismiss Trish's involvement with her dog than to be reminded of how much he misses his dogs.

Iowa college student Faye Nuddleman's friends also do not always understand. "I mostly have trouble going out at night with friends when I'm at home because I get distracted easily by the cats. It takes me an hour longer to get ready when I'm home than at school and most of my friends get upset with me. They have to come in when I'm getting ready so they can yell at me and tell me to stop playing with the cats. But my friend Emilee understands. She has the same problem with her dogs at home!"[41]

Teens who do not feel the need to "connect" with an animal tend to have a more self-focused lifestyle. They only have to think of themselves: what they want to do or what makes them happy. When teens develop a bond with a companion animal, however, their focus shifts away from themselves and onto their companion. Mary feels that shift actually marks an important milestone in transitioning from thinking like a child to becoming a mature adult. "I think that some of my friends who have never had a dog or are afraid of dogs are really missing out. Of course, they aren't aware that they are. But there's just something a dog or pet can give you that you can't get anywhere else."[42] Kristy Kosinski feels that caring for her birds has helped her become more responsible than many of her peers. "I have to be home at a decent hour to put them to bed and up at a reasonable time to wake them up. They're not as much work as a human child, but I'd say they're on par with dogs and the like, so at twenty years old I had four things to care for, while most of my peers were off living in dorms doing who knows what."[43]

YOU CAN DEPEND ON ME

Is it possible that taking care of animals helps prepare some teens to explore meaningful social relationships and eventually become parents? Growing up in a midsized city in Iowa, Faye feels animals helped her learn to nurture. "I never had any younger brothers or sisters, so I usually played with my dogs and cats as if they were my children. A lot of the kids I went to school with never thought of animals as being part of the family like I did."[44]

Kelli feels that taking care of an animal helps prepare teens for many of the responsibilities that come with parenting. "There are many people who think they can raise children, but they can't even raise a dog! Taking care of an animal is not as much responsibility as having a child but it's very similar. With both of them, there's someone depending on you. One difference is you can leave dogs in their crates for a while, but you can't do that with a kid."[45] Christina agrees: "Kitty has really taught me

Chapter 3

A mother models to her child the proper way to treat a puppy at an animal adoption event. Photos used with permission, Jeffrey Green, Total Recall Dog Training.

responsibility because I have to take care of her, feed her, clean her litter box, give her attention, play with her, and teach her right and wrong. At the same time, my experience with her has also taught me to feed myself right, keep good hygiene, and clean my room. I think having a pet is the perfect first step before having a baby, because then you can make sure you are able to take care of someone else. Plus, if you find out that you aren't responsible enough yet to take care of someone, it'd be easier to put a pet up for adoption than if you started with a child first." Although Christina doesn't think teens should get a pet with the intention of just giving it away if things get a little difficult, she adds, "A child's something you really can't just give away."[46]

Teens who are totally committed to their companion animal's comfort, safety, and care may have friends who are not responsible enough to be trusted with the safety and well-being of another living creature. It's challenging enough to be responsible for an animal when you live at home with other family members who are equally committed, but when you bring a pet into a college environment with roommates (and their friends)—especially ones not familiar with taking care of animals—the potential risk of danger to your pet increases.

SAFETY FOR ANIMALS ON CAMPUS

Choosing a college and finding suitable housing is a challenge for any student bound for higher education. Whether a student lives on campus in a university dorm or apartment, off campus in private housing, or commutes from home, one thing is certain: The college lifestyle can present dangers to companion animals. Items that pose a danger should never be left anywhere your pet can touch or ingest them. Some of these potential problems include:

- **Cans, bottles, and glasses from alcoholic beverages**
- **Makeup, medications, and other personal hygiene products**
- **Open windows with no screens, electrical cords, computer wires, etc., which are potentially dangerous for any animal that chews or become entangled in them**
- **Foods like chocolate, avocados, and onions, and many common houseplants that are harmless to humans but toxic to animals.**

BRIDGING THE GAP

Animals have an amazing ability to bridge the gap between different types of people. Instead of seeing other animal lovers as being a specific race, culture, or age, we instead perceive them as people with a common interest in animals. Is this because people who love animals tend to connect better to others, or is it because we have learned from our companion animals how to choose who we can trust?

Kyle feels it's a little of both. "For example, you might see someone walking down the street and judge them unfairly just from the way they look. But if you see that same person walking with a dog, that perception changes. Of course, while some people might think they can read what kind of person you are based on the type of dog you're with, just having an animal around you shows a certain level of companionship and compassion. Granted, there are also some species (like snakes)

Chapter 3

> **IT HAPPENED TO ME: THE BOND IN ACTION**
>
> Growing up with younger brothers and sisters, Trish Hampton was used to closing doors behind her and felt that caretaking and nurturing were just extensions of how she grew up. But when teens who have never taken care of anyone else or are still learning to become self-sufficient suddenly become responsible for an animal, it is often the animal that suffers from their lack of experience. One incident that changed Trish's life made this quite apparent.
>
> Trish had gone out and left her dog, Butchie, in her apartment, safely locked in the kitchen behind a baby gate, like she always did. Some time later, one of her roommates called to tell her that Butchie had just been hit by a car because the roommate's boyfriend had left the door open and the dog had gotten out, chased a squirrel, and ran into the street. Butchie's injuries were not life threatening; however, Trish was really upset because she was so far away at that point. She instructed her roommate to take the dog to the nearest emergency vet office and that she would meet her there as soon as she could. "I was so worried if Butchie was going to be okay, if she would need surgery or if she'd need a cast . . . basically if she was alive! I was crying and crying and crying. And by the time I got to the vet, I was furious." But her roommate hugged her immediately and told her how sorry she was—that it was an accident and that they didn't mean for this to happen. That calmed Trish down quite a bit. Fortunately, Butchie just had a few scrapes and bruises and a minor fracture in her pelvis. But Trish was definitely not prepared for the emergency vet care bill. Also, Butchie had only limited movement and couldn't navigate the stairs for about a week, so she needed to be carried everywhere, which meant Trish had to take time off from work. Although her roommate's boyfriend told Trish how sorry he was and that he didn't mean for it to happen, about a week later he left the back door open again right in front of Trish. "Butchie got up and started walking to the door. When she got about two feet from the door, he realized, 'Oh, my gosh! I have to close the door!' and he quickly went and closed the door."[47]

or types (like pit bulls) of animals that are scarier for some people. Not that there's anything wrong with the animals or the people, but because those animals can be more violent or aggressive, it would then take a more dominant and confident person to keep those animals in line. And there are also people who choose certain animals or breeds for reasons that have nothing to do with compassion but to reflect the kind of person they are or how they will look. For example, if I was walking down the street with a poodle versus two giant pit bulls, people will think totally differently about me. And if a girl was walking down the street with two giant pit bulls, people would have a different impression of her than if she was with a poodle."[48]

Friendship

Young people who are involved with animal activities may find they don't have to be as socially competitive as their classmates, because involvement with animals and animal-related activities also teaches fairness and respect for others. Teens already involved with companion animals take this to another level when they develop friendships from and through their involvement in animal sports. Brigitte explains, "I have what I call my 'horse friends,' who are a completely different group from my school friends. And then when you are at school you can have just five friends and that's completely okay because you don't have to worry 'Am I popular at school?' or anything like that. You know you're okay because you also have your horse friends. It's nice to know you have another group of friends you can depend on."[49] And those "horse friends," "dog friends," or "rabbit friends" not only vary in age, they also help blur cultural, economic, and other differences. In animal sports and shows, everyone is equal. There, it isn't about age, culture, or status; it's how you behave—how you treat each other and encourage and help each other out. From her numerous experiences in 4-H activities and rabbit shows, Richelle feels camaraderie can develop through competition. "At the rabbit shows, we talk the whole time because we all have a common interest with the rabbits. Plus, there is less of a gap between the people who show animals, no matter what their age or background, because we tend to also have the same problems in general." It's different in high school, however. There, Richelle sees a gap between people based on their neighborhood or race, whereas at the rabbit shows those barriers are already broken down between different people because their common interest makes these and other differences insignificant, so none of that matters.[50]

When Christina started college at Kentucky State University, she found herself in the minority, both culturally and racially. "I had a really hard time making friends, due to color, but when people would come to my dorm room to see my roommate they'd also see a picture of my cat that I had up on my bulletin board. And they'd start to talk to me and get to know me for me, instead of my color. With one girl, it reminded her of home and how much she missed her cats. It gave us a chance to bond and become friends because it was something we both cared so much about."[51]

Chapter 3

MAKING COMPASSION A LIFESTYLE

The sense of responsibility teens develop through their close bond with animals can also carry over into their relationships with other people. Christina says: "Having a close bond with Kitty also helped me with my coaching basketball to young kids. I learned to be more sensitive and understanding of some one else's needs; to give love and not yell at them."[52]

Richelle began visiting nursing homes with her animals when her 4-H leader initiated a service project. At the first visit, Richelle fell so in love with the people that her leader couldn't get her to leave because she was so busy visiting all the residents and hearing about their histories and lives. For example, a ninety-two-year-old lady in a wheelchair, who was being pushed by her seventy-year-old daughter, saw the bunny and started crying. When asked why she was crying, the daughter said her mother had never touched a rabbit. The woman's expression of joy touched Richelle so much, she decided that every person in that nursing home needed to touch her bunnies. So instead of staying in the community room with the rest of the 4-H volunteers, Richelle went door to door with her rabbits, taking them out of the basket and putting them in the beds with the patients while she sat and talked with them. She began visiting regularly, first with her rabbits, then with her dog and her duck, and she often visits without her animals because she enjoys the residents' stories so much.

Although many teens are self-centered and egocentric, those involved with animals exhibit compassion for all living things. And because of their actions, these teens and the animals they love can become role models in friendship for everyone around them. College graduate Reshoma Banerjee feels strongly that caring for an animal teaches you how to care for something outside of yourself and, in turn, teaches you how to be responsible. "Responsibility is a major issue when it comes to young people having pets. Pets are like an extension of the family, so you need to teach yourself how to care for them. But it's not just responsible guardianship. It's also a living example of the true meaning of love and friendship, which is to do everything you can to keep them surviving and sustaining a life that's worth living."[53]

NOTES

1. Christina Aviza, interview with the author, November 23, 2006.
2. Linda Blasser, "Make New Friends," *Buffalo Grove Countryside*, December 28, 2006, 61–62.
3. Merriam-Webster's Online Dictionary, "Friend," www.merriam webster.com/dictionary/friend (accessed April 14, 2007).
4. Kyle Fetters, interview with the author, September 2006.
5. Chase Herndon, interview with the author, February 2007.
6. Christina Aviza, e-mail to the author, November 23, 2006.
7. Dana Bouchard, interview with the author, September 2006.
8. Bouchard, interview with the author, September 2006.
9. Brigitte Mason, interview with the author, August 23, 2006.
10. Aviza, interview with the author, November 23, 2006.
11. Kelli Herbel, interview with the author, September 2006.
12. Herbel, interview with the author, September 2006.
13. Fetters, interview with the author, September 2006.
14. Andy Wick, interview with the author, September 16, 2006.
15. Tracy Glickauf, e-mail to the author, October 2006.
16. Karen McCoy, interview with the author, September 8, 2006.
17. Jessica Katz, interview with the author, December 2006.
18. Aviza, interview with the author, November 23, 2006.
19. Wick, interview with the author, September 16, 2006.
20. Herbel, interview with the author, September 2006.
21. Herbel, interview with the author, September 2006.
22. Katz, interview with the author, December 2006.
23. Richelle Hellpap, interview with the author, September 2006.
24. Mason, interview with the author, August 23, 2006.
25. National 4-H Headquarters, www.national4-hheadquarters.gov (accessed April 16, 2007).
26. Herbel, interview with the author, September 2006.
27. Robert Mason, interview with the author, August 23, 2006.
28. Brigitte Mason, interview with the author, August 23, 2006.
29. Hellpap, interview with the author, September 2006.
30. Fetters, interview with the author, September 2006.
31. Katie Green, interview with the author, September 2006.
32. Jenn Papa, interview with the author, October 2006.
33. Brigitte Mason, interview with the author, August 23, 2006.
34. Mary Dyrhaug, interview with the author, January 2007.
35. Fetters, interview with the author, September 2006.
36. Brigitte Mason, interview with the author, August 23, 2006.

Chapter 3

37. Fetters, interview with the author, September 2006.
38. Trish Hampton, interview with the author, September 2006.
39. Brigitte Mason, interview with the author, August 23, 2006.
40. Hampton, interview with the author, September 2006.
41. Faye Nuddleman, interview with the author, April 2007.
42. Dyrhaug, interview with the author, January 2007.
43. Kristy Kosinski, interview with the author, January 2007.
44. Nuddleman, interview with the author, April 2007.
45. Herbel, interview with the author, September 2006.
46. Aviza, interview with the author, November 23, 2006.
47. Hampton, interview with the author, September 2006.
48. Fetters, interview with the author, September 2006.
49. Brigitte Mason, interview with the author, August 23, 2006.
50. Aviza, interview with the author, November 23, 2006.
51. Hellpap, interview with the author, September 2006.
52. Aviza, interview with the author, November 23, 2006.
53. Reshoma Banerjee, interview with the author, December 2006.

4 Choosing Our Companion Animals

MAKING CHOICES

We all have to make decisions; it's part of being alive. A simple choice like which pizza topping we prefer is easy to make, but many other decisions may require more effort. Buying a car, moving to a new house, or picking the right college are all big decisions. In fact, young people may switch colleges and majors almost as often as they change their jeans. It isn't uncommon for college graduates to have attended two or three colleges or universities by the time they receive their undergraduate degrees!

Important decisions take time, commitment, and thought. While we usually don't make these types of decisions in haste, many people choose a companion animal based on impulse. A cell phone or car can be sold or traded in if it doesn't perform well or is quickly outgrown, but animals shouldn't be thought of as commodities. And unlike switching colleges or majors when we change our minds, it is not reasonable to assume that if a pet doesn't perform well or we outgrow our interest, we can just get rid of it or neglect it. It's a big step to bring an animal into a household, and there are big decisions that should be made before that happens.

Animals are a big responsibility. Depending on the animal, you may be taking on a ten- to twenty-five-year or longer commitment, with the inevitable changes in routine and living space or the noise and messes that can accompany the type of animal you are considering. Daily feedings, making sure the

"People shouldn't get pets if they aren't ready to care for them or love them."

—Natasha McDonald, suburban high school student[1]

Chapter 4

> ### A PERSONAL GLIMPSE
>
> **Communications major Kelli Herbel is a third-generation dog handler who has been showing dogs in AKC breed shows since she was a child. Beginning with handling her own dog as a "junior handler" at age ten, Kelli was showing other people's dogs in the show circuit by the time she was sixteen. But she always thought of the dogs as companions rather than just dogs to show as commodities. "They were *all* my friends! I never really understood the mentality of people who show any kind of animal as just a show animal. I mean, for you and the animal to show well, they just do better if you are both enjoying doing it and have some sort of bond."[2]**

water bowl is always clean and filled, daily dog walks, and cleaning cages, stalls, tanks, or litter boxes all take time and commitment. Is everyone in the family willing to adjust? Companion animals will need to adapt to humans and their rules, but that takes time and effort, especially with those that may be more independent or more dominant, or have instinctive needs or actions that conflict with what is acceptable to us. For example, large birds such as cockatoos and macaws not only need incredible amounts of social interaction with their human flock, they also have an instinctive need to chew, potentially creating lots of mess and damaging human possessions. They also are very vocal (read: noisy) and can be rambunctious or attention seeking at what might be considered by teens to be very inappropriate times!

Financial considerations such as food, equipment, bedding, vaccinations, spay/neutering, and routine vet care should be added in, along with the potential for additional vet bills due to illness or injury. Animals can accidentally get out of the house, ingest things they shouldn't, or develop diseases. As an example, routine teeth cleaning may cost around $300, but treating a dog for some types of cancer may cost more than $5,000. Broken legs, intestinal blockages, and other surgical procedures can add up in the thousands, as well. And with dogs

Choosing Our Companion Animals

> **THESE ANIMALS ARE REALLY SMOKING!**
>
> Research has shown that smoking is not good for our health, but have we also considered the impact of secondhand smoke on our companion animals? A young person may not smoke, but roommates, friends, or family members who smoke may place resident companion animals in danger. Not only do cats and dogs exposed to large amounts of smoke develop eye inflammation and chronic discharge, there seems to be another serious potential side effect. Studies conducted at the Tufts School of Veterinary Medicine have discovered a strong connection between secondhand smoke and cancer of the mouth in cats. An additional study at Colorado State University indicates that dogs may develop a higher rate of nasal cancer when exposed to the smoke, as well. For more information on these studies visit www.tufts.edu/vet and www.cvmbs.colostate.edu.[3]

living an average of ten to fifteen years and cats living fifteen to twenty years or more, these numbers can really add up over a lifetime! There is also the emotional investment of loving a companion animal and then having to eventually say goodbye with euthanasia, burial, or cremation.

The time you spend evaluating your situation and researching what animal or breed might best suit your lifestyle and personality will be time well spent. Bringing an animal into your life should not be an impulsive act or a decision made on a whim. Instead, the choice should be predicated on whether you and/or your family have the desire, ability, time, and resources that it will take to care properly for that specific animal throughout its lifetime.

ALLERGIES

Allergies can affect the type of animal you choose to live with. People allergic to animals are usually reacting to an animal's dander (dead skin continually being shed), saliva, or urine. While cats and dogs top the list, other animals such as birds,

Chapter 4

Puppy Love: Bonding with Tuxedo, a border collie puppy. Drawing by Katie Green, used with permission.

rabbits, or horses can also trigger reactions in humans. There may also be specific breeds or types within a species that cause more symptoms than others. For example, a person may be sensitive to golden retrievers but not to poodles. The amount and time of exposure can also play a critical part. While severely allergic people often experience symptoms within minutes of entering a home where an animal lives, others may show symptoms only when exposed for extended periods of time or if exposed to multiple animals in the same environment.

Although no one in Kelli Herbel's family is allergic to dogs, her boyfriend is. "He can be around some dogs, but not all of them. He has border collies and loves them, but they don't live inside his house. My German shepherd sheds a lot and bothers him the most, so that's been kind of tough. So we wind up spending most of our time at his place because there's dog hair everywhere in the air in mine. It's hard for me

Choosing Our Companion Animals

> **HAIR'S TO ALLERGIES!**
>
> Although there is no such thing as a 100 percent hypoallergenic dog, breeds with nonshedding coats cause fewer reactions because they produce less dander. What makes one dog breed less likely than another to trigger allergic symptoms? The answer is simple: Along with their minimal shedding, they have hair instead of fur, so many people with allergies can live quite comfortably with them.[4]
>
> Some breeds less likely to provoke allergies include:
> **Bedlington terrier**
> **bichon frise**
> **Chinese crested**
> **Irish water spaniel**
> **Kerry blue terrier**
> **Maltese**
> **poodle (all varieties)**
> **Portuguese water dog**
> **schnauzer (all varieties)**
> **soft-coated wheaten terrier**

to truly empathize with him because I really don't know what it's like to have allergies. I mean, growing up with dogs and being at dog shows, you eat food there and you know there's dog hair in it because there's dog hair everywhere at a dog show."[5]

Sometimes sensitivities to animals just develop. And they can develop at any age. However, people whose parents have allergies or who have sensitivities to other environmental substances are more likely to develop or exhibit reactions to increased contact with animals. Chase Herndon has experienced this. "I developed allergies around sophomore year of high school. Recently I've had to go see an allergist as it's become progressively worse. In a few years, I will probably end up just getting shots so I can continue working with animals without worrying."[6] Fortunately, Chase reacts to animals with fur and not feathers, so he is still able to maintain his close bond with his African gray parrot, Yoshi.

Chapter 4

Chase Herndon with Yoshi, an African gray parrot. Photo used with permission, Charles Herndon.

Jessica Katz has to take allergy medication. "And, since I am also an asthmatic, exposure to animals can cause issues." Jessica's allergies and asthma have also affected her choice of animals. "I grew up with fish because I was very allergic to everything else when I was young. I am still sensitive to cats and small animals and small animal bedding. But now that I am older we have more pets, including my Standard Schnauzer, Hobbs, who I luckily did not have allergies to. In fact, I attribute my love of animals to her. If we hadn't gotten her, I would have never walked into the pet store, gotten a job or be pursuing animal studies in school!"[7]

Teens who would like to have a pet but have allergy issues with furry animals might discover that fish or various types of amphibians and reptiles such as frogs, turtles, or lizards make good alternatives. According to Kyle Fetters, who has had reptiles growing up, "They are a more 'neutral' pet in that sense." Cats and dogs especially will leave traces of allergens throughout a home, but because reptiles usually live in containers that are confined and self-contained, the chance of allergic reaction with family members also diminishes.[8]

> ### KEEP ALLERGIES UNDER CONTROL
>
> There are ways to keep reactions to animals under control for you, your family, and guests.
>
> - Keep animals such as dogs or cats out of bedrooms, off the furniture, and out of the car, or use covers that are washed frequently.
> - Wash your hands after handling animals, pet toys, or bedding. Avoid touching your eyes or nose when handling them and do not allow animals to lick you.
> - Clean and vacuum often and run a portable HEPA air cleaner in rooms where there are animals.
> - Brush pets daily and, if possible, bathe weekly. Use an allergy-reducing spray on your pets after grooming. Feed your pets high-quality food with enough fatty acids to keep their skin healthy and prevent excess shedding.
> - Check with your doctor for allergy medications, shots, or other possible treatments.

WHAT'S YOUR LIFESTYLE?

When exploring the many variables involved in choosing a companion animal, we also need to consider different human lifestyles. Could variables such as living in an apartment versus a home, or living in the country as opposed to an urban environment, help determine what type of animal will best fit a young person's lifestyle? Jessica believes that choosing a pet is more than just preferring one type of animal. "It's also a matter of space and time commitment. For example, if you are a busy executive living in the heart of a large city, then maybe a desktop aquarium would be the best choice. But if you have acres and acres in the country you can basically choose whatever animal or animals your heart desires, as long as you take care of them properly."[9]

College grad Jason Green grew up in suburbia with dogs, but now lives in a multiple story building in a dense urban neighborhood. The condo building he lives in has a strict "no dogs" policy. "Yeah, my parents can't even bring their dogs to visit. It's kind of not fair because I'd like to have my dogs visit me, but on the other hand, it would be total chaos if everyone in the building had dogs. Not to mention the chance of messes in the hallways or a dog fight in the elevator!" There are no restrictions, however, on fish and other simpler creatures that live in a contained environment, so Jason has a large saltwater aquarium in his condo that he maintains diligently. "I've always been fascinated with the delicate balance of the coral reef, so it's been a real challenge, as well as a pleasure, keeping this going. And I'm considering adding a second tank, just because I enjoy caring for these creatures so much."[10]

An important factor to consider is the type of animal best suited to you and your personality. Although parental choices, space, allergies, and time commitments may determine the animals or breeds teens have close contact with, are there also distinctive temperament differences between young people who actively choose one type of companion animal over another?

Even a solitary goldfish in a bowl can offer companionship. Illustration by the author.

Choosing Our Companion Animals

SLEEP HABITS

Different animals have different sleep-wake patterns, depending on their biological clock. Although most wakefulness is naturally triggered by daylight, nocturnal animals such as cats, raccoons, and owls are more awake at night and prefer to sleep during the day. Does that sound familiar? Most teens would agree that they prefer to stay up until the wee hours of the night and then sleep until noon or later. Since most teens tend to be night owls, a nocturnal animal such as a hamster or cat might be a great choice!

Within different species, breeds exist that vary in traits such as independence and ability to be handled. For example, the bold, spirited Thoroughbred horse is a much different companion animal than the more docile, easy-to-handle American quarter horse. Is it possible we are attracted to a particular type of animal because our individual personalities mimic or mesh with that pet? For example, some teens are more socially active in groups or "packs," while others are more content with a friend or two or consider themselves as "loners."

Based on her own experience growing up with animals and working at a vet clinic, Kelli thinks there might indeed be a

Dogs and cats will usually sleep during the day while teens and other family members are gone. Illustration by the author.

correlation between temperament and the attraction of specific humans to specific animals: "Cats *are* very solitary and independent. I see cats as being more 'about me' whereas dogs are 'everything's about you.' I also learned from working at the vet clinic, dogs seem to be attached to people while cats seem more attached to places. And that actually kind of goes along with choosing dog breeds, too, because certain dog breeds are very independent. My grandparents bred Lhasa Apsos, which are a very independent breed. It really is all about them. I actually consider them to be the cats of the dog world. Whether they think they need you or not, they like to act like they don't. And a lot of cat owners may also think like that, kind of like they don't need anyone else."[11]

When we consider that dogs are pack animals, horses are herd animals, birds are flock animals, and so on, and that animals like cats, hamsters and reptiles are naturally more solitary, perhaps people who feel more comfortable with certain types of animals feel that way because it is easier to develop a bond with something that is familiar. As Katie Green states, "It is better to make the choice of having one happy Betta fish swimming around in his little 'Betta bowl' than to know you have failed an animal that is lonely and miserable because you made the wrong choice to be his guardian."[12]

Adapting is part of the survival instinct. Dogs learn to see their humans as their pack. Herd and flock animals, like horses and birds, also adapt to living with multiple people just as they would a herd of horses or a flock of birds. However, many people expect animals to just adapt to us without our help. Without it, many animals wind up in shelters. Jessica believes animals need to know what to expect when they live with humans. "People don't really understand what they are undertaking with a Malaccan Cockatoo or a full size macaw. It takes at least three or four interactive hours a day with a bird like this, and if you are not able to fully accept the bird into the family you are probably going to have an unhappy animal. Every animal needs routine in its life and the human owner needs to be consistent. No matter what type they are, companion animals need to look to the human for reassurance and know that is how they are supposed to behave."[13]

Kyle has some additional advice for young people. "If you're someone who's looking to do something worthwhile, definitely invest some time in animals. The biggest thing is you have to do whatever's right for you and your circumstances, but especially what will be best for the animal. Just don't overwhelm yourself with a bunch of animals thinking that's the answer to any problem you might have, because that could just be more stressful. That's the most important thing to remember, because many teens think it's either all or none . . . that you either have to have a lot of something or none at all. Our family happens to have four dogs and five cats. A lot of people would think that's a lot, but for us it is fine. And one dog or one cat or even one fish in a bowl can be just fine for other people. If you're looking for a good companion and loyalty, you really can't go wrong as long as you always offer the same back to the animal."[14]

THE CANINE-HUMAN BOND: MAN'S BEST FRIEND

> "When I first lived on my own I hungered for a strong bond with a dog. When I was having a bad day, it was comforting to come home to a being that had unconditional love for me. Also, I didn't have to explain myself to Risky; she was just there for me. Still is."—Tracy Glickauf, Beloit College graduate

Ask dog lovers why they love dogs and you will hear as many reasons as there are breeds. Like us, dogs are social creatures that love to play and interact. Dogs see us as members of their pack, while we see them as a member of our family. It is because of this instinctive similarity that dogs also possess the ability to fit right into different human household environments and situations. Whether it is because they make us feel safe, make us laugh, or just provide companionship, one of the main reasons people love dogs so much is that they give unconditional love.

Chapter 4

Rebecca Britz with a litter of puppies. Photo used with permission, Rebecca Britz.

As one teen put it, dogs simply "make us feel good because they are always happy to see us!"

Dog ownership responsibilities can mean different things to different people, depending on where they live as well as their specific circumstances. For example, owning a dog or several dogs in suburban or rural settings can be very different from owning a dog in a large city or other urban setting. One of the most significant factors involved is that of walking the dog. When young people live in apartments that have no yards or where dogs are not allowed to use the yard for a bathroom, walking a dog several times a day is a big responsibility, especially if they have to travel in elevators or up and down several flights of stairs, exit the building, and be escorted a block or more to a park or other area where they can relieve themselves. And the climate and the dog's health or age—as well as their owner's—are other variables that often play a large role in deciding on the size and type of dog to choose.

> **IT HAPPENED TO ME: THE BOND IN ACTION**
>
> Art student Andy Wick lived in an apartment in Chicago's south Loop while attending college when he chose to adopt a dog he named KB. It was a very difficult time for both Andy and KB while they learned to live with each other. "KB's only toys had been old tires and bricks, so he had to go through a complete change. He had absolutely no idea how to play or interact with humans. The first months were really nuts. But he finally got the idea that I was there to nurture him and he then adapted to that real fast. I had to walk two blocks just to go to the park and there was a lot of traffic and lots of noise, too. So he really had to get used to people and other dogs and all kinds of things going on."[15]

THE FELINE-HUMAN BOND: RELAX AND PURR

Second in popularity only to dogs, cats top the list as one of our favorite companion animals. Young people who may be gone from early in the morning to late in the afternoon attending school, work, and other activities often prefer having a cat. One of the downsides to owning a dog is that someone has to be there to let the dog out every few hours. Cats, however, do not

Chapter 4

> "Cats help me to unwind. Their presence is really just very relaxing to me and I feel really de-stressed whenever they're just rubbing against my legs or purring."—Kelli Herbel, University of Oklahoma student[16]

need to be brought outside or taken for walks to "do their business." And unlike many dogs that would basically eat until their stomachs burst, cats are very content nibbling on food throughout the day.

Another reason people choose to have a cat is simply that they are not allowed to have a dog where they live. Newlywed Jey McGahan adopted her cat, Dexter, from the Anti-Cruelty Society a few years before she got married. "I grew up with dogs, but I chose a cat because I lived in an apartment that didn't allow dogs. Dexter is pretty independent, but he has the spirit of a dog in him, so it was a pretty good choice. It was nice having someone who loved me unconditionally to come home to every day."[17]

Cats adapt to living in human households by learning about humans. This makes them very attuned to our moods and feelings. Cats can also help calm, which gives teens a sense of peace. In our stress-filled world, that ability to help relieve our anxieties and make us feel peaceful makes the cat a very valuable companion.

The bond teens can have with their cats can be just as intense as with any other companion animal. Christina Aviza comments about her cat, Kitty: "I love her so much; it's going to be the hardest thing in the world when she dies. She's not just a pet; she's family, too." Christina adds this advice for all teens who choose to have a close bond with a companion animal: "Love them no matter what. It's the best feeling ever when something loves you so much, especially when you don't have to do that much for them and you don't expect anything in return."[18]

Faye Nuddleman and feline friend at a cat show. Photo used with permission, Faye Nuddleman.

THE EQUINE-HUMAN BOND: POETRY IN MOTION

A companion animal can also be an animal many people consider to be livestock. Anyone who has ever watched a horse and a rider knows that there is no other animal that can command so much power and speed and at the same time share that experience with humans. Horseback riding is not the only activity that establishes rapport between animal and human,

Chapter 4

and teens who choose involvement with horses must do more with them than ride. Horses need a lot of care and are expensive to care for. Horses need to be groomed, fed, shoed, and brought out to pasture and back into the safety and shelter of their stables. In addition, their stalls need to be kept clean and fences kept in repair. Cleaning a horse's stall is much more time-consuming than cleaning a rabbit cage, for example, and may also involve lots of dust and mess. Teens who have made the commitment to horses, however, don't seem to mind these chores because it is often through these activities that a closer connection is developed.

Brigitte Mason has had horses for years and rides and shows her horses in competitions all over the country. A high school student, she still finds the time to maintain her horse caretaking as well as her school work and a busy social life. While Brigitte doesn't share the same interest in other tasks, like cooking, her parents totally support and encourage her in her involvement with her horses. Her father, Bob Mason, says, "And that's totally forgivable because of the way she applies herself through her horses and the way she conducts herself in school and in her extracurricular activities. It wasn't like we said, 'If you don't do

Brigitte Mason enjoys a beautiful winter ride with Cookie. Photo used with permission, Brigitte and Robert Mason.

this, then we'll take your horse.' She had the horses and she acted responsibly. We don't have TV and she can't get anywhere without our car so she is trapped enough right now!"[19]

Like other teens with animals that need to be cared for on-site, Brigitte has made the choice to not leave for any extended periods of time unless someone is home to take over her responsibilities. Instead of going on more traditional family vacations, Brigitte's family often plans trips that include the horses. But once in a while the Masons cannot incorporate their horses with their family vacations. Brigitte explains, "Then the horses stay behind. They're part of the family, but they stay behind then. I miss them, but it is a good break from being with them all the time and having to do stuff. And then, of course, I'm very happy to see them when I get back!"[20]

CHOOSING A BOND WITH BIRDS, RABBITS, SMALL MAMMALS, REPTILES, AND OTHER EXOTICS

Not all teens wind up bonding with dogs or cats. And sometimes what starts out as a casual interest can develop into something much more.

Although vet assistant Kristy Kosinski didn't have any pets until she was six years old, she has always loved animals and would spend hours looking out the window watching the birds and squirrels. Then she got a cockatiel named Spike. Although Kristi spent less time with him during junior high, by the time she was sixteen or seventeen years old, she snapped out of that "too cool for anything related to home" thing and decided to reinforce their earlier bond. "I realized what a treasure I had. He's very sweet and gentle with me, sings songs for just me, preens my eyebrows and eyelashes, and is in general just a great bird. And he is very strongly bonded to me."[21] After graduating high school Kristi adopted her second bird, Kiwi, a Greater Jardine (an African parrot), and then Peanut (a budgie that her aunt found outside), and Brutus (a cockatiel she fostered and later adopted from A Refuge for Saving the Wildlife). By the time she was twenty, Kristy chose to give the veterinary field a try and got a full-time job as a vet assistant at a small animal practice.

Chapter 4

Cockatiels are intelligent, social birds that often mimic the sounds they hear. Drawing by Katie Green, used with permission.

Some young people feel that animals such as reptiles, fish, rabbits, or hamsters may be perfect matches for them because they lack the time to devote to animals that need more attention. Ruth Toht, a high school student, decided to get a hamster instead of a dog because she is involved with extracurricular sports activities in addition to hours of homework each night. "Most people just think that because hamsters are just little animals, you don't care about it, but once you get a hamster you get really attached to them. I have a hamster whose name is Domino. I play with him a lot and pet him. If I'm having a bad day, I usually sit on the couch, get something warm to drink and have Domino just playing

> ### WHEN SOMETHING GOES WRONG: HOW SOCIETY VIEWS ANIMALS
>
> When we choose to have an animal that is protective or that society views as dangerous to approach, we sometimes are forced to make difficult choices we wish we didn't have to make. Whether right or wrong, many municipalities have ordinances prohibiting certain dog breeds that have the potential to harm through misdirecting or misinterpreting their instinct to protect. In 2006, Andy Wick finally received word that he had been accepted at the University of Oregon, a school he had really been trying to get into. But because the notice was last minute, he only had two weeks to find an apartment out of state, get packed, and move. His plan, of course, was to bring KB with him—that is, until he discovered how difficult it was to find a landlord willing to rent to him where the university was located. So even though Andy was now able to attend the school of his choice, it appeared that the dog he had rescued, lived with, and loved for four years couldn't come with him. "Basically what I've found was that no one wants to take on the responsibility for housing bully breeds. [Landlords and management companies] kept on saying their insurance wouldn't take him even if I have insurance for my dog. KB's got a whole résumé from the past landlords he's been with, and they still wouldn't accept him. What disturbs me the most is that any breed, including smaller dogs, can also bite. And small dogs cause just as much damage in an apartment. He's not a 'pet' to me. He *is* my life right there; he *is* my family. Like, he is what I was considering the very beginning of 'my' family, or at least my own branch of it. I wanted him to stay with me for the rest of his time and my time, that's the thing. But I have to go on with my life. I've got to do what I need to do in order to survive in this world, which means going back to school. And it's going to be very bad; it's going to be hurtful. He's just been so precious to me."[22]

around. That usually makes me feel better. He's kind of my little friend here at home."[23]

Sometimes our choices in companion animals are a direct result of outside influences. Kyle has had at least some type of reptile for as long as he can remember and is a perfect example of a teen whose choices were partly influenced by the media. "Growing up when Steve Irwin came out, made him a big part of my life and I really enjoyed doing the 'Steve Irwin' thing, kind of going out and trying to find reptiles in their real habitat and catching them. I wouldn't try to keep them or anything; I just enjoyed touching them and looking at them and all. Then I'd release them. Or, on occasion I'd come across some creatures that were being picked on and then I'd help them out."[24]

Companion animals can serve as noncritical, loving friends who patiently listen to us no matter what. They, in turn, can find purpose and pleasure interacting with humans who provide all the comforts they need. When we consider all these factors and choose our pets based on what is best for the animal, we take another step toward becoming responsible animal guardians.

NOTES

1. Natasha McDonald, interview with the author, December 2006.
2. Kelli Herbel, e-mail to the author, September 2006.
3. "Second-Hand Smoke Is Bad for Pets," *Pet Product News International* (October 2006): 41.
4. Nancy Muklewicz, "Allergies," Bichon Frise Breed Column, *AKC Gazette* (December 2005): 61–62.
5. Herbel, e-mail to the author, September 2006.
6. Chase Herndon, interview with the author, February 2007.
7. Jessica Katz, e-mail to the author, December 2006.
8. Kyle Fetters, interview with the author, September 2006.
9. Katz, e-mail to the author, December 2006.
10. Jason Green, conversation with the author, March 2007.
11. Herbel, e-mail to the author, September 2006.
12. Katie Green, conversation with the author, September 2006.
13. Katz, e-mail to the author, December 2006.
14. Fetters, interview with the author, September 2006.
15. Andy Wick, interview with the author, September 16, 2006.
16. Herbel, e-mail to the author, September 2006.
17. Jey McGahan, interview with the author, February 2007.
18. Christina Aviza, interview with the author, November 23, 2006.
19. Robert Mason, interview with the author, August 23, 2006.
20. Brigitte Mason, interview with the author, August 23, 2006.
21. Kristi Kosinski, interview with the author, January 2007.
22. Wick, interview with the author, September 16, 2006.
23. Ruth Toht, interview with the author, September 2006.
24. Fetters, interview with the author, September 2006.

Defending the Innocent: Animal Abuse and Environmental Concerns

FROM JOY TO SADNESS: ANIMAL ABUSE

The majority of people who invite animals to share their lives treat them with respect and compassion. But while responsible breeders, animal shelters, and rescue organizations are usually very careful to place animals in suitable homes, many other sources treat purchasing an animal solely as a business transaction. Basically, anyone with minimal financial resources can obtain an animal from sources as varied as puppy mills, online brokers, and "free giveaways" in store parking lots or flea markets.

Not only do most people spend more time deciding which car to buy than they do when considering getting a pet, they must also pass both a written and a driving test, obtain a driver's license, and, in many states, have mandatory insurance coverage. But acquiring an animal—a living creature that can live with us longer than we own most vehicles—requires nothing more than a person simply being able to obtain it. And the reasons are not always for companionship.

Family services major Katie Green recalls when a college student she knew told her about a decision he had recently made. "He had had two gerbils and when one had died, he didn't want to buy another one. And since he had heard somewhere that gerbils couldn't be happy by themselves, he decided to just let the surviving gerbil out in the wild to have 'one last good fling.' That was a horrible thing to do! You can't just let a domesticated prey animal out in the wild like that to

"I don't understand how people can have absolutely no compassion toward an innocent and often defenseless animal. It irritates and frustrates me to no end."

—Kaylah Dodd, former San Diego State University student[1]

Chapter 5

fend for itself! That was a certain death sentence. Why didn't he just take it to a pet store so it could have a chance to get a new home?"[2]

Christy Anderson and her sister learned early on that not everyone views animals with the same compassion they felt. One year, when Christy and her sister were young, her parents invited some friends and their two young boys to their summer home in Door County, Wisconsin. While walking on their beach, the children spotted a dead, partially decayed fish. The boys immediately started throwing rocks at the fish while girls hysterically begged them to stop. Neither the adult friend nor her boys could understand why they were upset about throwing rocks at a dead fish. These boys may not grow up to become animal abusers, but children who have been taught to have compassion for all creatures can grow up to make a tremendous difference for living animals that need compassion.

Teens and young adults who bully others often mistreat animals, as well. Rich Weiner, founder and executive director of the avian rescue organization A Refuge for Saving the Wildlife,

---

A PERSONAL GLIMPSE

Iowa college student Faye Nuddleman has witnessed animal abuse firsthand, and it infuriates her. "One of my brother's old friends deliberately swerved to hit a cat in the road instead of swerving to miss it. He actually had a couple of my girlfriends in the car with him at the time that he hit the cat and all he did was laugh when he did it. I also had a neighbor that never let his dog outside so he was constantly sleeping in his own waste. I would go over there every day to feed the dog, water him, and bathe him. I absolutely can't stand hearing about animal abuse. I don't even like hearing about friends going hunting. One friend at school likes to talk about hunting and says cats are meant to be thrown up in the air and shot at. I always get defensive when people here talk about hitting cats with cars or shooting them. They usually bring it up when I talk about spoiling my cat. Then they say cats are pointless and they talk about abusing them. They don't realize that pets have feelings just like humans and they also don't realize they have needs like humans also."[3]

sees many birds that have been mistreated. "Many times we get birds that have a tough time with young adults and teens because of their background. The fact is so many of these teens are not taught to respect animals as feeling, living, breathing creatures or even perceive that they can be a source of enjoyment. They're just something that's a bother. And it takes a long time for these abused birds to get beyond that. It takes a minimum of three years to turn around a bird that's been abused for a year."[4]

Sometimes teens act out, especially if they are being abused at home by their parents. Because they view an animal as beneath them in status, they, in turn, begin abusing it. Rich, a police officer for many years, is very familiar with this pattern. "It's a cycle of violence that we see time and time again. It's actually the whole history of violence. If violence is what someone is taught to do, that is what you are going to do. Most often the abuser will go after the animal in the household to make the other people in the household fearful, especially in situations where they can't go after the other people. But the animal will cower and run in fear. It's a very difficult thing to erase."[5] Clinical grief counselor Laurel Lagoni adds, "In general, teens who abuse animals are likely to have been abused themselves and the cycle of abuse and violence continues and escalates. Teens who abuse animals choose them as victims for the same reason that adults choose children—they are easier victims and can be controlled."[6] The likelihood (and consequences) of being caught abusing an animal are also less significant than if the victim were human.

Although the strongest survive in nature, with fights to the death for food, water, territory and mates, the cycle of violence and abuse does not exist in the animal world. Sadly, this is one of the main differences between animals and humans, because we are the only creatures that perform abusive acts for pleasure and justify them as being "okay."

When we think of animal abuse, we usually think of animals that have been beaten, starved, or tortured. But animal abuse actually comes in many different forms. Something as common as tying up a dog and not providing water or shelter may not seem like abuse, but it is if it is done out of intentional neglect

Chapter 5

or if it causes the dog discomfort or pain. Tying a dog outside in the yard for a couple hours on a beautiful autumn afternoon is not the same as chaining a dog in a yard for hours or days at a time without shelter or social interaction, and in all types of weather. Newspapers, television, online news sites, and other media are filled with stories about starving animals, dogs wearing collars so tight they cause open wounds, and horses standing in filthy stalls and in pain from stones and festering sores in their hooves. Sadly, Animal Planet's *Animal Cops* never runs out of real-life abuse and neglect situations to film. And in both the programs and in real life, the stories don't always have happy endings.

It would be impossible for most of us to fully understand the scope of animal abuse nationwide. We only know about the ones that are discovered. So many animals that end up in shelters, rescues, or foster care are victims of neglect or abuse—or worse. Some of them don't survive the torture.

In January 2007, a disturbing and graphic video was posted on the website MySpace by the seventeen-year-old Texan who filmed it. In it, the teen encouraged his pit bull to attack and maul a stray cat. The teen's statement was equally disturbing. When questioned by the police as to why he did this, the teen answered that he got a "rush" seeing the animals fighting and one animal killing another one.[7] In a similar story reported by WGAL news, three young men and a seventeen-year-old girl in Cumberland County, Pennsylvania, received a free cat from a newspaper ad. They subsequently trapped it in a basement, poked it with broomsticks, and then used a pit bull to kill it. Police only discovered this abuse after the girl brought a videotape they made during this torture killing to school and showed it to a classmate.[8]

The March 26, 2007, issue of *People* featured an article about Dr. Melinda Merck, an Atlanta-area veterinarian who is one of only a handful of veterinary forensic specialists in the country. The article describes a scene of torture involving a three-month-old puppy. After its muzzle and paws were duct-taped, it was cooked alive in an oven. The article notes that people like Merck are making a difference in helping to fight crimes in which animals are victims of abuse and torture. Because of Merck's vivid reconstruction of the events that involved the helpless puppy, the seventeen- and nineteen-year-old defendants pled guilty to aggravated animal cruelty and were sentenced.[9]

Universally, people who love animals may experience discomfort watching any form of animal abuse or suffering, even if they know it is make-believe. Movies like *Bambi* or *Babe* brings tears to the eyes of young and old alike. While some teens seem to be perfectly comfortable watching movies that depict animals being shot, drowned, or trapped in a fire or other frightening situation, many young people find it very difficult to comprehend that anyone would do anything intentionally to harm an animal. Is it possible that peer pressure may influence much of the mainstream response to pop culture's depiction of animals and suffering?

College student Kaylah Dodd witnessed an incident that suggests this could be the case. "One of my friends had a new puppy. It was like only five or six months old. Well, the puppy was playing and got a little rough and bit one of his friends. My friend slapped the puppy really hard, to the point where he wobbled when he tried to walk. That really upset me and I told him that beating the dog wasn't going to make him understand what he had done wrong. I'm just hoping what I told him made him think before he acted again." Some abusers start young. Kaylah feels that "little kids can be pretty mean to animals, too. I remember one time I was walking with my grandma and these little kids were stuffing a kitten into a tiny lunch box! My grandma walked over immediately and told them to stop."[10]

Kyle Fetters adds, "There are so many sad situations that happen, you just want to be a vigilante looking for people who do these kinds of things. I've heard so many twisted stories through the shelter (where my mom volunteers) about people abusing these little tiny dogs. I mean, they have no reason to be doing that other than maybe it makes them feel better about themselves. Personally, I've never been able to associate causing harm to anyone else, let alone especially an animal, as a way of making me feel better about myself."[11]

Chapter 5

People who harm animals may also harm people. So whether you care about animals that are neglected, abandoned, or abused because of a moral obligation to care for those who need our help, or because cruelty to animals is illegal in all fifty states, or just because it's the right thing to do, helping to stop animal abuse actually winds up helping everyone.

WHY THEY DO IT

In order to get an animal to trust them, teens must learn to avoid certain types of behavior, especially rough, violent, or hurtful actions that animals might perceive as a threat to their safety. While most teens learn positive social skills from parents and family, others may not. Teens who exhibit hurtful behaviors with animals have either never been taught to inhibit their impulses or deliberately choose to do so because it makes them feel powerful. And not all teens respect living things or think that animals have any feelings.

Whether abuse is the result of intentional mistreatment, neglect, or an act of cruelty resulting from ignorance, animals need our protection. Fortunately, there are many ways young people can help make a difference. Kelli Herbel lives in a rural area and grew up with animals, so she has always respected them. "Teens can help a lot because many of animal abuse cases I hear about actually involve teens. The very violent ones usually involve those teens who are just one step away from hurting people. I'm not saying all are hurting animals, but there have been some terrible stories about dogs being tortured and abused, and usually it's by teenagers. And, you know, that's definitely not a good situation. Especially while I've been in college, I have seen so many people who just have dogs as status symbols or because they look tough or it makes them look tough. I know it's probably dependent on the area of the country you live in, but there are a lot of people here who like to have big scary-looking dogs in the back of their pickups because it makes them look cool. That's partly why everyone is afraid of my one dog, my great big teddy bear German shepherd who loves everyone and only wants to give you the biggest lick on the face that you've ever got. Everyone's afraid of him because of those people that think it's cool to have mean dogs."

Defending the Innocent: Animal Abuse and Environmental Concerns

Katie grew up in a suburban environment and has had dogs almost her entire life. She comments: "Perhaps having a mean looking dog becomes an extension of themselves or maybe they are just trying to overcompensate for something that they don't have. Or maybe they are so scared themselves, they have to have a dog that looks even scarier. Having a dog that appears to be scary can help compensate for their own fears or feelings of being powerless."[12]

Kelli observed something interesting after her internship experience at the American Kennel Club headquarters in New York in 2006. "I think it is much harder owning a dog in New York City, so if you do own a dog there, it's because you truly appreciate that dog. It's much easier to go buy a dog and just throw it in your back yard here (in a rural area) than it is to own one there (in an urban area) where you have no yard and have to walk the dog in all types of weather. That takes real dedication."[13]

IT HAPPENED TO ME: THE BOND IN ACTION

Reshoma Banerjee volunteers with a rescue organization that makes a difference for abused animals. She recalls one specific story about a husky named Mooney. "I immediately felt connected to him because both my college and middle school's mascot had been a husky. I was terribly saddened by his story. Mooney's former owners had neglected him. They did not feed him properly and left him outside all the time. So because he was devoid of any human care and love, flies had chewed off his ears. He also tested positive for heartworm. Mooney wound up getting adopted by a wonderful couple with a beautiful home and another husky. Not only is he in a much better place where he is loved and cared for, he also has a playmate! He'll never be lonely again."

Chapter 5

MAKING A DIFFERENCE: THE POWER OF THE INTERNET

The Internet influences all of us by spreading information and knowledge and bringing together people from all over the world and from all types of situations. We can learn almost instantly about topics like responsible pet ownership, various animal breeds and species, and new breakthroughs in veterinary science. It is also a marvelous source for people seeking adoptive pets, purchasing animal-related products/supplies, or just as a means to share photos of pets with other online buddies. The ability to share so much information to so many, however, can be a double-edged sword. While some people may use the Internet to search for the perfect dog to adopt, others use it for questionable, unethical, or illegal purposes. The Internet may be a very important and powerful tool for disseminating an endless amount of positive information, but it also has a dark side.

The anonymity of information disbursed on the Internet has made it the perfect breeding ground for stories and graphic displays on many controversial subjects, including pornography, racial hatred, religious cults, adult predators, and, unfortunately, various forms of animal abuse. The rapid growth of peer-to-peer networks such as YouTube and MySpace has created even more opportunities to expose teens to disturbing stories and graphic depictions of animals that are tortured, abused, neglected, maimed, or killed. While teens may easily exchange harmless information with other teens through these networks, they have now also become the innocent recipients of upsetting images and information.

In addition to this visual assault on the unknowing, the power of the Internet is coupled with failed efforts at policing online sites and lack of control over the type of content displayed. As a result, animal abusers can find and communicate with others who have similar tastes. Some people also use sites such as MySpace or YouTube to promote the violent abuse of animals as "entertainment." When you consider that MySpace alone hosts millions of users worldwide and appeals especially to teens, it is apparent that displaying animal abuse there can potentially target young people. Even more horrifying is that it also exposes how many young people are actually turned on by explicit depictions of animal abuse. The reaction of getting a "rush" watching one animal kill another can translate into other perversions and crimes. One of the latest Internet fads is that of "crush videos," where animals are tortured and killed using sexually explicit forms of torture.

Is it enough for teens to know that animal abuse is wrong and that not everything displayed online is acceptable, or can teens actually use their own unique resources and abilities to make a difference? While the easy, instant dissemination of information via the Internet seems to be a substantial part of the problem, it may also be the solution. Many young people feel they should harness the power of the Internet to counteract the negative ways it is being used—by enlisting that very same tool to spread the word that animal abuse is wrong. Online websites from organizations such as In Defense of Animals (www.idausa.org) use the very same peer-to-peer networks to spread awareness and encourage people to report animal abuse to the proper government regulatory agencies. Until a solution is found to better control the content displayed online, many humane organizations are choosing to use MySpace and other high-volume sites to promote a very different message. By posting videos and other graphic illustrations with a strong message about why animal abuse is wrong and displaying them on the same sites that exploit animals, their collective goal is to help educate people to the horrors of animal abuse.

Reshoma Banerjee suggests that teens who love animals and are interested in eliminating animal abuse and neglect should harness the power of the Internet to help spread the word individually to all their friends, online groups, and chatrooms. She feels that teens and young adults can make a difference by just being aware of the world around them and by seeking aid for animals in need.

Chapter 5

STOP ANIMAL CRUELTY: WAYS TEENS CAN HELP

While this book is primarily concerned with adolescents from the United States and Canada, teens across the globe can help stop animal abuse by following some of these suggestions:

- Learn to identify and recognize animals that have been or are being abused.
- Get help. If you see someone hurting an animal or see any animal who looks sick, injured, or deprived of adequate food, water, or shelter, contact the police, local animal care, control agency, hotline, or an adult you can trust. Write the facts down while they are fresh in your mind so nothing will be forgotten or left out. Do not try to help the animal yourself, because you might get hurt, especially with an animal that is injured or fearful.
- Educate family, friends, and others about animal cruelty and its connection with human violence and other forms of abuse by sharing information from organizations such as the American Society for the Prevention of Cruelty to Animals (ASPCA), the Humane Society of the United States (HSUS), and local humane organizations in your area.
- Be a responsible pet owner. Show others how to properly treat animals by caring for your own pets with kindness.
- Report websites that encourage animal abuse to their service providers so the sites can be removed.
- Start an animal protection club at your school or get involved in the HSUS Teen Network, a free online service that provides members with e-mail updates on animals and environmental topics. Other humane organizations and animal registries also have online chats and blogs.

For more information, check online at www.aspca.org, www.akc.org, and www.hsus.org.[14]

High school student Ruth Toht has a real bond with her hamster, Domino, and doesn't understand how people can hurt animals. "All animals do is make you happy. But there are times I can kind of see the reason why they might want to. I'm not at all saying it's right, but maybe they're just in a bad situation themselves and wind up taking it out on the animal. Or, like, the kind of thing that happened to me in 2006. I was just walking my grandma's dog and a loose dog attacked. It bit my grandma's dog, but luckily it didn't get me. This is one of those situations that make me understand why some people can fear animals or react by hurting them because they're afraid of them or afraid of what they might do."

ANIMAL ADOPTION AND RESCUE

> "Rescuing an animal is more than just giving them somewhere to live. It's taking that innocence and giving it back to them because then they're not living in fear again and wondering 'Am I going to be able to eat tomorrow? Am I going to be hit tomorrow? Or am I going to be beaten or shot . . . or whatever it might be.'"—Kyle Fetters, suburban Illinois teen[15]

Animal companions can enrich our lives in many ways. But without the proper awareness and knowledge of how to be a responsible pet owner or animal guardian, adding an animal to a household can have disastrous consequences instead.

Sometimes the best intentions don't always turn out to be the right solutions. When she first started college, Kelli was faced with an unexpected dilemma. "My dad came to visit me during my freshman year in college and he showed up at my door with a kitten he found in the middle of the road! He had actually stopped traffic in this four-lane road, got out of his car, and picked up this tiny kitten. It was the size of my hand! Even though that was a very noble thing he did, I'm standing there thinking, 'What am I going to do with this cat, 'cause I've got dogs!?'"[16]

Many people make poor decisions about the types of animal they bring into their lives. Mismatches between pet and owner often result in the neglect or abandonment of the animal, as

Chapter 5

> **A PERSONAL GLIMPSE: HELPING ABUSED ANIMALS**
>
> Kyle Fetters's family has adopted dogs and cats for many years. "We're just kind of an 'out-there' family, kind of open and loud. The dogs we have right now come from a shelter. These are dogs that had been abused, but over time you can see them coming into their comfort zone being around us. And it's great to see that! I mean, here you have this dog that when you adopt them and bring them home, you're not really sure if they're ever going to open up to you, let alone anyone else, and it's just so great seeing that happen! Whether it takes a couple months or longer though, they really do open up. It makes their lives so much better by just being good to them."[17]

well as damage to homes and property. There are thousands of animals in shelters or rescues and foster care that have been given up by owners who cannot care for them properly or have been humanely removed from abusive and/or neglectful environments. In addition to dogs and cats, there are also many rescue organizations specializing in other types of pets, including birds, ferrets, reptiles, monkeys, horses, and rabbits.

The intense compassion for animals that Christy Anderson demonstrated at a very young age eventually impacted many lives in multiple ways. While attending college, she began Wright-Way Rescue, an animal shelter run solely by college students (with high school and adult volunteers). Within just a few years, the privately run southern Illinois shelter demonstrated one of the top adoption rates in the state and caught the attention of the PETCO Foundation. Since 2004, Christy and her dedicated staff have made the eight-hour trip twice a month from the southern tip of Illinois to a far northwestern Chicago suburb with a van full of adoptable dogs and cats for adoption weekends at a PETCO store. In 2007 they planned to open a second facility in one of Chicago's northern suburbs.

In high school, Christy began working with rescue groups as well as finding homes for stray dogs she brought home. After graduation, she moved to Carbondale, Illinois, to attend college at Southern Illinois University (SIU). Christy describes herself as

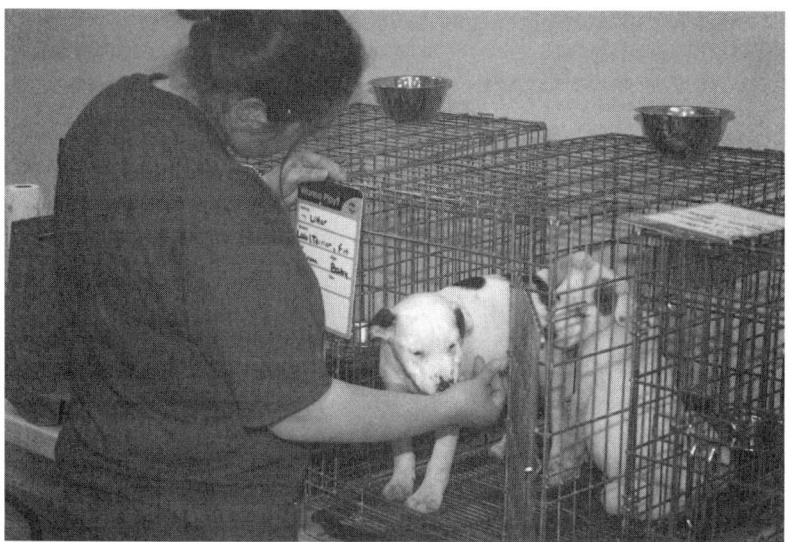

Christy checks the information on a puppy available for adoption at a PETCO-sponsored adoption event. Photo used with permission, Jeffrey Green, Total Recall Dog Training.

just being a "normal" college student at first, involved in studies and the SIU Equestrian Team. But when a friend living off campus decided he wanted to get a puppy, the two of them went to the local animal pound to adopt a puppy. Although Christy had been to a similar facility in Chicago, this experience proved to be much different.

"When we got to Animal Control, they were going around and checking off dogs that were scheduled to be euthanized later that day. I wanted to take each of them, but we couldn't; we could only take one. I couldn't believe how many animals were just being put to sleep, because most of the dogs there were very adoptable." And Christy knew that given enough time, she could find homes for each of them. But these dogs weren't going to be around the next day. That's when Christy decided this was what she wanted to do with her life. When she rented her first place and began the "official shelter," she had no idea it would become anything other than a way for her to fulfill her love for animals and help them find homes. "I didn't picture it getting big. When I first started the shelter, I was doing five or six adoptions a year. Now I am responsible for twelve hundred adoptions a year! And it grew that way in only three years."

Chapter 5

And with that amazing growth, Christy had to learn many different skills, including fund-raising, managing employees, administrative details, and every aspect of running a not-for-profit business—skills that also help her in other areas of her life. Because Christy and the other shelter members are so young, they weren't taken seriously by the rescue community until their adoption numbers were included in PETCO and Petfinder's statistics. "Then people started asking, 'What's going on? Who *are* these people? Who are these *kids*?'" As the shelter grew, Christy knew she needed a larger facility. The twenty-two-year-old purchased a former bar and grill, using money she had personally earned and saved along with money loaned to her by a family member. Wright-Way Rescue is currently housed on a three-acre property with three buildings, walking paths, and trails. In addition to the animal shelter and isolation area used to monitor new or ill animals, Christy plans to open a dog park and turn the third building into a low-cost spay/neuter clinic to service the counties of southern Illinois and offer club-style obedience classes where people pay an annual fee for unlimited time, so students in the area can afford to participate. "If we provide a fenced-in area so they can give their dogs exercise and wear themselves out, the animals will be a little better behaved and the students are then more likely to keep their animals."[18]

Christy is also exploring the possibility of a career in animal behavior and continuing with studies in that field. This would only help the animals she cares so much about since it would equip her even further to be able to handle the rescue animals that come into the shelter and need to be worked with in order to become adoptable.

Kelli has sound advice for teens who are thinking about getting a dog: "Think about adopting one that doesn't have a home before going to a breeder. Breeders almost always have homes for their puppies because they have the resources, but there are so many dogs that don't have a home. It goes back to people not seeing dogs as individuals and beings that also have their own personalities and feelings."[19]

IT HAPPENED TO ME: THE BOND IN ACTION

Jessica Katz had life-changing experiences volunteering at the avian rescue organization A Refuge for Saving the Wildlife. This no-kill parrot rescue, rehabilitation, and educational adoption shelter is nestled in a quiet suburb in the Midwest. "There is as much diversity in the domestic birds at the Refuge as one would find in people walking the streets of a large city. Personality wise—the birds can be as sweet as Peachy—a born cuddler—or as unsocial as a recluse. I loved the variation in birds and their personalities, especially the challenge of working with the larger 'toos.' Needless to say, my cage-cleaning skills have skyrocketed, as well as my ability to do so with minimal damage from the beaks of birds who despise women for one reason or another. Many birds at the Refuge have preference to the sex of their human handlers, and I believe this preference is tied into how they were raised, or is the result of negative experiences. The turn-in sheets in almost every bird's file explained their presence at the Refuge: divorce, death of an owner, an owner's illness, a bird's aggression towards a member of the family, a birth in the family, or even the paltry excuse of not having enough time to care for a remarkable avian. It was heartbreaking, and through reading and compiling the information for each individual bird, I was able to associate behaviors with trauma, discover remarkable vocal or trick abilities that merely needed the right trigger, and even a bird's favorite foods. The biographies posted at http://rescuethebirds.org are something I am very proud of, and by letting me into the lives of his birds I could see I had also gained Rich's trust—another invaluable commodity. The conclusion is simple: they let me into their lives. 'They' being the birds, Rich, Karen (volunteer coordinator), the other volunteers—they treated me like family. In TV shows or movies, the intern is often represented as a very young person (usually referred to as the 'kid') who is always sent out for coffee, or given the least-desired tasks. At the Refuge, however, other volunteers would thank *me* for lightening their load! I would feel like arguing with them over their gratitude—teaching me about their experience with birds made *me* feel just as grateful, and humble. Then again, anyone treated to a large Military Macaw's fully extended wings flapping up a storm might feel a bit insignificant."[20]

Chapter 5

Not all teens live in families that share or even encourage their love for animals. The reasons for this can vary from simple practicality—such as household members with allergies or living where pets aren't allowed—to more complex issues. One or both parents might work long hours, travel often, or have other time commitments that make them unavailable to supervise or care for an animal. They may never have experienced positive interaction with animals, or they may have been frightened by one when young and never outgrew their fear. And if their own parents didn't encourage compassion for animals, they might not want to make the adjustments necessary or even understand why their teens want to have an animal.

Growing up in homes that do not allow pets or with family members that feel animals are too much work or just a lot of mess can make teens who love animals feel lonely, isolated, and misunderstood, sometimes making them feel angry and resentful or that something is missing. However, there are several things such teens can do to overcome the imbalance between their desire to interact and bond with animals and their inability to do so in their own households.

Young people willing to adopt or who volunteer at shelters can make a tremendous difference in the lives of these animals. Photo used with permission, Jeffrey Green, Total Recall Dog Training.

> **RENT-A-FRIEND!**
>
> It's not always possible for teens to have their own companion animals. But by "adopting" a "surrogate" pet, they can still connect with an animal in a very meaningful way. Although she wasn't allowed to own a dog growing up, Reshoma Banerjee began volunteering for a local animal shelter called Illinois Humane (www.illinoishumane.org) shortly after she moved to Springfield, Illinois. Many pet stores around the country sponsor weekend animal rescue/shelter adoption events, so Reshoma went to one of the pet adoption sites in Springfield, introduced herself, and told the agency that she wanted to volunteer. "I went in the very next day and did a shift, and have vounteered there pretty much every weekend since. I am making a huge difference for the animals because I spend time with them and give them some of the care and love they need. It gives me a lot of satisfaction knowing that I am helping animals find better homes. Through this organization, I have met many other dedicated volunteers who also want to stop animal abuse. It's a perfect way to network with people because you share the common bond of loving animals. It doesn't depend on age, race, [or] economic or politial status. No one judges you; they just know you love animals."[21]

Animals who wind up in shelters are often very scared, lonely, and confused. And shelter staff members are often overworked and understaffed. It may be difficult for them to give one-on-one attention to the animals because they are so busy handling paperwork and following legal guidelines. By volunteering in a shelter, you help both the staff and the animals by keeping cages clean and water dishes filled, and taking dogs outside for brief walks and play. You can have a positive impact in animals' lives this way and, at the same time, have the opportunity to interact and bond with them. An added perk is that you might also meet and become friends with other teen volunteers at the shelter.

Chapter 5

ANIMAL RESCUE AND FOSTERING

In addition to animal shelters that house multiple animals in an institutionalized setting, there are also animal rescue groups that place individual animals with individual volunteers in foster homes. Every dog and cat breed has at least one rescue group that focuses on finding homes for animals of that specific breed. The dedicated people involved in rescue and foster care are usually very familiar and knowledgeable about the particular species or breed they work with, making them better equipped to work through any behavioral issues that might be specific to that type of animal. There are also general animal rescue groups and individuals that provide volunteer care for injured animals or mixed breeds. Much like their human counterpart, foster homes can offer animals specialized one-on-one care to help make them more adoptable.

When a neighbor asked Julie Kisman's mom if she would be interested in another collie, she initially declined, since the family already had two collies. But when she heard the dog's owner was going into a nursing home, she agreed to foster the dog and help find him a new home. Patrick, as Julie's family later called him, slowly became a part of their family and dog pack. About two weeks later, sixteen-year-old Julie was surfing online and came across a website for the organization Collie Rescue of Greater Illinois. She e-mailed the organization about Patrick and explained how her family had come to foster him. Collie Rescue sent someone to the Kisman home to evaluate Patrick and explain more about their process of fostering and adopting, and offered to post a photo of Patrick on the group's website so he could find a new home. About a month later, Julie's mom got a call that someone was interested in adopting Patrick. Although Julie was thrilled, a part of her was also very sad. "After having him so long, my heart started to ache and tears flowed. A part of me didn't want him to leave and go to a new family! But I did what rescue groups refer to as a 'home visit' where I could check out the people who did eventually adopt him and he really fit the new family very well."

With the approval of her parents, Julie fostered several other collies through Collie Rescue over the next few years. Each dog

Defending the Innocent: Animal Abuse and Environmental Concerns

has a different story, including one who wound up going into rescue at the same time she was undergoing heartworm treatment. Although the dog had to be kept quiet and crated for three to four weeks, her treatment was a success. But Julie and her family did not adopt her out right away. Although taking in animals like this can be very labor and time intensive, especially with medical issues needing special care, these animals often touch their foster "parents" in a very special way. Julie found it especially difficult to give her up after forming such a close bond. "Colleen stayed with us for a good six months until she got adopted. Giving her to a new family after forming such a close bond was very difficult, especially bringing her through the treatment and not really knowing if she was going to make it in the end. I still keep in touch via e-mail with the family who adopted her."

While young people who choose to help foster animals that need extra medical attention may be more extraordinary, the rewards of helping in any capacity with rescued, abused, or abandoned animals is huge. Julie offers advice for teens who might want to help animals but don't know where to begin. "Just look online. There are *tons* of different sites for animal rescue groups all over the country. Or look in your local newspaper or phone book for local shelters and call to see if they need extra help. Although most of the work that needs to be done is volunteer and not always glamorous, doing what you can to help will at least get you started. I enjoy helping sick and unwanted animals and feel it is very rewarding in the end. It really helped me get through my teen years. Whenever I felt my parents weren't listening for whatever reason, I would be able to turn to one of my dogs. I figured they can't talk back!"[22]

BIRDS AND OTHER ANIMALS IN NEED

Although most people think of dogs and cats when they think of animal rescue, many other types of animals that have been abused or abandoned, or are no longer able to be cared for by their human owners, also need help. Animals such as ferrets, horses, birds, reptiles, and other "exotics" often find

Chapter 5

themselves in the care of people who did not realize what they were getting themselves into when they first acquired the animal. People may think it would be "cool" to own a parrot, sugar glider, or tortoise because they are unusual pets, but after the novelty wears off and they discover how much time is really required to care for the needs of these wild animals, they often think differently.

For example, cockatoos and macaws require tremendous amounts of attention and interaction. These intelligent birds have long life spans and a natural propensity to create messes, noise, and damage when bored. And, like dogs and cats, they can develop behavioral issues during adolescence that can escalate and challenge even the most attentive owners. Chase Herndon and his parents have an African gray parrot named Yoshi. Chase offers an example of just how intelligent these birds are. "I am real strong with Yoshi because I work with him the most besides my dad. We get along well, and Yoshi and I talk to each other. African grays can have *huge* vocabularies, and he communicates with us quite well, way more than people expect. My friends are always amazed that Yoshi actually knows what he's saying. And I mean actual words. For example, when the phone rings, he'll say, 'Hello' as soon as someone picks it up. If you do the "charge" whistle, he'll say, 'Go Bears!' He'll imitate the dogs and cats. He'll imitate my mom's voice and say my dad's name in her voice. And he's always learning new things all the time. Frequently we don't even know where he picks it up!"[23]

Dogs and cats have been domesticated for centuries, but birds are not domesticated. Their wild tendencies are still there. While many people think they can leave birds alone in a cage all day or just throw some birdseed in and say hi once in a while and they'll be okay, that is not the case. When birds are deprived of social interaction, they eventually develop behavior problems. Parrots and other birds require human guardians willing to learn about bird behavior and dedicated to meeting those needs for a lifetime that may exceed their own. Most people are unable or unwilling to give these birds the attention they need, so when birds develop problem behaviors, their owners get rid of them—or worse, they lose interest and neglect or abuse them instead. However, birds—especially those in the parrot family—can live for decades, and once they develop unsuitable behaviors it can be very difficult to make them suitable for someone else to adopt.

Rich Weiner depends on numerous volunteers to help with the dozens of birds he rescues. Many of these workers are teens and young adults. "Volunteers come to us for different reasons. Sometimes it's because they need something to do, or something to connect with. Maybe they have a love for animals but have no idea about birds and are curious. Or sometimes they actually have birds and then they'll start to volunteer to get more experience. When they come to work with us, they get to handle many different kinds of birds and see which type works out best for them. Whether the teens volunteer every day, weekly, or only once a month, it still takes time to really understand how to care for a bird, the long term commitment involved, and why it is so important to learn. That is the greatest impact."[24]

Some animals may not require the same daily consistency and interaction that birds need, as long as their physical needs are taken care of. For example, horses may not need to be ridden each day as long as their basic survival needs (food, water, clean stall, etc.) are met. And if they are allowed some interaction with other horses and/or humans, they won't develop behavioral problems. Birds in captivity, on the other hand, consider humans as their flock. When the owner is gone, the bird is isolated from its flock. Rich explains, "That's what makes them fearful. In the wild, they live in flocks of hundreds, so it makes them feel isolated if they are alone even for short periods of time. When they are taken out of their natural environments and into captivity, you have essentially set yourself up as a substitute for their natural flock. It is detrimental to their well-being to deprive them of human contact, especially if they are the only bird in the house. And it's harder to keep a bird as a companion animal because every day you need to re-create the bond. Every day is a blank slate. You have to keep creating and reestablishing that bond daily so they understand that you are their flock mate."[25]

Chapter 5

The Refuge does not usually place birds with teens or college students because most young people are too busy for the commitment a parrot needs. While birds like cockatoos and macaws may not be the best pet for even the most patient teen, there are teens and young adults who successfully have other types of birds, such as parakeets and cockatiels. And involvement with birds may also lead to a lifelong love for all types of animals. Teens interested in becoming involved with birds should work with them in order to first learn what the birds are all about. Otherwise, the bird pays the consequence. Rich states that his goal is to put himself out of the rescue business by getting the word out and helping educate the public so one day there will no longer be birds in need of rescuing.

MAKING A DIFFERENCE: POLITICAL AND ENVIRONMENTAL ISSUES

In August 2005, the United States experienced one of the deadliest hurricanes to make landfall in our recorded history. According to Wikipedia, Hurricane Katrina was also the most costly national disaster on record, causing extreme devastation along the north-central Gulf Coast. Portions of the greater New Orleans area were completely destroyed when levees and canals breached, flooding 80 percent of the city and surrounding areas. Nearly two thousand people and untold numbers of animal companions, wildlife, farm animals, and others lost their lives in Hurricane Katrina, and countless animal companions were lost or separated from their human families.[26]

No matter what part of the country we live in, none of us is fully prepared for the devastation natural disasters can cause to the environment. Unless you experience it firsthand, there is no way to accurately describe the fury of a hurricane, the suddenness of a tornado, or the shock of an earthquake. While some parts of the country regularly have to deal with these and other natural disasters—including wildfires, flooding, avalanches, blizzards, and ice storms—most teens never experience any of these until they go to college in another part of the country. In addition to the effect these powerful natural

Defending the Innocent: Animal Abuse and Environmental Concerns

forces can have on pets and other domestic animals, the impact on regional wildlife can be intense, since each of these natural disasters can damage or destroy the ecology of the area and may require different responses.

So what can teens do to help with environmental and ecological issues? And what kind of impact can just one teen make? Kaylah has a real passion for ecology and feels there are many ways that teens and young adults can make a difference in the world when it comes to environmental and ecological issues. "There are endless opportunities! Write letters to your representatives, start recycling programs at school and at home, and tell your friends about what they can do to help. You can even go online and adopt a whale! Educating ourselves about environmental causes is most crucial as we get older, including spreading that knowledge to our peers. While natural disasters are devastating to the area, I also think it's also nature's way of reminding us we can't control everything. Disasters like Katrina may destroy the ecology of that area for a while, but you can look at it as a clean slate. People can build in the area again and hopefully be more sensitive to the environment."[27] Chase also feels teens can make a huge difference by just getting involved. "Look around your community for ways to get involved. There are plenty of animal shelters and environmental clubs ready to serve and be served by passionate teens. In addition, teens have unparalleled energy for topics that combine with their love for animals. When nurtured by the right organizations and mentors, teenagers can contribute proactively in many causes. While teens may find it difficult to make an impact with legislation when they are too young to vote, it is important that teens develop their own values to bring to the polls or to their jobs if they decide to get involved in government later on in life."[28]

For teens interested in animal-related social or legal issues, there are many ways to get involved and help make a difference where age and experience won't matter. Alert the news media to the problem by contacting local TV news stations or programs such as *60 Minutes*. Contact your local newspapers. If possible, search for reporters who have done other animal-related stories

Chapter 5

> ### Pop Culture—*Legally Blonde 2*
> The movie *Legally Blonde 2* addresses the subject of animal abuse and clearly shows how young people can make a difference in the lives of animals when they put their mind to it. In this movie, the heroine (played by Reese Witherspoon) introduces a bill to stop animal abuse and testing on animals ("Bruiser's Bill") and leaves her law firm to work in Washington, D.C., as a lobbyist for animal rights. Witherspoon's character goes through a long, laborious process to uncover information about various politicians and the dogs they've owned so she can subsequently play on their emotions and love for dogs to secure votes for the bill, which, predictably, wins out in the end.
>
> Of course, that is Hollywood's version of how things turn out happily every after. Unfortunately, initiating and passing legislation is usually a long, complex process that involves a great deal of work, finances, and support. For teens interested in careers in law or politics, working in the area of animal rights or environmental issues can be an ideal way of combining a career with a love for animals.

and may be animal lovers themselves. You can even express your views by attending town or village meetings or writing to local, state, or other governmental officials about the issue. The important thing is to *do something*!

There are many national organizations and advocacy groups involved in legislative issues. If they are made aware of the problem, they might be willing to lend a hand and use their voice and funds to help. At the very least, they might be able to suggest another course of action that you might not have thought of. There are also an increasing number of colleges and universities offering courses on animal ethics and animal welfare issues. Even a number of law schools, including the law schools at Rutgers, Indiana University, and University of California–Berkeley, offer courses, as well as specialties, in animal rights law.

Faye Nuddleman lives in a city that has an overabundance of stray cats. "We have problems with people not spaying and neutering their cats, and then they end up with kittens. When the kittens' eyes aren't even open yet they dump them in a box and set them outside of the Humane Society. I used to be a part of the Humane Society; however, recently I have been doing some research online to see if there is a way for me to do anything to help increase the punishment in Iowa for animal abusers. I would really like to see harsher punishment for people that are abusing or neglecting animals."[29]

One of the differences between generations is how each one sees and responds to the world in general. Unlike any generation before them, people born between 1981 to 1995, referred to as "Generation Y," have grown up with all kinds of computer technology, from the Internet and video games to iPods and text messaging. It is as natural to anyone in this demographic group to communicate via podcasts, IMs, or blogs as it is to see blue skies and green grass. Just the sheer amount of information accessible to teens from all over the world is staggering!

Kaylah feels it is this technology that enables teens to speak with other teens throughout the world, learning from their peers in the process. While many young people may never experience a close bond with a companion animal, Kaylah believes that respect for life is imperative for everyone. "I sincerely hope anyone who has ever had a dog or cat—or basically any relationship with any animal—can see and understand how special they are. It is important they also broaden that thinking and realize *all* animals are special and deserve a healthy life, preferably in their natural environments, and will want to preserve the wildlife we have, as well as take steps toward bettering the earth's condition. Relationships with their pets should not only be an inspiration for teens to open their homes and hearts to all animals, but also to encourage

Chapter 5

them to learn what they can do to help keep all animals safe and healthy." And the media, as well as other entertainment venues such as SeaWorld, can help educate people on environmental issues. "Pairing a show featuring trained marine mammals with a powerful message can have a great impact on the visitor's lives and help everyone realize the importance of keeping our planet healthy. Hopefully that message gets across to teens."[30] And in making a difference in the environment, Kaylah feels teens are making a difference for their own future as well.

Not only is Kaylah interested in the environment, she is also interested in political and social issues that involve the environment. She's trying to make a real difference by becoming involved in politics and the legislative process and feels that teens definitely need to get involved in the legislation to get things changed.

IT HAPPENED TO ME: THE BOND IN ACTION

Kyle Fetters's fascination with turtles transforms into empathy when he finds one that needs help. His neighborhood has a couple of lakes nearby, and one day, he spotted a rather large leatherback turtle casually crossing the street at a turtle's pace in the middle of the busy road. "I was riding my bike when I saw him crossing the street. This was a rare species and I had to do something to get him out of danger. They're pretty low to the ground and not that visible, so he could have gotten run over very easily. I wound up picking him up and carried him in my arm while riding my bike all the way back home. I had to hold my handlebars so I carried him almost like a Trapper Keeper or a book or something on my side. Leatherback turtles have really long necks and can reach really far. He reached behind and tried snapping at my arm a few times, but I got him to my home safely. It wasn't a big deal because it was only about a mile ride. I do remember getting a couple of *really* strange looks from people, however, as I rode by! He actually wound up doing pretty well, so I let him go toward the end of the summer so he could get ready for winter"[31]

Defending the Innocent: Animal Abuse and Environmental Concerns

There are also internships available for teens interested in political or environmental issues. By 2006, Kaylah had already had the incredible experience of participating in several internships programs involving marine animals, and she continues to look for additional internship experiences. One internship program she has been investigating is with Greenpeace, an organization known worldwide for its work with marine environmental issues. In addition to career opportunities, it has a student network that offers many opportunities for teens to get involved in global issues.

Teens can also get involved in environmental and ecological issues by joining school-supported clubs or groups. Chase participated in his school's Environmental Club, where high school students helped clean up their local environment and encouraged riding bikes instead of driving cars to school. "Sierra Club is a great place to start, either by joining or just checking out information on their website. It's a huge organization that provides tons of information as well as opportunities to work hands on. Working as a volunteer with local forest preserves is great too."[32]

Once teens turn eighteen, there is yet another powerful tool at their disposal: They can vote. Frequently, it is the environmental issues that inspire Chase to actually get to the polls, because he feels he can tell a lot about a politician's character by the way he or she treats the things that can't vote, such as the environment or animals.

Regardless which area of concern they are interested in, it is possible for young people to make a difference for animals. Kyle sums up why he believes so strongly in helping abused or abandoned animals, as well as all animals needing our help: "In a way, it's all about loyalty. It's about showing [the animals] and giving them a reason to trust you and to trust people again. And just giving them a reason to trust is a great thing!"[33]

Although love may be the primary impetus in the human relationship with animals, there can be no real love without responsibility. It takes dedication as well as being caring and compassionate. That's all it takes. But involvement in the welfare of animals is considered by many to be just a small token of gratitude for their contribution to the welfare of humankind.

Chapter 5

NOTES

1. Kaylah Dodd, interview with the author, September 2006.
2. Katie Green, conversation with the author, December 2006.
3. Faye Nuddleman, interview with the author, April 2007.
4. Rich Weiner, interview with the author, November 11, 2006.
5. Weiner, interview with the author, November 11, 2006.
6. Laurel Lagoni, e-mail to the author, April 17, 2007.
7. In Defense of Animals, "Teens Make and Post Video of Dog Killing Cat," *IDA Newsletter* 6, no. 5 (January 31, 2007), www.idausa.org (accessed September 18, 2007).
8. "Men Accused of Taping Pit Bull Killing Cat Appear in Court," WGAL, June 1, 2006, http://www.wgal.com/news/9305091/detail.html (accessed May 10, 2007).
9. Ellen Shapiro, "Animal CSI," *People*, March 26, 2007, 113–14.
10. Dodd, interview with the author, September 2006.
11. Kelli Herbel, interview with the author, September 2006.
12. Green, e-mail to the author, March 2007.
13. Herbel, interview with the author, September 2006.
14. Tip Sources: www.aspca.org, www.akc.org, www.hsus.org (March 30, 2007).
15. Fetters, interview with the author, September 2006.
16. Herbel, interview with the author, September 2006.
17. Fetters, interview with the author, September 2006.
18. Christy Anderson, interview with the author, August 19, 2006.
19. Herbel, e-mail to the author, September 2006.
20. Jessica Katz, e-mail to the author, December 2006.
21. Reshoma Banerjee, e-mail to the author, December 2006.
22. Julie Kisman, e-mail to the author, March 2006.
23. Chase Herndon, interview with the author, February 2006.
24. Weiner, interview with the author, November 11, 2006.
25. Weiner, interview with the author, November 11, 2006.
26. Wikipedia, "Hurricane Katrina," http://en.wikipedia.org/wiki/Hurricane_Katrina (accessed April 14, 2007).
27. Dodd, interview with the author, September 2006.
28. Herndon, interview with the author, February 2007.
29. Nuddleman, interview with the author, April 2007.
30. Dodd, interview with the author, September 2006.
31. Fetters, interview with the author, September 2006.
32. Herndon, interview with the author, February 2007.
33. Fetters, interview with the author, September 2006.

6 The Bonds of Trust: How Animals Help with Emotional and Social Issues and Interactions

As humans, we all have a basic need to be loved. However, it's also important to be accepted for who we are. The relationship between a teen and a companion animal is much less judgmental than one with difficult family members or peers. This is not to say that a human-animal relationship should become a substitute for healthy human-human social interaction, but rather that the human-animal bond can serve as a catalyst for riding through difficult times, a "time-out" stress buster without heartbreak, rejection, or failure. And because that bond remains consistent and unconditional, animals can provide a feeling of stability when everything else around us is not.

Vet assistant Kristy Kosinski feels that animals can definitely help teens who are having problems. "But it also isn't fair to the animal if it was purchased purely for 'Hey kid, you're sad, have a kitten.' I'm very pro-responsible-ownership first. And by responsible pet ownership, I mean adopting/rescuing when possible, and providing proper nutrition, as much enrichment as possible through mutual companionship, and adequate veterinary care."[1]

GETTING ALONG WITH PEOPLE: FAMILY SUPPORT

Most young people who have a passion for animals and eventually get involved in some sort of animal-related career or hobby do not suddenly wake up one morning and decide they like animals. Many of these teens have just always had a heart

Chapter 6

> **A PERSONAL GLIMPSE**
>
> "None of my friends really understood what I was going through. They thought I was just being moody. Although they tried to cheer me up by cracking jokes and trying to get me to do stuff with them, they never really did or said the right thing. Oh, I went along with them because I didn't want them to think I was a total dork. But I was only going through the motions and pretending to be having fun. I was too depressed to enjoy anything. And I don't think they even realized that. The only one that really knew what to do to make me feel better enough to laugh and cry was my dog. He just took one look at me when I felt down, cuddled up next to me and slowly kissed me. Then he'd roll on his back, put on a silly grin, and make the funniest sounds that sounded like "Row, woo, row," like he was trying to tell me everything was going to be all right. And he made me feel like it really was."—Katie Green[2]

for animals, while others were brought up with animals or had parents or grandparents who encouraged them to pursue the human-animal bond.

Brigitte Mason has had a tremendous amount of encouragement and parental support when it comes to her involvement with horses. "My mom shows her mare, too, so we always go to the [horse] shows together. I'm *very* close to my mom and also to my dad. I think I have such a close relationship with them because they do support me."[3]

In addition to being influenced by Steve Irwin, Kyle Fetters believes that an early common interest in nature gave him a closer bond with his grandmother, who was instrumental in his involvement with reptiles. "My grandmother was my driver when I was young. She'd take me to different nature places after work or on her days off. I'd just walk around the lake with my net, finding all sorts of creatures with her."[4]

FAMILY CONFLICT

Not all teens get along with their parents. Or they may experience conflict with one parent more than another. In these

How Animals Help with Emotional and Social Issues and Interactions

> "I think I had always loved animals but when Maggie came into my life, everything just changed for me. I needed the unconditional love an animal gives. I mean, it's comforting to have someone that loves you unconditionally and for who you are."—Reshoma Banerjee, college graduate[5]

situations, animals can help smooth some of the rough spots. Reshoma Banerjee has experienced family conflict, especially when she was in high school. Although Reshoma's parents would not allow her to have a dog of her own, she found another option. "There had been a lot of difficulties between

Animal companions can make us feel loved no matter how we feel, how we look, or how our day is going. Drawing by Katie Green, used with permission.

Chapter 6

me and my mother, a lot of issues with trust and everything. Then my neighbor's dog Maggie came into my life. It was a miracle and she was amazing. Maggie became my surrogate pet. She was such a wonderful dog! Every day, she would wait by the fence for me to come home and, since she was outside a lot, I began to go outside a lot, too, regardless of how or what I was feeling. She gave me such a sense of tranquility. Whenever I was having problems with my parents, I would burst outside crying, hoping Maggie would be there just so I could just play with her and pet her. That had such a calming effect on me. I could just relax and forget about my troubles. She was like an angel."[6] Jey McGahan also remembers some very rough moments living at home. Fortunately, she had her dog, Rowan, to confide in. She feels that having a companion animal definitely gives teens someone to turn to if they don't feel comfortable talking to parents, friends, or other people about what is going on with them.

While these two examples are typical during teen years, some young people may actually live in family situations that are extremely painful. For these teens, positive contact with animals can make the difference between survival and total defeat. With teen suicides at an all-time high, it's important that young people who are abused, neglected, or depressed find someone they can trust. For many, working with animals is the perfect solution. The bond that develops between teens who have known abuse or neglect and an abused or neglected animal can be extremely intense. One reason may be the empathy these teens feel for the animal, while, at the same time, they feel the animal truly understands how they feel. With the animal-human bond, teens do not have to feel alone; instead they feel needed and loved.

By working with animals that need our help, we can also benefit from helping them in unexpected ways. In addition to being with creatures that will not judge or criticize, teens who get involved in volunteer work at animal shelters or other animal-related organizations also have opportunities to interact with other compassionate humans. For some, these chance encounters with people that demonstrate kindness can become life changing.

How Animals Help with Emotional and Social Issues and Interactions

Rachel G. lives in Manhattan and had a close friend who spent most of her time during high school volunteering at the American Society for the Prevention of Cruelty to Animals. The friend had a lot of family issues, struggled academically in school, and was depressed, but didn't have any pets of her own. However, instead of seeking solace in drugs, alcohol, or other choices with negative or self-destructive results, this teenager sought a different path to help ease her pain. Like Reshoma, she discovered that interaction with animals could help her deal with her depression and difficult family situation. Rachel explains, "So my friend volunteered at the ASPCA almost every weekend or as often as she could. She was so unhappy most of the time, but when she was at the ASPCA and when she talked about the animals, she was so happy."[7] Reshoma suggests, "Teens and young adults who might be going through difficult times with their parents, but don't have pets, should do as I did, and find some kind of surrogate pet to relax them and calm them. It will really ease up on their stress. Or just find a place to volunteer at, like an animal shelter. The animals there need your love just as much as you need theirs."[8]

Teens who grow up in emotionally or physically abusive homes with parents that are critical, prejudiced, or use harsh punishment instead of encouragement and understanding learn that humans can be very judgmental. They can also lie, leave you, or hurt you. Many troubled teens seem to connect better with nonverbal animals simply because they don't judge or criticize. And animals give love unconditionally, something that may be missing in the lives of many troubled teens. What is certain is that troubled teens who find positive ways of interacting with animals wind up doing something positive for themselves in addition to helping these animals.

Richelle Hellpap says, "Animals actually do help. I have seen it myself. One of my friends was very depressed. Then she got a pet and that helped her. It's like she now has someone to explain things to and she has someone to take care of. The animal needs her so she feels needed. Now she has a *reason* to live."[9]

Chapter 6

WHEN IT ISN'T YOUR FAULT: DIVORCE AND OTHER FAMILY PROBLEMS

> "There's a dark side to everything in life. But if you bring the light side out, it tends to overpower the dark. It's amazing how animals always know how to do that."—Kyle Fetters, suburban Illinois teen[10]

Can having pets help teens in other family situations as well, such as divorce, parents fighting with each other, dealing with siblings, and underage drinking, drug abuse, or other issues? Jessica Katz's family went through some major changes during her parents' divorce, but her standard schnauzer, Hobbs, was there for her. "She is a very big part of my life. When everything in my family moved around she was the only thing that kept me confident. About ten days before I moved to college, my parents told me they were getting a divorce and one of them was moving out. It was terrifying when I came home for that first Thanksgiving break, and basically walked into an empty house. But the one rock in the ocean was my dog. I love her so much and I am so grateful for her."[11]

Dana Bouchard has experienced that trauma herself, but was helped through those tough times by her animals. She says, " During my parents divorce, I would hear them fighting all the time late at night and it hurt to hear. It was a very rough time in my life. And those times when I needed somebody right then and there, my dog, Angel, would always be there."[12]

After a teen's parents divorce, subsequent dating or remarriage can create difficult situations as well. Christina Aviza had major adjustments to make after her parents divorced and her mother remarried. "Although I didn't have Kitty yet when my parents went through their divorce, I did have her when my mom married my stepdad. Although my

How Animals Help with Emotional and Social Issues and Interactions

family always said that there won't be repercussions, there always were. But I could 'talk' to Kitty and she would never lash out. I could yell with her, I could cry, and she would never get angry. She would never ground me. I could tell her how I felt about my stepdad and she wouldn't tell me that it was wrong. So instead of getting angry at them, I could just sit with her and mellow out. I'd listen to her purr, feel her heartbeat, and it would calm me down. Kitty gave me a total feeling of peace."[13]

DATING AND OTHER SOCIAL ISSUES

> "Every human being needs some form of consistency to obtain some kind of normalcy in their life, whether it's a parent, sibling, or significant other. Mine just happens to be my dog."—Mary Dyrhaug, college graduate[14]

The teenage years and the years that follow, as young people explore various social relationships including dating and long-term relationships, broken hearts, and breakups, can be very rough. At the same time, teens are dealing with the academic challenges of high school and college. Peer pressure is at its peak, as choices move from parental control to the teen's control and are often based on what their friends choose. These changes and choices include lots of difficult decisions, some of which can lead to danger or trouble.

Kyle feels high school can be a very hostile environment for teens. "You're on the brink of becoming an adult, where you're trying to figure yourself out and everyone else is trying to figure themselves out. A lot of times people will just do what they think benefits them, without hesitating or even thinking how it could affect someone else. So when you think about it, a teen that has a good loyal cat or dog or other pet would actually

Chapter 6

Companion animals can help smooth the rough times when family tensions are high. Illustration by the author.

wind up with a much-needed comfort zone. I mean, the animal's not going to apologize or anything, but they can be your companion and spend time with you regardless of whatever you might have done or not done. Basically, animals will appreciate you no matter what. This is the opposite of a person, who, if you don't do a certain thing or act a certain way or whatever, may stab you in the back without hesitation. Not literally, of course!"[15]

For teens going through tough times or dealing with issues in their lives such as drugs, sexual orientation, low self-esteem, learning disabilities, or even just struggling with certain academic subjects or classes, animals can provide friendship in a way that people often cannot. One of the great things about animals is that they don't fool around and avoid communicating the truth the way humans do, nor do they attempt to manipulate and lie.

Christina has also experienced how feeling connected to an animal can help get through tough times. "I had a lot of social problems in high school, mostly freshman year. I had few friends, so sometimes, when I felt lonely, I'd grab a shoelace and just play with Kitty. With her, I could just be myself. It eventually became a habit, and, in a way, she also taught me not to be as shy as I was."[16]

Another difficult experience young people have to deal with is breakups. In fact, one of the main reasons Mary Dyrhaug decided to get a puppy during her last semester in college was that she was going through a breakup with a boyfriend. She had always wanted a dog, and this seemed like the perfect timing. "The relationship just wasn't working out, but Mackenzie took my mind off of it completely. Instead of constantly worrying about whether or not he was going to call that day, I had my dog to keep me busy and have fun with. It sounds corny, but it worked!" She also made a startling discovery from her experience. "Honestly, I love my dog more than any boyfriend. She gives me more of what I need emotionally and can sense what I'm feeling better than any guy. She'll give me a kiss on the cheek or come up and just cuddle at just the right moment."

While on the surface, it might appear that Mary basically chose to substitute a dog for her boyfriend, there is really much more that has grown out of her bond with Mackenzie. She also considers her dog to be a form of consistency in her life, since she has discovered over time that human companionship is not as predictable in duration or quality. "My friends are friends. I love them, of course, but they're not family. Friends come and go. Some of the best friends I've ever had are no longer in my life for one reason or another, and it's really depressing. It's kind of sad because you think they'll always be there, but then you go your separate ways, away to different colleges, sometimes you drift apart, or sometimes it's more than that. Boyfriends are slightly different because eventually they could possibly become family. Or they can break your heart. But I know my dog's not going anywhere. And she won't disappoint or hurt me. She's my most dependable friend. And I really think a lot of people would say that about their pets."[17]

Christina says, "After my first boyfriend and I broke up was the time my cat and I bonded the most—mainly because the ex-boyfriend had cheated on me. I didn't tell my mom. Instead, I just took Kitty into my room and cried. She appeared to be listening, but never judging or reacting negatively. Kitty lay on my lap, licked my hands, and just purred. Even though it didn't take *all* the pain away, it eased it quite a lot."[18]

In addition to helping teens become better able to interpret body language, caring for and interaction with animals may also help them understand other people's feelings and emotions as well. Jenn Papa relies on her companion animal for advice. "I talk to my dog about everything. I have a boyfriend but we have a lot of difficulties sometimes; we may agree on one thing, and then not agree on another thing. But I just have to talk to my dog about it. By the end of the conversation, I know what I have to do."[19]

THE HEALING POWER OF THE HUMAN-ANIMAL BOND

> "As a teen, it was very calming for me to just go and sit with my rabbits or dogs. I would wipe my tears off with my rabbits' ears or I would go horseback riding. It was where I could get away from stress and just relax. Today I can just sit with one of my birds and it takes me away from everyday life."—Karen Stoner, bird refuge volunteer coordinator[20]

Current social trends in the United States and other Western countries have made the need for pets and interaction with animals more important than at any other time in history. More people live by themselves, without consistent human companions, because of the increasing numbers of broken families and increased mobility, with family members scattered across the country. Teens may often feel they are alone, an illusion fostered in many suburban and urban environments by impersonality and alienation. In addition, teens, as well as adults, are always searching for identity, for something that confirms their uniqueness.

How does this impersonal, isolated lifestyle affect us? Or *does* it affect us? Human beings have an innate need for touching and being touched. Electronic technology has given us many advantages, but at the same time it has removed much of the sensory experiences we need in order to feel "connected" to our world. Instead of going to movie theaters and watching a movie with dozens of other people, we now watch that same movie on our computer or on any of a hundred cable, satellite, or digital TV stations—without ever leaving our bedrooms! However, in our isolated high-tech society, it is still possible to meet some of those sensory needs by hugging and stroking a companion animal.

PLAY AND THE HUMAN-ANIMAL BOND

Animal companions do not disappoint us. When we're feeling blue, a cat or dog or horse won't yell at us for sleeping until noon. Instead, they poke or bark or kiss us. They do something silly and we respond by laughing. Unlike the human approach, animal antics often make us laugh when we're feeling down, which is *exactly* the thing we need to improve our mood. As Katie Green puts it: "How can I feel depressed about a test when my dog has just kissed me for ten minutes and is now rolling around in my dirty laundry with a smile on his face that shows pure joy? How many of my friends or family members

> **A PERSONAL GLIMPSE**
>
> While Jessica Katz was interning at A Refuge for Saving the Wildlife, she learned that her mother had breast cancer and required surgery. When her mom came by the Refuge just after learning of her condition, she was promptly deemed acceptable by a few of the birds. Jessica wrote in a journal, "On my Refuge days, I would return home and cheer her up telling her about the antics of seventy birds. The Refuge has become a haven for me; I am able to set aside all of my outside worries in favor of devoting myself to the birds. It is cathartic, and both the birds and I benefit from such complete attention. They seem to sense that something is different about a person who is ill (even when not visibly so), and avian compassion shines through. I suppose the latter half of my internship hasn't seemed like an internship at all; it's really avian therapy. Therapy dogs are a fixture in canine culture; perhaps the next new thing will be therapy birds. I, for one, would be enthusiastic to see if it could be done."[21]

would roll around in my dirty laundry to make me laugh? Okay, how many would roll around in my dirty laundry and truly enjoy it?"[22]

Play has a whole new meaning when you engage in it with a companion animal. Humans often play to win, but animals' main purpose is to have fun. With animals, the whole point of play is to engage, and play is initiated for its own sake. It also has the potential to elevate our mood, especially when our companion animal's joy merges with our own. In making our pet happy, we forget our problems and worries and focus instead on someone else who has the ability to live in the moment.

With the increasing number of busy dog owners comes the need to find outlets for our pets to engage in play, especially when they may be cooped up all day while we are at school or work. Nowadays, people can drop dogs off at a doggie daycare center, hire a dog walker, or take their favorite pooch to a dog park, where they can engage in play with other canines as well as their owners. Janet Carhuayano lives and walks dogs in Manhattan. "Here in the city we have quite a few areas referred to as dog runs or dog parks, where dogs can run and play, meet different people and dogs, and where we can also meet different people from the neighborhood. I spend pretty much all my free time at the dog run!"[23] Tracy Glickauf lives with her border collie, Risky, in the trendy River North area in the heart of Chicago. Like Janet, Tracy takes her dog to the dog park for a regular romp and also to meet other dog owners. "After going to the dog park on a daily basis, it's inevitable that you develop acquaintances with other neighborhood dog owners whom you consistently run into. I've gotten to know many of my neighbors, ranging from young adults around my age to those who are retired. However, we all have an obvious commonality in our love and bond with our dogs, that immediately makes it easy and natural to create a friendship based on that foundation."[24]

ANXIETY, STRESS, AND THE EMOTIONAL BOND

Even if a teen has a loving, caring family, the world we live in today is one filled with an ever-increasing amount of stress. College costs continue to rise. Fluctuations and uncertainty in

How Animals Help with Emotional and Social Issues and Interactions

> "I think everybody could use a pet because of its unconditional love, and everybody needs a little of that."—Christina Aviza, former Kentucky State University student[25]

our economy often make it difficult for teens to earn enough gas money to get to their jobs! Suicide is the third leading cause for death in teens,[26] while, as a nation, we are currently just coming to grips with the nationwide epidemic of stress-related obesity.

In an ideal world, schools are supposed to be safe and parents loving and wise. No one should be judged or ostracized because of the color of their skin or the type of clothing they wear. However, events like the Columbine High School shootings on April 20, 1999, where two students murdered

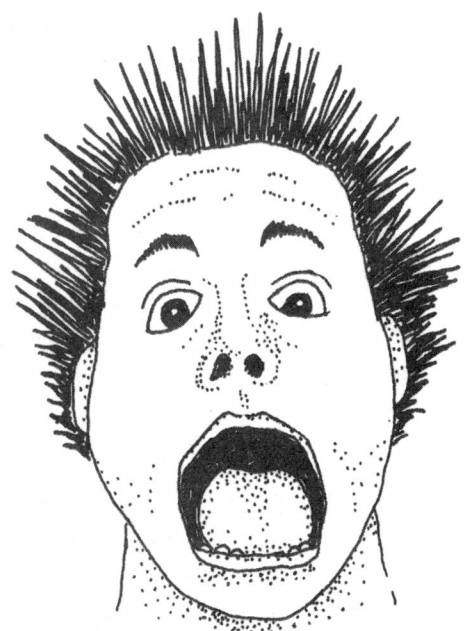

Stress and how we react to it can affect teens' health, mood, and ability to succeed. Illustration by the author.

twelve classmates and one teacher and injured an additional twenty-one students, or the April 16, 2007, shootings at Virginia Tech, suggest a different world. Events like these also remind us that school can be potentially much more dangerous when teasing and bullying, cliques, and exclusion and social hierarchies based on economic, racial, or cultural criterion are accepted as part of teen culture. In addition to natural disasters, we, as a society, now have to worry about terrorist attacks, gang violence, and urban drive-by shootings, as well as the "normal" daily stresses of school, family, and job. Unfortunately, anxiety and fear are now part of daily life in America after the unimaginable events of 9/11. In fact, post-traumatic stress syndrome from that event is still being evaluated as to its full effect.

Research has shown stress to be a primary factor in many of the health problems in our high-pressure society. But people of all ages turn to their animals in times of emotional distress. In addition to helping us learn valuable life skills, companion animals can also provide much emotional assistance, especially as a focus for emotions that family members don't feel safe expressing to one another. In trying to reach teens traumatized or abandoned by society and/or family, therapists use animals to help heal the pain and break through the defenses that lead to unacceptable behaviors. Animal-assisted therapy is also used to help put lives back together for those who have been the victims of teen violence.

Positive interaction with animals can help young people in many areas including, but not limited to, social/emotional confusion and isolation stemming from family problems; physical, emotional or sexual abuse; sexual orientation; peer relationships/social standing; racial, religious, and cultural prejudices; personal or family member substance abuse; and learning/self-esteem issues. College student Chase Herndon comments, "First off, taking care of an animal—whether volunteering at a rescue or having your own pet—keeps teens busy. And when someone is busy thinking about taking care of someone else, it takes their mind off of other stressors while also providing a sense of companionship, responsibility, and success."[27]

How Animals Help with Emotional and Social Issues and Interactions

Jason Green enjoys a relaxing moment, away from the everyday stress of school, work, and social pressure. Photo used with permission, Katie Green.

Even an animal as small and simple as a fish can evoke feelings of calmness in those suffering from anxiety, especially in situations such as waiting in the oral surgeon's office for wisdom teeth extraction or when a family member has been hospitalized. Many hospitals, clinics, and dental and doctor offices have fish tanks in their lobbies or waiting rooms because of the calming effect they have on people.

GETTING INTO TROUBLE

Sometimes life just isn't fair and we don't get what's best for us. But the way we respond to stress, family issues, and other problems may also not be the best for us either. While most teens never get in trouble with the law, some teens do. They can either make bad decisions or make decisions based on what they learned from their environment—or, as typical teens pushing the boundaries, they push just a little too far.

Whether it is because of drug use and underage drinking or shoplifting, curfew and traffic violations, teens who get into trouble may be ordered by the court to perform community

Chapter 6

IT HAPPENED TO ME: THE BOND IN ACTION

Katie experienced anxiety when she transferred from a small, local liberal arts college to a large state university. Not only was she moving into an unfamiliar environment with a population of thousands where she didn't know anyone and where the campus was large and confusing to navigate, her dogs were now more than a hundred miles away. At first, Katie didn't realize the university dorms allowed fish, since they did not allow other types of pets, so her goldfish, Melody, stayed at home in her dad's care. Katie eventually purchased a new tank system and brought her fish to school, but the new pump was too strong and poor Melody was sucked up into the filter, got injured, and died. "I felt guilty that she died, like I had failed as a pet mom. I thought it was my fault for taking her to school." Katie purchased two other goldfish when she came home for the summer, but they died too, making the college student feel she was "just one big failure."

The academic year that followed was extremely stressful. Katie found herself struggling in a program for a field she had wanted to be in all her life. It was her dream, but she was now dealing with daily anxiety and worry, not knowing if she would pass her exams and if she had made a mistake in this career choice. Her self-esteem was at an all-time low. She began coming home on weekends as often as she could just to spend time with her dogs. They eased her anxiety and helped her cope as she eventually made the difficult decision to change majors and find a new direction. Fortunately, she experienced success with the classes in her new major, but she missed having a companion animal. Both her roommate and her best friend had recently gotten Betta fish. After Kate saw how well they were doing, she figured if they could do it, so could she! So she decided to take the plunge and get another fish. A Betta fish turned out to be a much better match for her, since they are easier to maintain and require no complicated equipment or filtration system. "Saying hi to my fish and feeding him makes me feel wanted and needed. When I'm gone all day at class, the first thing I think about on my way home is how my fish is doing! And since he's still swimming happily in his little bowl, I now feel like a success!"[28]

How Animals Help with Emotional and Social Issues and Interactions

service. One of the ways teens can perform these community service duties is by volunteering at a place like Crossroads Animal Rescue, a facility in Georgia that combines helping animals in need with helping at-risk teens.

One of the abused animals coaxed back to health at Crossroads was a boxer named Frank. According to Crossroads executive director Rebecca Carey Sowers, "We have had many abused animals throughout the years, but he came here malnourished and weighing only thirty-seven pounds. Frank's head on top was sunk in, and you could see every rib in his body. I fed him sandwiches loaded with mayo, and, of course, regular dog food, and *all* of our leftovers! In one month's time he gained thirty pounds! It took three months to get all the weight back on Frank so he could be neutered and put up for adoption. But he left Crossroads after nine months to live in a home that was selected very carefully for him. We don't know where he came from, but Frank wound up being taken care of not only by me but by all the teens that came here on the weekends."

Crossroads works with the Forsyth County, Georgia, court system, which is in one of the wealthiest counties in the United States. The teens Rebecca sees are all issued community service from the juvenile court system, which can be anywhere from eight to one hundred hours. "The teens we see at Crossroads get into trouble, get caught, go to court, and then get put on probation for things like truancy, being unruly, drug related problems, vandalism, traffic violations, etc.—but nothing extremely violent. And no teen is allowed here with a history of any animal abuse whatsoever!" The teens that are at Crossroads from 8:00 a.m. to 4:00 p.m., Saturdays and Sundays, except for major holidays, perform various types of duties, including cleaning up after dogs, rabbits, goats, pigs, horses, and other animals as well as cleaning the pasture, water troughs, bowls, and feed dishes. They may also be assigned to build things like fencing for the animals, or they may paint fences and help around the farm. Teens who feel comfortable handling the animals are given additional tasks, including walking or washing dogs and grooming horses. Rebecca emphasizes that "every teen is treated the same here and assigned similar tasks."

Chapter 6

Involvement with animals such as rabbits or ducks, which are not normally thought of as pets, can help teens develop empathy and improve the way they interact with others. Photo used with permission, Teresa and Richelle Hellpap.

According to Rebecca, each teen who performs community service at Crossroads receives a pass/fail report card. And sometimes they do not pass for a variety of reasons, including poor attitude, trying to hide and smoke (which is not allowed), refusing to work, or failing a drug screen. If they do fail, they are assigned additional replacement hours. She adds, "Some teens actually get put into courtroom detention and then reassigned here as well. I utilize work as a consequence for negative behavior, and those teens who are not interested in working with the animals are assigned labor like cleaning the pasture. I never want to force a teen to work with an animal." As far as working with the animals and how it helps the teens, Rebecca has seen lots of positive results. "Even though this is a consequence to a negative behavior, most kids enjoy coming here and being outside. It also does appear to help the kids by caring for an animal that has been hurt or neglected. We see a lot of empathy here and have a very low rate (8 to 10 percent) of recidivism."[29]

Although college student Kelli Herbel has never been in trouble herself, the teens she has observed in her area who do get into trouble often do so simply because they don't have enough to do. "So they're going out and finding things to do that they shouldn't be doing and that gets them into trouble. How animals can help teens dealing with self-esteem issues or learning disabilities, however, is something that relates back to how dogs always give back. And, any time you have that type of bond, it's going to help someone like that."[30]

Juveniles in detention often lack empathy. That's why Crossroads and similar programs across the country are so crucial: They help teens learn to empathize with animals that have experienced some of the same things they have. In addition to the programs that work with teens who have been convicted of milder, nonviolent offenses, there are also programs in various parts of the country that combine caring for animals with teaching violent and at-risk teens to be caring and responsible.

Project Second Chance is a program in New Mexico that gives troubled teens in detention centers a chance to do something positive by pairing them with dogs from local shelters in need of adoption. Since many of these dogs are literally on "death row," these teens learn valuable lessons about life and death while also identifying with these dogs. Much like teens who have committed crimes, ranging from petty theft and drug possession to rape and murder, many shelter dogs are not easily adoptable because of inappropriate behaviors. These behaviors may develop for a variety of reasons, including genetic predisposition, poor socialization and lack of training, and owner abuse or neglect. And since many troubled teens who exhibit inappropriate behaviors come from similar environments and experiences, they can easily identify with these animals and possibly even learn from their suffering. The program matches these teens with dogs that not only have similar tendencies, such as aggression and violence,

Chapter 6

but that also face uncertain futures. In turn, these teens may feel safer with the dogs as well, since animals do not judge. It is a win-win situation. Essentially, these teens lose the stigma of being criminals or "losers," because the dogs don't care if the teens training them have been in trouble. And the teens need to work hard to establish and maintain trust with animals that have themselves been in trouble.[31]

In addition to running the Crossroads Animal Rescue and working with the teens sent to her through the county courts, Rebecca Carey Sowers has also taken in and fostered a number of troubled teens over the years. "Most of the teens I've fostered have been very helpful in assisting with the care of animals. However, one specific foster teen we'll call 'Mandy' was especially crazy about any and all animals. She even rescued a squirrel once!"

According to Rebecca, teens who are abused often develop reactive attachment disorder and subsequently have difficulty attaching emotionally to anything. "They try really hard to push everyone in their life away because, to them, getting close to anyone or anything is not okay." Mandy was with Rebecca for about six months and found a way through this disorder by attaching to animals. "She had been severely sexually abused and turned to animals as a way to achieve comfort without being asked for something in return. Mandy asked to be the one who got up early to feed the horses. She would get up before 5:30 a.m. and feed them and then groom them right after school. And she'd ride as well. Even when she got thrown off, she would get right back on. She had no fear and a huge passion. She even rescued a pregnant dog that slept in her bed and had pups there too! Unfortunately, once her family got it back together and she was on her way to becoming an adult, she died in a car accident in September 2006."[32]

HUMAN AND ANIMAL DELINQUENCY

Some of the reasons teens wind up getting into serious trouble, eventually resulting in arrest and placement in juvenile

A PERSONAL GLIMPSE

When she was eight years old, Amanda Nelson's parents left her with her baby brother and sister in a K-Mart parking lot after the parents got busted for stealing. Amanda and her siblings grew up living in a series of foster homes. "I have definitely had some hard times. I was living in a group home for two years. I did not trust people or want to have anything to do with them, I felt hurt, lonely, abused . . . didn't feel like I was worth being on earth." Then she was fostered by Crossroads director Rebecca Carey Sowers. Amanda says, "The animals were like me. Abused. They had been hurt like me. They had to trust me to help them. That's actually how I learned how to trust people. And I am okay to talk about it now because I know it was in my past and not everybody is like that."

At one point, Amanda adopted a dog of her own that became a very special friend. She felt having her dog made the moves and transition much easier for her during the three years she had him. "I was passed around a lot to foster homes in different states. But I had my dog, Sneakers. We had each other and him being with me made me feel better because new places were so hard for me. I had no family, and Sneakers did fill that hole in my life. Animals love you no matter what." Unfortunately, Amanda eventually had to give him up. "I hated to have to give him up. But I didn't have anywhere to live and I felt bad for him always moving him from place to place and different states. I felt he needed a family and to be in one place. So he went to the Humane Society, where they could find him a good home. It was the hardest thing I have ever had to do. It was like giving away my kid."

Although she had already turned twenty-one, Amanda made the choice on her own to return to Crossroads and her former foster mom in 2007. "I wanted to get my life together because I was going down the wrong path." And she feels that being in an environment with all these animals—and, of course, her foster mom—is helping her get her life back. "Since I have been here I have gotten a full-time job and am saving for a car. I really don't know how to explain it, but I am just more relaxed here." And Amanda has also developed a bond with Benjie, a dog at Crossroads. "He's just a small gray-and-white dog. I am not sure what kind he is. My mom found him in a box a long time ago before I knew her. But he sleeps with me every night."[33]

Chapter 6

detention facilities, are the same reasons why many animals also wind up in shelters. Adolescent dogs and cats are being given away or abandoned in disproportionate numbers because of their out-of-control behavior. Many difficult or aggressive behaviors that begin as puppies or kittens usually reach their peak during adolescence, when hormones rage and animals push owners to the limit.

The average pet owner, however, is usually not equipped or knowledgeable enough to handle problem animal behavior. Pet owners must be able to maintain the respect and leadership position within the family, pack, flock, or herd, but must not abuse the animals in order to maintain it. It's a fine and often difficult balance. Most pet owners do not understand that principle, nor do most people know how to establish and maintain themselves in that position, especially if they have an animal that exhibits dominance, aggression, or other problem behaviors.

People themselves often give confusing and mixed signals that can create behaviors that are the opposite of what they want. For example, bite inhibition in animals is a lesson taught by mother, father, and/or siblings in the wild. All puppies have the instinct to bite and the need to chew during the teeth-cutting months, so they must be taught by us, their surrogate parents, what they are allowed and not allowed to put their teeth on. Many humans, however, will play "rough" with their young animals, encouraging them to be "mouthy" by grabbing clothing, arms, or hair "in play." That only teaches the animal to associate placing their teeth on humans as something fun to do—a behavior that only escalates as they get older. What started out as a cute puppy antic of grabbing your arm becomes unacceptable behavior when that cute little puppy has grown into a hundred-pound Rottweiler!

According to people who have worked with troubled juvenile delinquents, many of these young people come into the system with serious social behavior problems, and they often come from abusive or neglectful environments. Add the hormone fluctuations adolescents experience along with the pressures of school, peers, and other external forces, and you have a recipe for trouble. Teens and young adults will often act out how they feel internally in inappropriate ways, which can include abusing siblings, strangers, or animals.

Most teens grow up in environments where they feel cared for and safe, with parents who bond with their children as soon as they are born. The bonding process itself is very complex and involves a combination of instinct, sensory stimuli, cultural practices, and learned behaviors stemming from the parent-child relationship the parents had with their own parents. Babies are also born with instinctive responses to various stimuli. For example, the scent of a baby's head or the sound of an infant cry can trigger a response in the parent, while the touch of a mother's breast will trigger an instinctive rooting and suckling reflex in the baby. Although the relationship may be challenged during the teen years, the bond between parent and child usually continues throughout childhood, into adolescence and beyond.

For many teens, however, human interaction has not been so positive. Victims of abuse as well as adolescents with behavior problems, physical disabilities, or other problems may have difficulty forming and maintaining positive human relationships. According to a special report in the October 2006 issue of *Pet Business*, a pet industry trade magazine, most physically abused children and adolescents who enter therapy programs have problems with healthy touch. However, when psychiatric and other therapies are combined with "nontraditional" therapies using animals, amazing things can happen. And it is because of the bond created between these abused young people and animals, plus the unconditional love shared in this unique nonverbal communication, that healthy touch can be reinitiated.

Places like Inner Harbour in Atlanta, Georgia, a facility that provides multiple levels of psychiatric care for children and teens under eighteen years old, combine traditional therapies with nontraditional animal therapy programs. Children and adolescents with behavioral problems or who have experienced physical or sexual abuse benefit from a grant program that funds and provides various animal therapy programs for medical staff, therapists, and volunteers. These various therapies include an equestrian program as well as the Pet Care

Chapter 6

Trust Foundation's Animals in the Classroom program. More recently, Inner Harbour's equine program has been expanded to a multispecies program that also includes dogs, cats, birds, reptiles, amphibians, and fish, plus a nature program focusing on a nearby forest and lake. Although dogs and cats are the most common animals used in animal-assisted therapy, the combination of school classrooms, nature center, and barns on the twelve-hundred-acre campus has allowed Inner Harbour to expand the typical therapy boundaries. Various exotics, such as frogs, snakes, and bearded dragons, along with animals like rabbits and guinea pigs, are now a part of the therapy program, as are animals such as butterflies or deer.[34]

And the impact these animals have on the children and teens is pure magic. Because many of them may not have had a loving family, these animals become their family. The animals provide and receive love, require food and care, and introduce compassion and responsibility into the lives of children and adolescents who may never have experienced that before. These animals provide play and laughter; they also provide companionship for teens who have never experienced real friendship.

Animals can invoke feelings of safety and comfort with touch, as well as the pure pleasure and joy found in watching and interacting with them. They can also be a great motivation for success in school. As many of the teens have stated, when animals also become your friends, you have someone outside of yourself to care for. And when you have a friend, you have a sense of hope. You are not alone.

NOTES

1. Kristy Kosinski, interview with the author, January 2007.
2. Katie Green, interview with the author, January 2007.
3. Brigitte Mason, interview with the author, August 23, 2006.
4. Kyle Fetters, interview with the author, September 2006.
5. Reshoma Banerjee, e-mail to the author, December 2006.
6. Banerjee, e-mail to the author, December 2006.
7. Rachel G., interview with the author, January 2007.
8. Banerjee, e-mail to the author, December 2006.

9. Richelle Hellpap, interview with the author, October 2006.
10. Fetters, interview with the author, September 2006.
11. Jessica Katz, e-mail to the author, December 2006.
12. Dana Bouchard, interview with the author, September 2006.
13. Christina Aviza, interview with the author, November 23, 2006.
14. Mary Dyrhaug, interview with the author, January 2007.
15. Fetters, interview with the author, September 2006.
16. Aviza, interview with the author, November 23, 2006.
17. Dyrhaug, interview with the author, January 2007.
18. Aviza, interview with the author, November 23, 2006.
19. Jenn Papa, interview with the author, October 2006.
20. Karen Stoner, interview with the author, November 11, 2006.
21. Katz, e-mail to the author, December 2006
22. Green, conversation with the author, December 2006.
23. Janet Carhuayano, interview with the author, October 2006.
24. Tracy Glickauf, e-mail to the author, October 2006.
25. Aviza, interview with the author, November 23, 2006.
26. Teen Suicide: Adolescent Suicide Statistics and Prevention, www.teensuicide.us (accessed April 16, 2007).
27. Chase Herndon, interview with the author, February 2007.
28. Green, conversations with and e-mail to the author, December 2006.
29. Rebecca Carey Sowers, interview with the author, March 22, 2007.
30. Kelli Herbel, e-mail to the author, October 2006.
31. Keith Oppenheim, "Troubled Dogs and Troubled Teens Try to give Each Other New Life," CNN, July 9, 2006.
32. Sowers, interview with the author, March 22, 2007.
33. Amanda Nelson, interview with the author, April 2007.
34. John L. Pitts, "Natural Therapy in Special Classrooms," *Pet Business* (October, 2006): 152–55.

7 Life Changes: College, Country, and Careers

GOING TO COLLEGE

Making decisions about college can be difficult enough, but teens who are closely bonded with their companion animals face additional choices. Besides individual social needs, academic goals, and career plans, students must decide whether to go to school in state, out of state, or attend a local commuter college—and whether to include an animal in those plans. How does this critical issue affect their ultimate decision?

High school student Nichole Freeman has definitely thought a lot about this dilemma. "I have been trying to find a college that allows me to live off campus my freshman year so I can have a pet. My parents would never let me take my dog with me because everyone in my family loves him, but I don't think I could live that long without a companion animal. I just can't imagine coming home to nobody."[2] Janet Carhuayano chose to attend a commuter school in New York because she felt she couldn't live without her dogs. "When I'm gone for just two or three days, I miss them terribly. How could I stand it for two or three months? Maybe dogs don't have a real sense of time like we do, but they know when they haven't seen somebody for a long time. If they haven't seen you in days and then they see you again, they are truly happier than any person would be."[3]

College choices are normally based on many variables, including academic programs, affordability and/or available scholarships and grants, campus size, student body demographics, social activities, and campus location. For teens

"College bound now and learning to live on my own, far away from my fuzzy friend and everything else I've known."

—Katie Green, college student, Northern Illinois University[1]

165

Chapter 7

who want to include companion animals in their plans, there may be other considerations, including restrictions imposed by the colleges themselves.

High school student Richelle Hellpap is just beginning to prepare for college. She has already found that school activities take up much of the time she used to spend with her rabbits. "Being in school takes away time to play with them at night and feed them. They don't get to see me as much as when I was in eighth grade. Sometimes I feel kind of bad about it, like they

A PERSONAL GLIMPSE

Once she made her college decision, University of Vermont student Jessica Katz was unable to take her dog with her to school because school policy does not allow animals in the dorms. "I miss Hobbs more while I'm at school than I miss my family. I can talk to them on the phone to find out how they are, but I have to actually see her to know how she is." Jessica feels, however, that having a pet in the dorm can create tension between roommates, in addition to subjecting an animal to the college lifestyle. "It can be dangerous with all the substances such as makeup and medication and other things. On my campus there actually are no apartments, so for my situation, it's more a matter of space and time. Of course in an apartment you also have to think of noise restrictions."

But after completing her internship at a bird rescue organization, Jessica discovered she could still be involved with birds when she was home on breaks. "Of course, no animal-related internship is complete without learning the hardest lesson of all—as a college student it would not be feasible for me to adopt. Since I own no other birds, and refuge birds must be tested vigorously for a variety of communicable avian diseases, however, I was the perfect candidate for—drum roll—*fostering*! Taking care of Drake, a male Indian Ringneck, one summer completely made up for not bringing anyone home permanently. It was the most intimate experience I had that summer, and when a family disaster occurred, there was even a feathered friend waiting for me to cuddle with him when all was said and done. Drake's entry into my life marked the first time I have ever had a bird in my house, and as a result have been privileged to a whole host of learning experiences!"[4]

kind of know that I am getting older and things change."[5] And college life definitely changes the amount of time and money students have to devote to an animal. Without the safety net of family, students can find themselves with problems and an animal that ends up neglected or not taken care of properly.

Animal-loving teens who consider themselves to be close to one or more of their parents or grandparents usually have family members and role models who also love animals. Chase Herndon says, "I consider myself close to both my parents and grandparents. Both my parents have been supportive of all our animals and each has their own preference/passion (dad—dogs, mom—cats). I probably got most of my passion for animals from my mom, as she's loved animals since she was younger too. And also, my dad grew up on a farm, so he is quite familiar with animals of all kinds. I pretty much grew up with a zoo at home, including having two black labs, two cats, a bird, three aquariums, a bunny, and a man-made pond that I maintain and stock with koi [a type of fish]. I've also had turtles, lizards, and other dogs and cats over the years. I miss all my animals while I'm at college, but I do have an outside bird feeder here at school."[6]

Once teens make their decisions and move to college—with or without their companion animals—they often have trouble adjusting. Even though they want to become independent and prove how grown-up they are, they are often surprised at how much they miss their families—or at least how much they miss their pets.

Kyle Fetters decided to attend an out-of-state school in Boston and could not take any of his pets. Although he got used to it, there were definitely times when he missed the simplicity and loyalty of animals, as well as their friendship. "It was very strange to me, because growing up, I can't remember a single day when I didn't have a dog, cat, or something animal coming up to me and meow or bark. And leaving that was definitely a little strange. I mean, I loved going away to college. I met a lot of new people, and that was nice, but it was also really a lot different for me. It was lonesome not having any animals around."[7] While Kyle was not allowed to have any animals other than fish in the dorm, he still managed to find a way to get his "animal fix" at school. "Whenever I would walk down the path, there were always people walking with their dogs. You couldn't go outside without seeing a dog or bumping into a dog. I actually learned a lot more about dogs because I was around all kinds of different breeds I'd never seen in person before."[7]

Jessica Katz also needed interaction with an animal, so she got a Betta fish. "That's basically the only thing we are allowed to have in the dorms here. I have had him since moving in and owe him so much because he's just hilarious."[8] Northern Illinois University student Katie Green also has had fish throughout college. "Even though I'm in an apartment now, I'm in one that doesn't allow dogs so I'm glad to have my fish. But I can't wait to graduate and get back home to my dogs. It's been a long six years!"[9]

Sometimes students transfer to schools back home after a year or two instead of "toughing it out." Before Jey McGahan got her cat, Dexter, she had an incredibly hard time adjusting to being away at school, especially since she couldn't have any pets in her college dorm. "It was so hard for me to be alone all the time. I hated it. I ultimately ended up moving back home and transferring to Columbia College, where I could live in an apartment in the city [Chicago]. Having my own place and being able to have an animal there for me really helped me get through that difficult period."[10]

Like other teens making college decisions, Brigitte Mason is taking everything into consideration, including her ability to bring her horses with her and find suitable housing for them. While her primary focus is to find a school that meets her academic needs, to help her become an equine geneticist, she knows that her ultimate decision will not only affect her ability to continue showing her horses but also prevent or enable her to just be with them. As a high school junior, Brigitte was carefully looking into several different universities, both in and out of state. While she would actually prefer to go out of state, she feels that would present an added challenge and test the bond she shares with her horse. "If we're going to have to travel a long distance, she'll have to get used to a whole new environment. So if I do go out of state, it will kind of test our relationship to see just how much she really *does* trust me in that new environment. But I'm very emotionally attached to my horse and my horse is very emotionally attached to me, so I don't think it will be a problem. Instead it will be more like just another step in stuff that I do with him."[11]

College graduate Mary Dyrhaug waited until her last year of school before getting her Shih Tzu, Mackenzie. "I felt the timing was right my last year of school because I lived in a townhouse close to campus. Some of my neighbors were close personal friends of mine, so it worked out well. We were very tight-knit and everyone just loved her." Because Mackenzie was just eight weeks old when Mary got her, she also had to deal

---

DILEMMAS IN BRINGING COMPANION ANIMALS TO COLLEGE

The decision to include pets at college can also pose problems with things many of us take for granted. Kelli Herbel, an Oklahoma college student and third-generation dog show handler, grew up with animals and cannot imagine living without them. "I was always fortunate to live in the country, because when you live in the city, they can tell you what you can own or build and how many dogs you can have. I mean, that's really tough! But I was fortunate enough to live out in the country in a rural area, so we didn't have to deal with any of that." Once Kelli left for college, however, she found it wasn't only in the city that restrictions on dog ownership existed. "It was kind of tough going away to college, because already there are a lot of places that won't rent to college kids anyway because they feel they aren't responsible enough. But when you tack on dogs as a college student, no one wants to rent you anything!" It took Kelli a while to find a solution to this dilemma, but she persisted. "I don't live on campus, but I live very close to it in a trailer that a very nice man rents to me, who lets me have my three dogs inside. I've lived in other trailers before, but I've just now found a really good place. However, it took me *three* years to find this one!"[12]

Chapter 7

with a puppy that needed to be taken to the bathroom many times a day and didn't understand basic commands, chewed everything, needed a puppy-safe environment, and couldn't be left alone for very long. But Mary didn't feel that Mackenzie interfered at all with her class schedule or social life. "At that point, my classes were only a minute away, so she was never alone for more than a half hour. If I was gone longer than that, she stayed with my friends. And I had a lot of friends who volunteered to watch her! I got Mackenzie in April, so in reality, I only had a month or two of school left before graduation. She was my graduation present to myself!"[13]

Vet tech student Rebecca Britz also has a dog with her on campus. She feels that having a dog with her at school was not a luxury, but a necessity. "My dog definitely helped with my emotional ups and downs as well as my stress level. He will sit next to me while I am studying for a test and just lean on me. However odd it may sound, it makes me feel safe. So, no matter

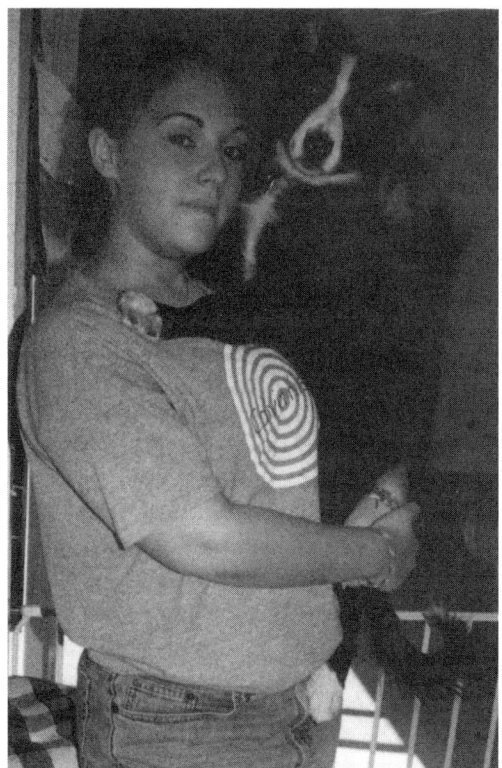

Katie Green says good-bye to four-month-old Shady before she leaves for school. Photo used with permission, Jeffrey Green, Total Recall Dog Training.

Life Changes: College, Country, and Careers

how bad the stress level gets, he is always there to make me feel better. Unconditional love combined with a selfless appreciation for each other. I wouldn't have had it any other way."[14]

Another very important consideration in bringing a companion animal to school is the logistics of traveling home for school breaks. In addition to the expense of maintaining your animal, can you afford to hire sitters or board your pet while you are gone? Or will you choose to stay at school during breaks? Many university-owned dormitories, as well as the privately owned dormitories and other types of housing, often close for cleaning, repair, and other maintenance during breaks. For teens with vehicles on campus who attend schools within a reasonable driving distance from home, bringing animal companions home for weekends and the long winter, spring, and summer breaks can be a reasonable option. However, if teens need to travel by plane, bus, train, or other forms of transportation—or if they cannot bring their pets into their family home—having companion animals on campus can pose unanticipated problems for both students and the animals. With the tight restrictions airlines now impose on the types of liquids that can be transported, even transporting a Betta fish on a plane is impossible.

There is no doubt in Brigitte's mind that her horse will be accompanying her to college, even though many universities

A PERSONAL GLIMPSE

Dilemmas can also offer opportunities. As strange as it may sound, Jessica Katz's fish ultimately became responsible for choosing her current boyfriend. Once she realized she wouldn't be able to bring her fish home for the summer because she was flying home from out of state, she was desperate. "I asked a friend on the floor if he would take my fish over the summer and he did, and now we have been dating for about a month. He is compassionate person and he's just wonderful! Plus he's a 'dog' person like me."[15]

restrict where freshmen are allowed to live. "I'm thinking of living on campus and then boarding him off campus if I have enough money to do that. Plus, I may not have a car on campus, which could be a big problem. Fortunately, a lot of schools have campus barns where they allow their students to board their horses. That would make it a lot easier and probably not be as expensive as it would if I had to take my horse to someone else's place, because that could easily be $600 a month. And that would be a *lot* to pay. Actually getting into another schedule with them is going to be harder, plus being able to balance all my studies. And then I would also like to hang out with friends in addition to doing things with the horse. So if I do bring my horse with me I would like to do something with him, like competitive equestrian teams, stuff like that. It will be hard physically, but I'm not worried about taking him. I think it will just make our relationship stronger."[16]

MOVING TO A DIFFERENT COUNTRY

Not all teens attend college. And sometimes jobs or other family needs cause teens or young adults to move to places

Brigitte Mason and equine friend. Photo used with permission, Brigitte and Robert Mason.

where taking their pets is not possible or practical. When people temporarily or permanently move from their native country to another, they usually are able to take their children and spouses with them. But what happens to their companion animals? What is involved in bringing the family dog or cat across borders or across the world?

Since she was married, Yoko Ageta has moved from country to country with her husband and her son, Toshihiro. They moved from Japan to the Netherlands and then to the United States in 2004, with plans to return home to Japan in 2007. During their stay in the United States, their yellow lab, Kai, lived with them in a rented house in a suburban subdivision. Through all their moves, they never once considered giving up Kai because he is considered as much a part of their family as each of them. And with the family's continual moves from country to country, Yoko's teenage son needed some stability. In situations where families move to different locations, such as military families or businesses that require transfers every couple of years, teens have difficulty initiating and maintaining friendships. They no sooner invest in a friendship when they must leave. Kai was the one friend that remained constant for Toshihiro, no matter where he called home. However, bringing a dog from one country to another is more than just a casual experience, and bringing Kai into the United States was not only very expensive, it was also very stressful. According to the U.S. Embassy, the requirements for bringing a dog into the United States are very specific and detailed, including having a rabies vaccination at least thirty days before entering the United States, and all cats must be free of evidence of communicable disease. Animals entering the United States from some countries may have to stay in quarantine for up to thirty days.[17] Exceptions to these strict rules exist only if you have a service animal, which only allows you to be placed at the front of the screening line. International travel itself can be extremely stressful for animals, since animals must not only be separated from their families, they must also be confined for many hours within a cargo area of the plane, a situation that can be frightening to some animals and equally stressful for their

Chapter 7

families. And as with all travel, there always exists the potential for injury or escape.

It is not always practical or even possible to bring a dog or other pet from one part of the world to another. Because of finances and other reasons, young people who move to the United States from other countries may have to leave their best friends in their home countries. Both Katarzyna Szymanska and Marta Masiewicz came to the United States from Poland when they were in their late teens or early twenties. Katya came here to find work, while Marta came to the United States to be with her boyfriend. Both young women had to leave their dogs behind with family members who remained in Poland. And both had no choice. Even if their families had agreed to part with their pets, it was simply too expensive to bring the dogs here.

Marta hasn't seen her dog, Dina, for almost two years. She feels confident, however, that she is in good hands with her parents and sister. "For my dog, I was the most important person. I miss my dog, too. When I call home, I always ask my mom about my dog—how she feels, what funny thing happened, etc."[18] Katya describes her dog, Sara, as being like a sister to her. But the four-year-old dog remained at her parents' home in Poland because they loved Sara so much they wouldn't let her take the dog with her. What Katya remembers most about the day she left was that "I was so sad, and my dog was, too. But, my sister said 'Don't worry! I'll send photos!'"[19] Although these two young women miss their dogs, they both feel they wouldn't have had time for them if they had brought them to the United States, and that would not have been fair to the dogs.

Tina Swinkels's immediate family moved to the United States from Australia for a year so they could experience American culture, but decided to leave their dog, Patches, in Australia with a trusted relative. Tina, a high school junior, feels Patches is happy where he is because he is living on sixteen acres with three children and another dog to play with. "I really loved the way he would always make me happy. If I was in a bad mood I would just go for a walk with him. Yeah, I missed him a lot at first, and it was sad saying good-bye but I know he is happy where he is."[20]

CAREERS

Imagine waking up each morning totally excited about going to work! That's the goal of every career counselor in advising students on career paths that meet their individual needs. One way for teens who love animals to accomplish that goal is to tie the two together. Career choices should involve more than education and academic expectations; they should also include natural talents, interests, character traits, and temperament.

ANIMAL-RELATED CAREERS

The following are just some of the many career paths teens who love animals can choose:

- Veterinarian, technician or assistant, animal massage therapist, chiropractor, pet grief counselor
- Manufacturer or retail salesperson for animal related products such as food, clothing, accessories, bedding, and grooming supplies
- Breeder or trainer for animal assisted therapy programs, service/guide animals, search and various law enforcement/military dogs, or for entertainment
- Groomer or other worker at boarding kennels, doggy daycare, spas, camps, pet transport service, dog walking, or pet waste removal services
- Dog writer, photographer, portrait painter, or dog show handler, groomer, or judge
- Scientific research in animal husbandry, genetics, food, or medicine
- Environmentalist, political activist, animal rescue/shelters, animal welfare

Chapter 7

Possibilities for including animals in a career are as varied as pursuing a law degree focusing on animal rights advocacy or becoming a hair stylist and working as a groomer or dog show handler.

Besides a passion for animals, what other factors might motivate a teen to choose activities or careers directly related to or involving animals? High school student Ruth Toht feels that an individual's unique personality, environment, or even a single event might also play a part. "If you have a love for animals from a young age, you're likely to pick a career working with animals somehow. And while a person's personality has to do with how and why they like animals, an event or series of events with enough impact can also be the reason why a teen would fall in love with working with animals."[21]

Brigitte Mason and Julie Kisman are both very close with their parents. Julie feels that while her parents are very loving, caring people, her passion for animals is something she was just born with. "My parents love animals, but if it wasn't for the love and passion I have, our family wouldn't have had companion animals. But they have always been very supportive." Early experiences with her grandfather also influenced her. "When I was younger my grandpa would take me to the pond to feed the ducks. He *always* talked about animals and how much he loved them!"[22] Brigitte was influenced by both her mother and her grandmother, and her passion for horses has completely influenced her future career choice. While her dad doesn't feel he's as much of an animal lover, Bob Mason is extremely supportive and wants to do whatever he can to make her happy. He says, "If having horses and doing competitive sports with them makes her happy, I'll continue doing what I can to encourage her. And if she chooses to go into equine genetics for a career, I will also support her decision 100 percent."[23]

Combining your love for animals with a career, however, is more than just combining a degree with some experience around a family pet. You should have a passion for it. Like many other teens, Rebecca's passion for animals was obvious at a very young age. "Not all children grow up being told by their parents they can be whatever they want to be, but both my parents would tell me that on a daily basis. I remember wanting to be a part of the animal field when I was five years old. Some children grow out of the veterinarian or vet tech phase; I just never did. Once my parents realized I was truly in it for the long haul, they took me to as many animal type places we could find. We were *always* hitting local zoos or aquariums on vacations! My parents were very supportive in all my endeavors, and have helped me reach my goals."[24] Trish Hampton is studying for a career in forensics in the civilian sector, which will include visiting crime scenes and collecting evidence, and she hopes she can eventually combine her love for her dog with her profession. If she chooses, she could eventually train to handle bomb- or drug-sniffing dogs or become a forensics specialist.

It can be difficult for young people to make major decisions about their future without knowing what their possibilities might be. After all, college decisions are made when a teen is only seventeen or eighteen years old, when most teens have had only limited job experience or might not have an aptitude for the types of classes they might need for certain majors.

Faye Nuddleman attends Kirkwood Community College in Cedar Rapids, Iowa. She didn't declare an "official" major as a freshman in 2007, but she was already preparing to become a veterinarian. Although she had wanted to be a vet as a child, she changed her mind several times in high school, including entertaining choices as far flung as becoming an engineer or a pilot. The turning point, however, came when a family cat had kittens. "Tekila had an infection while she was pregnant with her kittens, and one kitten (a little red one) ended up failing when he was a few months old. I stayed home from school that day and held [Riley] while he died in my arms. That's when I really started thinking again about becoming a vet."[25]

It is also common for students to begin in one field of study and then change direction—and majors—in the middle of their college education. Chase wants to pursue an animal-related career but isn't sure what he wants to do. Although his current major, outdoor recreation, will prepare him for careers dealing with animal ecosystems, he would prefer one involving hands-on interaction with animals. Chase comments, "In retrospect, I may have made a mistake not doing a biology major, but I'm currently exploring the option of doing an animal behavior minor."[26]

Because of her varied experiences, Rebecca has developed an appreciation for many different animal-related fields and the animals involved in them, making it difficult to narrow down which field she wants to pursue. "I plan on staying in the animal medical field. However, if I could lump all animals into a group and work with them in different ways all at the same time, I would be in heaven!"[27]

IT HAPPENED TO ME: THE BOND IN ACTION

After taking time off from college to decide what career direction she wanted to pursue, Janet Carhuayano took a reception job in New York City and not only found a stray dog wandering around the streets, she also found her calling.

The dog was picked up by the local shelter, but it had mange, a highly contagious skin disease. Janet was also told the shelter only takes care of strays for a few days and then they're put down. "*That* just devastated me! I decided right then to start looking at shelters to find out if I could work at one. I felt so horrible [about that little dog]. I needed to help these animals in any way I could so they could be adopted and not put to sleep." She was relieved to discover a no-kill shelter nearby and applied for the first job opening available—cleaning kennels. Although this job may not seem glamorous, Janet discovered she really got to know each of the individual shelter dogs and was able to alert the vet tech if she saw anything unusual or if a dog became sick, since airborne infections are easily passed in such close quarters. "When new dogs came in they'd be scared, so they didn't always eat. I got to know what kind of things they liked and what kind of food they wanted so they wouldn't go hungry. I also gave each of them quality time, getting them out with the various volunteers to learn to connect again to people so they would open up to humans again and be adopted. That was the most rewarding thing for me."[28]

Life Changes: College, Country, and Careers

Animals in shelters benefit from teen volunteers willing to spend time just playing with them. Drawing by Christa Baker, used with permission.

Many teens that develop a lifelong passion for animals have had bad experiences with animals. But that negative experience doesn't seem to change their perception and love for animals. Julie once found a stray dog when she was younger that bit her on the face, right near her eye. "You would think after that I would not like dogs, and even be afraid of them, but that sure didn't happen. I still love them!"[29]

Chapter 7

VOLUNTEERING

Choosing a career is a little like buying a car sight unseen and without taking it for a test drive. It can take years to be academically prepared for a field before students ever have hands-on experience to know if they've made the right decision. With all the possible choices, how can a teen know which career direction is right for them?

Volunteer work is one of the easiest ways a teen can experience different types of jobs and get real hands-on experience in the field. The advantage of volunteering is that teens not only experience real job situations, they also have opportunities to learn from people who have already been educated and trained to perform many types of skills in that field. For example, physical and occupational therapists treating patients at a therapeutic riding stable perform various forms of therapy while the teen volunteers assist with tasks. Not only do these teens see the results of the therapeutic riding, they also have the advantage of being part of an actual clinical experience, something that is usually only experienced in higher education.

High school student Natasha McDonald began helping out at a therapeutic riding stable because she wanted to work with children and horses, and this was a place that allowed her to do both. While there, Natasha performed a variety of different tasks, including leading horses during riding sessions, "side walking" (walking on the side of the horse while someone else leads so the child does not fall), cleaning horse stalls, grooming and feeding horses, and teaching private riding lessons. She feels her experiences there have mostly been amazing. "The kids have benefited so much from their experiences with the horses and riding. When they ride, the horse and the kids develop a special bond. You can just tell they have one because you can see it in their faces and hear it in the way that they talk about the horses." One of Natasha's fondest moments occurred while teaching a six-year-old girl who was blind. "When she got off the horse, I would let her groom it. When she was brushing her horse, her face was just so calm and peaceful. You could tell she was just so in love with that horse. And normally when we try to groom him, he goes crazy. But the horse was just standing there, calm and still, letting her brush him. It was amazing to see him letting her do this. It was like he could sense she was okay and wasn't going to hurt him."

Although Natasha had never considered a career with children and animals prior to her volunteer work at the riding stable, her current plan is to become a physical therapist and work with disabled children. She also wants to include therapeutic riding in her career, something that she is already gaining experience in through her volunteer work. "Horses and animals are just always going to be part of my life. I don't see how they couldn't be."[30]

IT HAPPENED TO ME: THE BOND IN ACTION

While most animals turned in to rescue groups require only basic health care, such as treatment for parasites or mange, many require more extensive medical treatment and care. Rescue organizations depend on foster volunteers, financial contributions, and volunteer veterinarians. Julie Kisman has been volunteering and providing foster care for many years through Collie Rescue, especially helping dogs that need a little extra care.

"Lucy was a collie turned in by her owner because of 'family issues,' but it soon became apparent she could not go up and down the stairs very well. After X-rays and a whole bunch of tests, the vet discovered Lucy needed double hip replacement surgery, which is expensive and involves a lengthy healing." Julie and her mom picked Lucy up only two days after her surgery. They had to use a walking harness just to help the dog relieve herself. Julie slept with her on the laundry-room floor for the first few nights and checked every two hours to make sure she was okay. She kept a night-light on so the dog could see and not be afraid. Over the next few months, Lucy got stronger and regained her muscle strength through treatments at a veterinarian rehab facility and learned to walk on her own again. The dog had a very sweet disposition and eventually found a new, loving home with a family in a neighboring suburb. A year later, Julie saw Lucy again at the Collie Rescue picnic and was asked to speak to the group about her experience fostering a dog healing from major surgery. "Although it had already been a year, it was still hard for me to talk about it without tearing up. Everyone who had been involved helping Lucy was in tears, too, after hearing my story and seeing how far she had come along. I'll always have a special place in my heart for her."[31]

Chapter 7

INTERNSHIP PROGRAMS

Young people can also explore different career possibilities by applying for internships, where teens get a real glimpse into the reality of different career choices and fields, and benefit from the advice of those who already are in those fields. Teens who love animals and want to pursue a career directly or indirectly involving animals can benefit from programs available in fields as varied as veterinary studies and journalism to animal-assisted therapy and marine biology.

Communications major Kelli Herbel had the incredible opportunity to jump right into a real-world publishing environment before completing her education, an experience that would never have happened if it weren't for her passion for animals. A dog lover her entire life, Kelli applied to and was accepted as an intern at the American Kennel Club headquarters in New York City, where she actually got to do editorial work on the two magazines published by the AKC—*AKC Gazette* and *Family Dog*. Kelli had already been involved for many years in showing dogs as a junior handler at AKC-sanctioned dog shows. At one of these shows, a woman working with junior handlers and the internship program suggested Kelli apply to this nationwide program, which involved filling out an extensive application form with questions about the various dog sports and their histories. It also included a phone interview. "That was probably the worst thing for me because I don't know what's happening in the silence, like if they're writing or if they're waiting for me to say something or what. And, of course, I can't see their facial expressions, something that is actually very nerve-wracking for me."[32]

Once Kelli was notified she had been accepted into the internship program, she found lodging in New Jersey with some dog obedience people her parents knew from their involvement in herding trials. Kelli was unable to take her dogs with her and missed them terribly, but because the people she stayed with had dogs, she still had daily interaction with canines. The AKC publishes dog-related magazines and other publications, and Kelli was placed in the publishing department, which is closely related to her field of study. Kelli soon discovered that not only did her prior experience with dogs help her with the articles she was editing or proofreading, but her familiarity with breeds and terminology also allowed her to add input when needed.

Volunteer work and internships can even be part of a school curriculum. Jessica, an animal science major at the University of Vermont, was able to use internship experience at A Refuge for Saving the Wildlife for college credit, paving the way for other students to participate in internship programs with this organization. While looking for internships she remembered being told about a local bird refuge. She looked it up on the Internet and gave the director a call. His initial response was "Are you serious?" He had never contemplated the idea of having an intern before. As a result of her internship with this organization, Jessica definitely knows she wants a career that directly involves animals. She states, "I am very grateful to them for this experience; it is honestly probably one of the highlights of my life. I would love to do welfare work and that comes with my deep interest in animal behavior. I've always wondered why animals do what they do. That's why the birds are so interesting to me. I'm more interested in caring for the animals then making a profit."[33] While Jessica's primary interest is in working with birds, she is also interested in working with other exotics, like reptiles and ferrets, in localized shelter settings. She feels lizards are often mistreated and as misunderstood as birds are. However, because she suffers from animal-related allergies, she is considering working on the administrative side rather than in direct contact with the animals.

LEARNING TO BECOME FINANCIALLY SELF-SUFFICIENT

With college costs continuing to rise and many four-year degrees taking five years or more to complete, it's no wonder

Chapter 7

> **IT HAPPENED TO ME: INTERNSHIP AT SEA WORLD**
>
> When Kaylah Dodd's parents took her to the Indianapolis Zoo as a young child, she fell in love with the dolphin show and decided she wanted to become a dolphin trainer. As she learned more about the ocean and the creatures that lived in them, she decided instead on a career in marine biology. After visits to SeaWorld Adventure Parks in Florida and Texas, Kaylah decided to visit the website and discovered that SeaWorld offered an internship program. She applied and was accepted to the spring 2002 session. One of the intern activities involved feeding the dolphins. "It was *so* much fun! After we were done feeding, we got to play with them using huge rubber balls. We would throw the balls in and they would push them around and try and get them out again. At one point I started playing 'hide and seek' with the dolphins. I would run down the side and duck, then crawl away a few feet and pop up again. They were all following me and vocalizing. It was *so* awesome!" However, some activities also involved jobs that were not as much fun. "We had to clean *a lot*! More than I ever thought. All that cleaning made me really realize how much work being a trainer is, let alone being a parent. Feeding the sharks was fun too, but we had to stuff vitamins into fish chunks, and it smelled horrible! I swear I smelled like fish for two days after I left the camp!" She also got to touch the animals, something she had never done before. But mostly, she came away from her internship experience more focused and certain about her career choice. "I liked touching the beluga whales' bump on their head; it's squishy. The dolphins feel like rubber and their skin kind of peels off, which surprised me. We also got to touch the killer whales . . . and one was named Kaylah! I fell in love even more with the idea of researching their habitats. My internship made me realize I didn't want to become a trainer. I'm not sure I have the patience that is needed to become a trainer. I would rather be out in the open every day, and that discovery also opened my eyes to the idea of doing research with sharks."[34]

that students are strapped financially. And young people do need to take that into careful consideration when they bring an animal into their lives while they are still in school. On the other hand, when responsible teens and young adults have companion animals, financial lessons learned can be invaluable.

Life Changes: College, Country, and Careers

Kelli feels that caring for animals has helped her become a more responsible person with her finances. "I pay for everything. A lot of college kids still have their parents paying for everything but they're not even going to class. They don't appreciate their education and are messing up their lives. There are just so many kids my age who want to be adults, want to make all their own decisions, but they still want—and expect—Mommy and Daddy to pay for everything. So you can choose to not grow up and stay dependent, or you can grow up and pay for everything. I decided to be independent *and* responsible!"[35]

Because Brigitte has already decided on a career path involving animals, she feels she'll have a definite advantage over many of her peers. Meanwhile, she plans to compete in equine breed shows and is in the process of purchasing a top-quality horse to show. "The entry fees are a large amount of money. The horses that go there are the best of the best, and my quarter horse just isn't good enough or competitive enough to do quarter horse shows." But while Brigitte's parents agreed she could purchase a new competition horse, they aren't footing the bill for this new venture. Not only has Brigitte paid for all her show entry fees for years, she also plans to pay for her new horse using money she has earned and won. "I'm not the girl who goes out to the shopping mall and decides she needs to spend $300 on a T-shirt, so I don't spend my money like that. I work at a local stable and have also been saving my money for years, so it just accumulated from there."[36]

Brigitte and Kelli aren't the only teens whose parents have encouraged them to become financially responsible. There was a point in Richelle's life where she had both her horse and her rabbits and was traveling to rabbit shows with entry fees alone totaling up to $200 a weekend. But with her brother in college, Richelle's parents needed to cut something out of their budget. They gave her the choice to either sell her horse or stop going to the rabbit shows. This was a difficult decision for the teen, but she chose the rabbit shows. Richelle sold the horse, however, to someone who lets her and her mom ride her whenever they want, plus the new owners pay the vet bills! They couldn't have asked for a better situation! And Richelle still gets to show her rabbits, obviously the closest thing to her heart.

Chapter 7

MAKING WISE CAREER CHOICES

When choosing a career with animals, examine the difference between "humane careers" and careers that exploit animals. According to the Humane Society of the United States, there are some concerns teens should have when investigating potential careers. It is important to realize that some jobs may involve work that might also inflict various degrees of suffering on animals, from mild stress to extreme pain. Although these concerns may not always arise, the potential for them exists in areas such as research, testing, and breeding; zoos, aquariums, amusements (such as animal fighting or pony rides), and circuses; and businesses that use animals in the production of food, clothing, cosmetics, and drugs. Careers involving the exploitation and consumptive use of animals can create many difficult emotional situations for people who care deeply about animals, so it is especially important to keep in mind the possibility of potential emotional distress as you research and interview for jobs in these fields.

SPORTS AND OTHER ACTIVITIES

Volunteering, interning, and working in a job involving animals are fantastic ways to learn, but there are also many animal-related recreational activities students can participate in that can help prepare them for later careers. Just a few of these include science fair competitions, county and state fair activities and competitions, various animal sports, and therapy animal programs.

Both Brigitte and Rebecca participated in science fair activities that brought them to the state level in competition. Brigitte's interest in horses and equine genetics formed the basis for her project on paying for her new horse, while Rebecca's project developed as a way to help a brood of baby birds. Since Brigitte was planning to get another horse, she decided to base her project on economics, which wound up winning both Grand and Best at county level as a Financial Champions entry. The project may have had nothing to do with animals but it did demonstrate some very real issues of animal ownership, including how Brigitte might pay off the entire horse and how long it would take. A friend's mom raised parakeets, and when some of the young were not taking to their mother the way they should, she and her friend decided to hand raise them and teach them what they needed to know. They turned the endeavor into a science fair project demonstrating the differences between birds raised by their natural mom and those that are hand fed by humans. "Raising the birds gave me a strong sense of purpose, as well as a great amount of responsibility, because I was the birds' sole source of life. It was up to me to make them who they were to become. And although it made me feel successful, I never felt the pressure behind it, just the importance of doing the job right. I also loved raising these baby parakeets because it put some light on my dream of being a vet tech and reassured me that that is what I truly wanted. Every experience with young animals is good experience for the future."[37]

Where a student lives or attends school makes a difference in the type of sports, volunteer activities, and internships that are available. Aside from participating in certain dog sports, Kelli felt her geographic location limits her. "It's kind of tough for me, because in rural Oklahoma you don't really have the opportunities to participate in a lot of the other activities, like agility or therapy dog. There's very little of that in this area, although I did train and compete in herding, obedience, and junior showmanship competitions. One program I learned about from my internship at the AKC was the Reading Education Assistance Program, where therapy dogs go into elementary schools and the children read to the dogs. I think it's a great program, but getting my dog registered as a certified therapy dog and starting a program in my area would cost a lot of money. Plus, I would need time to devote to it. But if someone were already a teacher or librarian, that might be nice to add to your existing programs, as well as an interesting way of combining your career with animals. Like, if someone wanted to go into education or library science, and they loved animals, they could actually combine the two. And that's

Chapter 7

actually not a bad way to start the day . . . going to work with your dog!"[38]

While she's still in school, Jessica has found yet another outlet to make animals' lives better. In addition to volunteering at an avian rescue organization when she is home on breaks, she has also begun working as a volunteer with a therapy dog group. Many high school or college students do not realize programs like these are available, but teens who have the heart for working with animals can benefit greatly by getting involved in these types of campus activities. Jessica explains: "I am part of a group here at the University of Vermont that takes greyhounds to visit rehab centers and nursing homes. It is very interesting to interact with these people. A lot of them are very old and rather sick but they want to share their stories. The dogs are a great gateway to conversation and interaction. It's really very fulfilling for everyone."[39]

A teen's love for animals might also lead to career choices taking unexpected turns. Although Kyle Fetter's original dream was to become a vet, after he decided to leave college and pursue a different career track, his dream took a different form. No matter what Kyle eventually does, he plans to be involved with animals for the rest of his life. "We've gotten all our dogs from a shelter, and something I've always considered is that if I ever do become financially successful, what I'd really like to do is to help finance an animal shelter. I feel like right now I've got a lot to prove because I did leave school. I'm not saying that's great, but basically when I left, I also wanted to prove I could still do it well and make good money. I think I can accomplish that if I can start a good business. And any way that I can connect those two goals would be great! I would love to be able to support good causes. People don't think about being a philanthropist when they're growing up. You actually don't realize how many animal-related jobs there are. Everyone's first assumption is you have to become a vet. But it would be great if I could just write a million-dollar check for someone who's going to just take every dime of it to help animals. I'd *love* to give money to that; I feel that's a *very* good cause. You know, there's a lot of other good causes out there, but because this is something that has had such an influence on my own life, it's something I'd feel very good about being a part of."[40]

At Your Service: Hot Careers

The explosive growth in the pet industry has given rise to several new ways to combining a love of animals with a career. Some of the hottest careers involving companion animals can actually be found in the service sector, and places like doggie daycare, bakeries, spas, and camps catering to four-legged "children" are now part of the economic landscape from coast to coast. Add in growing franchises for mobile vets and groomers, animal transport services, personal dog trainers, dog walkers, pet sitters, and waste removal services, and you have a better idea of the types of services that have become necessities rather than luxuries.[41]

Additional career opportunities reflect new technologies such as microchipping and maintaining recovery databases. Not only are lost pets with microchips more likely to be reunited with owners, they also save animal control agencies time and expense. Many towns and cities are considering and passing ordinances requiring pets to be microchipped. For example, because of the increasing dog and cat population, city officials in Evansville, Indiana, proposed an ordinance that offered a substantial reduction on the city's annual licensing fee for all pets that were spayed/neutered *and* microchipped. The ordinance passed and took effect December 16, 2006. According to a January 3, 2007, report in the *Evansville Courier Press*, the drastically increased number of microchipped pets demonstrated a very positive public response to the ordinance.[42]

One perk in service sector careers is that many of them do not necessarily require formal schooling beyond a high school diploma, or perhaps classes at a junior college or accredited vocational facility. You can even be trained on the job in some fields, like vet assistant or dog bather. And many programs for careers like groomers, trainers, and animal massage therapists can be completed in two years or less.

Chapter 7

According to the American Pet Products Association, one of the nation's fastest-growing job and career sectors in pet services involves some form of pet sitting.[43] Taking time off from college has given Janet a new perspective and a chance to really experience being a dog walker. She plans to return to school for a business degree so she can run her own dog-walking business. Janet explains that she chose this career for several reasons: "First of all, I live in Manhattan. In the financial district, where I am, they're turning a lot of the buildings into residential, so now there are now twice as many dogs down here. We have quite a few dog walkers, but there's still so much more business still coming in because there are *so* many dogs!" The public transportation system makes it possible for Janet to travel from one end of Manhattan to the other, wherever her dog-walking clients are located. "When I was nineteen, I worked for a pet-sitting business that took care of animals from dogs to fish. Our company wanted their clients to meet us before we took care of their pets, and you get different clients that are not in the same area. So I'd jump from downtown to the East Side or the West Side or the Village. I'd be all over the place." This is an ideal job for teens who love animals, are physically active, like to be outside in all types of weather, and want a job that keeps them physically fit. Because Janet still needs to walk from the subway or bus to her clients' homes, she stays in good physical shape as well as in good spirits. "The dogs I walk are just so happy to see me each day!"[44]

In contrast to urban living, where dog owners walk dogs along city streets and at dog parks, most suburbanites live in houses with yards where dogs are let out to do their business, giving rise to yet another thriving business—dog waste cleanup. In suburbia, dog walkers and pet-sitting services are also thriving. However, in these areas, a reliable automobile is required, because clients are often spread out and public transportation does not suffice. Julie lives in a growing suburban area in the Midwest. She is currently a pet sitter and dog walker for people in her area and is also considering going to school to become an animal massage therapist. "I really enjoy pet sitting. Of course, some nights when I'm tired, I wish I didn't have to go back to let them out again but that's just part of the job. I mean, it's not like they can let themselves out to go potty. But once I'm on my way I'm happy about going to see them again. And knowing I make such a difference in their lives is very rewarding."[45]

WORKING WHILE IN SCHOOL

Whether they initially decide to pursue animal-related careers or simply careers that can involve animals at a later point, young people can find opportunities to work in entry-level jobs in animal-related fields while they work on their academics. Rebecca is doing just that. "I did not get a job until I was eighteen because I knew how hard it was to get into any type of veterinary career. I decided to focus on school first and get the best grades possible. And my first job was at a local veterinary practice!" Although her official title was "kennel girl," Rebecca was also allowed to assist in the exam rooms. While she did receive a lot of experience, she still wanted to get the full experience of what it would be like to be a vet tech. When a position for a vet assistant opened up, Rebecca jumped at the chance, since that position allowed her to be trained on the job. "I worked at that vet clinic for a little over two years while getting my college Gen Ed classes done, and I loved it! I had always known what I wanted to do all of these years, but to be living it even slightly for those couple of years just reinforced and amplified my goals."[46]

Vet assistant Kristy Kosinski suggests, "Volunteer, volunteer, volunteer! Some vet clinics really need volunteers, too. It's a *great* way to get your feet in the door and make sure it's a field you really want to enter."[47] Kristy adds that teens interested in veterinary careers should read a lot, too. But, she cautions, be sure to only read up-to-date texts. Between increasing numbers of scientific discoveries and the ability to share communication so quickly, the field continues to change rapidly, so books, articles, and websites need to be current for accuracy.

Doing something you love involving something you feel passionate about is the most satisfying choice anyone can make.

Chapter 7

It is up to each person to walk his or her own path, but with encouragement and determination, most young people can find a way to combine their love for animals with a career or outside activity. Rebecca sums it all up: "If there is any advice I can give to younger students it would simply be to keep striving for your dream and start planning *now*. If you can learn a large chunk of the science and math, it will help tremendously in college. Also, get involved with animals wherever you can. You can help out at animal shelters or even with a job like tending the kennels at a local vet clinic. All of these things helped me to get where I am today and I couldn't be happier."[48]

NOTES

1. Katie Green, excerpt from poem "My Pal," e-mail to the author, January 2007.
2. Nichole Freeman, interview with the author, December 2006.
3. Janet Carhuayano, interview with the author, October 2006.
4. Jessica Katz, e-mail to the author, December 2006.
5. Richelle Hellpap, interview with the author, October 2006.
6. Chase Herndon, interview with the author, February 2007.
7. Kyle Fetters, interview with the author, September 2006.
8. Katz, e-mail to the author, December 2006.
9. Green, e-mail to the author, December 2006.
10. Jey McGahan, interview with the author, February 2007.
11. Brigitte Mason, interview with the author, August 23, 2006.
12. Kelli Herbel, interview with the author, October 2006.
13. Mary Dyrhaug, interview with the author, January 2007.
14. Rebecca Britz, e-mail to the author, October 2006.
15. Katz, e-mail to the author, December 2006.
16. Mason, interview with the author, August 23, 2007.
17. U.S. Customs and Border Protection website, www.cbp.gov; and "Travel to the USA," U.S. Embassy, Tokyo, Japan, website, http://aboutusa.japan.usembassy.gov/e/jusa-faq-travel.html#107 (accessed May 24, 2007).
18. Marta Masiewicz, letter to the author, October 6, 2006.
19. Katarzyna Szymanska, letter to the author, October 6, 2006.
20. Tina Swinkels, interview with the author, December 2006.
21. Ruth Toht, interview with the author, September 2006.
22. Julie Kisman, interview with the author, April 2006.

23. Robert Mason, interview with author, August 23, 2007.
24. Britz, e-mail to the author, October 2006.
25. Faye Nuddleman, interview with the author, April 2007.
26. Herndon, interview with the author, February 2006.
27. Britz, e-mail to the author, October 2006.
28. Carhuayano, interview with the author, October 2006.
29. Kisman, e-mail to the author, April 2006.
30. Natasha McDonald, interview with the author, December 2006.
31. Kisman, e-mail to the author, April 2006.
32. Herbel, interview with the author, October 2006.
33. Katz, e-mail to the author, December 2006.
34. Kaylah Dodd, interview with the author, September 2006.
35. Herbel, interview with the author, October 2006.
36. Brigitte Mason, interview with the author, August 23, 2006.
37. Britz, e-mail to the author, October 2006.
38. Herbel, interview with the author, October 2006.
39. Katz, e-mail to the author, December 2006.
40. Fetters, interview with the author, September 2006.
41. "Too Busy to Drive Your Dog?" *Pet Product News* (August 2006): 22.
42. Jimmy Nesbitt, "Animal Ordinance Support Cited," *Evansville Courier & Press Courier Press*, January 3, 2007, www.courierpress.com/news/2007/jan/03/animal-ordinance-support-cited/ (accessed November 26, 2007).
43. Marjorie Wertz, "Pampered Pets," *Pittsburgh Tribune-Review*, July 17, 2005, www.pittsburghlive.com/x/pittsburghtrib/s_353188.html (accesed May 24, 2007).
44. Carhuayano, interview with the author, October 2006.
45. Kisman, interview with the author, April 2006.
46. Britz, e-mail to the author, October 2006.
47. Kristy Kosinski, interview with the author, January 2007.
48. Britz, e-mail to the author, October 2006.

Overcoming Health Problems, Pet Loss, and Other Adversities

The lifestyle of most twenty-first-century teens is anything but healthy. Statistically, there are more overweight teens and young adults in the United States today than at any other time in history. Besides poor food choices and the prevalence of the fast-food lifestyle, teens do not exercise enough or get enough sleep. Too many hours spent on a chair in front of a TV, computer, or video game and driving everywhere instead of walking have taken their toll in creating a sedentary generation.

"Exercise can be a very lonely thing to do, but when you're with a dog, you're never really lonely doing it."
—Katie Green, college student, Northern Illinois University[1]

OBESITY: AN EPIDEMIC IN THE TWENTY-FIRST CENTURY

Our pets have not escaped this serious trend. Like their owners, they take in more calories than they use and wind up with less exercise because we, their human guardians, are too tired or pressed for time—or simply too lazy. However, unlike people, our pets don't choose to be obese. They don't connect the cause and effect. In the wild, animals weren't guaranteed a meal each time they were hungry. If they wanted to eat, they had to do something about it, from running and flying to hunting and foraging. Modern-day pets have effortless and endless supplies of food and treats from the hands of their humans. All they have to do is travel from their napping spot on the couch to their food bowl. How can they possibly maintain a healthy body weight or physical condition?

In the summer of 2006, Katie Green found out one of her dogs was overweight. "Our vet said he had to lose weight or it

Chapter 8

will take its toll on him, especially since he was eleven years old. I decided to walk him a lot more, so we basically became exercise partners. Not only did the two of us lose weight, we were also more energetic. Plus, we got to spent a lot of extra time together on our walks, which was great since I miss him so much when I'm away at school"[2] Kelli Herbel comments, "I don't really like to exercise. I know it's important, however, that you should be active and everything like that. Well, the only way I can get myself to exercise is if I walk my dogs. I know *they* need the exercise, and I'm the only one who can give that to them. My college has a new wellness center. It costs a lot of money to go to college here and I'm paying for that wellness center through all my fees and tuition, but I never use it because my dogs can't go inside! I walk outside around campus instead."[3]

Overweight pets can develop many of the same types of diseases humans do when overweight. Increased strain on the heart and joints can contribute or add to the development of joint and back problems or heart disease. And the larger and more overweight animals and teens are, the less physically active they may ultimately become, resulting in reduced physical exercise and ability to enjoy many activities. Kelli adds, "It amazes me that people don't realize their dogs are obese or visibly unhealthy because they have so much extra weight. And they have no idea; they just keep on feeding them Pop-Tarts or whatever. They shouldn't do that; they don't understand what a health risk it is for an animal with such a short life span. It's really going to take its toll on them but people aren't as conscious of this because we have such a long life span."[4] Obesity can seriously jeopardize your pet's health in other ways, too. Fat animals are at higher risk for serious disease, high blood pressure, and increased risk of diabetes, as well as a higher risk of complications during routine surgeries and anesthesia. So what steps can we take to help both humans and pets maintain a healthy weight and lifestyle?

What we eat is as important as when and how we eat. For many types of animals, such as hamsters, birds, or finicky cats and dogs, "free range" feeding, where they always have access

Overcoming Health Problems, Pet Loss, and Other Adversities

to food, is essential. For overweight pets, however, this only perpetuates the problem because it allows them to eat more food than they need. Eliminating the constant source of food prevents overeating. Other solutions include changing to a lower-calorie food, reducing the amount of food offered, and supplementing with low-fat cooked or fresh vegetables like green beans, carrots, or celery so the animal feels full but isn't taking in as many calories. For some pets, such as cats, better-quality food with a higher protein and reduced carbohydrate content can help shed pounds. Diet changes, however, must be introduced slowly and increased incrementally over a period of time. Putting pets on starvation or crash diets for quick weight loss does more harm than good. Safe weight loss should be slow, occurring gradually over a period of time that may vary from weeks to months. Crash or fad diets affect teens just as adversely as it does their pets. Young people who skip meals, don't consume enough protein, or suffer from eating disorders like anorexia or bulimia wind up losing lean muscle mass along with body fat at a time when their bodies are still growing.

Feed your dog or cat once or twice a day and measure the amount of food offered at each feeding according to the advice of your veterinarian. This helps you know exactly how much your pet really wants to eat for a single meal so you can adjust the amount you feed it accordingly. Eliminate extra calories by omitting treats or only offer occasional low-calorie, nutritionally sound treats like small pieces of raw apples, carrots, or other easy-to-digest veggies.

Evaluate what your companion animals do most of the day. Do they lie around snoozing or do they have the opportunity to run and play? It is up to you to provide them with the environment they need for physical activity. Provide climbing apparatus and interesting objects for birds to engage their minds and keep them active. Supply hamsters and gerbils with a running cycle and house them in modular living habitats connected with tunnels and tubes so they can run from nest to nest, as they would in the wild. Or do you have animals that need human interaction to be active and play? If so, make a conscious effort to increase your active physical interaction with them. Get safe, interactive toys to play with and engage your cat in active play sessions. Make a game of Frisbee or a brisk walk with your dog a part of your daily routine. If your dog is still overweight, try adding additional walking time or increasing your walking speed. When the weather won't allow outdoor activity, find creative ways to exercise indoors. Walking up and down the stairs and around the rooms in an unpredictable path is a great way to burn calories as well as mentally challenge your pet. Put on some music and use basic obedience commands and movements to try to dance with your dog.

Before initiating any of these suggestions, however, have your vet determine the best dietary changes to make and whether your pet is healthy enough to engage in increased physical activity. You will find the more you get up off the couch, push yourself away from the computer, and start exercising, the better both you *and* your pet will feel. As an extra bonus, the additional time you spend with your animal will only help foster that human-animal bond.

A curious cat can often entice even the most sedentary teen to play games involving some form of movement. Illustration by the author.

WALKING WITH DOGS

According to a 2005 study conducted by researchers at the University of Missouri–Columbia, daily walks with dogs encourage people to get more exercise, which can keep us in good shape and help us lose weight. The economically disadvantaged and disabled participants in the study were encouraged to walk researchers' and faculty members' dogs, offering these non-pet-owning participants an opportunity to be responsible for a pet and also enjoy some of the positive benefits of that relationship. The study found that having a pet can result in more weight loss than many recognized diet plans. So find a dog and get walking![5]

KEEP THEM HEALTHY!

Prevention is the key to keeping animals healthy. Make sure companion animals have fresh water, noncontaminated food, and clean food containers, housing (crates, cages, stalls, etc.), bedding, or litter. Also clean and sanitize outside run areas several times a year. Although many people are concerned with risk factors, vaccinations can prevent many deadly diseases that can be caught from unvaccinated domestic and wild animals. In some cases, such as rabies vaccinations, the law requires that your pet have up-to-date vaccinations.

Chapter 8

CARING FOR ANIMALS THAT ARE ILL

While some teens have never experienced illness or medical conditions with their companion animals, other teens are well acquainted with caring for animals that are sick. Animals can also suffer from conditions humans develop, like heart murmurs or epilepsy. Both Katie Green and Annalies Kocourek have experience with dogs that had seizures. Annalies recalls, "One of our dogs had a grand mal seizure before she died. She lived through it but was [permanently] paralyzed from the neck down, blind, and deaf. We had to put her down. That was pretty sad, but it was probably better than keeping her paralyzed, blind, and deaf like that."[6]

Katie had a dog that had frequent clusters of seizures. "Madison would have three to four grand mal seizures in a twenty-four- to forty-eight-hour period. And he'd come out of them like Annalies described, but he was only temporarily paralyzed, blind, or deaf. And sometimes he'd have heightened senses, which is the opposite, like the intensity of scent was increased. He'd try to do things like chew through walls or climb under pipes. He'd bite our face because he thought our breath was food. It is very tough watching a dog seize." Katie remembers a time when she was home alone and Madison began to have a seizure right at the top of the stairs. "I was so afraid he'd fall down the stairs while his body was spasming, so I had to think quickly. I grabbed a couple of bed pillows and placed them between him and the stairs. There were also times when he had seizures in the middle of the night. My bedroom is close to where he slept, so I could hear the unmistakable sounds. One summer night he had a seizure while my parents were asleep. But since I was still awake, I just brought him outside after he was done and cleaned him up. It was kind of spooky being alone in the yard hosing him off at 3 a.m.!"[7]

WHEN PEOPLE ARE ILL

Unless a friend, neighbor, or family member gets sick, most teens rarely think of debilitating diseases or illnesses. Why should they? Their bodies are just developing into their new adult shapes, hormones are raging, and they have their whole lives ahead of them. Although most diseases are relatively uncommon among children and teens, there are others that strike humans of all ages or appear during childhood or teen years. Leukemia, brain tumors, and juvenile diabetes are just a few of the conditions that typically strike young people.

Children and teens who develop these diseases feel isolated from their peers, which can add to their fears. And because of the mystery surrounding cancer, people often hesitate to touch anyone with cancer, partly out of fear they will catch it and partly out of fear they will hurt the person who is suffering with the disease. Healthy touch, however, can often comfort and soothe. Without it, an ill person might feel even worse. Pets can help fulfill that need, since they often know intuitively to be gentle or less exuberant when their humans are ill or in pain. Animals don't see tubes and wires or the physical appearance of a teen that is sick; instead, they sense someone in pain who needs their help. As Marty Becker states in his book *The Healing Power of Pets*, much of the fight against cancer is the "debilitating fear and loneliness of a diagnosis that feels like a death sentence. As with so many experiences with our animals, when you have your pet alongside you, you not only don't feel so alone, you feel alive."[8] Teens who are ill can also feel something paramount to survival: feeling loved and needed.

Animals not only inspire us to get up and get moving, they can also help take our focus off our pain and lift our spirits. The way we feel about or view our situations is also a result of our brain chemistry. Many naturally occurring "feel-good" chemicals are released or increased in our bloodstream as a result of the human-animal bond. Stroking a pet, watching fish swimming in a tank, or feeling the hot breath of a pony tickling your leg can trigger a chemical cascade of mood-altering biochemicals such as dopamine, beta-endorphins, prolactin, and oxytocin, which make us feel happy, calm, relaxed, safe, or joyful and block our processing of pain.

Chapter 8

> ### IT HAPPENED TO ME: THE BOND IN ACTION
>
> Katie Green witnessed exactly how a dog could help when her mom was recovering from surgery in 2003. "We have four active border collies. After my mom had outpatient surgery for breast cancer, we did not let the dogs anywhere near her because we were afraid they would hurt her. They could see her but were kept securely gated in another room. On the third day after her surgery, we allowed Shady, the dog my mom is very bonded with, into the room on a leash. We wanted to see if he would know what to do or if he would just be his normal bundle of energy greeting her, which would include putting his front legs on her chest so he could smother her in kisses. When he got into the room, he immediately raced to my mom and jumped on the couch. But then he froze, as if he had just been given a command to stop. Because he *is* so in tune with my mom, he must have understood he could hurt her. Instead, he approached my mom slowly and gently rested his head on her lap, kissing her hands and knees instead of her face, and avoiding her upper body, which was in pain from surgery. A week later my mom had a second surgery, but this time we allowed Shady into the room with her right after she came home from the hospital. Again, he demonstrated the same gentleness as before, never moving closer to her face than her lap and content to just lay with her on the couch. Being able to stroke his soft head, while his tail thumped out his feelings, was better for my mom than any painkiller! In fact, she didn't need anything stronger than Advil after that second surgery."[9]

Dogs and cats can also provide companionship for those suffering from AIDS or other diseases with social stigmas attached, since many of these sufferers are abandoned by family and friends. Teens with physical disfigurements or who suffer from illnesses, conditions, or diseases that physically disfigure them often relate to animals with similar problems. Animals can develop or be born with other medical problems such as encephalitis, epilepsy, heart conditions, diabetes, cleft palette, blindness, or deafness. Or they may develop conditions from abuse or neglect. A dog with three legs or a cat missing an eye may look horrible to many people, but teens who look beneath the superficial not only learn empathy by developing a

Overcoming Health Problems, Pet Loss, and Other Adversities

relationship with these animals, they can also learn to accept people for who they are instead of how they look.

CANCER: THE DISEASE THAT KNOWS NO SPECIES

While diseases such as multiple sclerosis or Parkinson's are ones that only affect humans, cancer is a disease that does not distinguish among species. Cancer strikes dogs, cats, and other mammals with an increasing regularity. Some cancers are treatable, with good prognosis for remission, while others are not. Since animals mask their symptoms when they are ill, it may not even be apparent a pet has cancer until it has reached a less treatable stage.

In January 2005, the Englewood/CO/PR Newswire reported that nearly 50 percent of natural deaths in older cats and dogs are attributed to cancer. Brigitte Mason notes, "My older horse has cancer in his eye. He's already had it once before and he had surgery but they can't remove it all, so now it's come back ten to twelve years later. I have to put ointment on his eye every day."[10]

KEEP IT SAFE!

Although many common household items and human food or ingredients are good for our pets, others are not. Some of these include:

- Chocolate
- Grapes and raisins
- Macadamia nuts
- Onion and garlic (high doses or concentrated)
- Avocado
- Foods containing Xylitol, an artificial sweetener
- Foods containing caffeine or theobromine (tea, coffee, cola beverages, etc.)
- Cooked chicken and turkey bones
- Uncooked yeast dough

Chapter 8

ALERT! EMERGENCY PLAN FOR YOUR PETS

According to an article in the August 2006 issue of *Pet Age* magazine, the Pets Evacuation and Transportation Standards Act (referred to as the PETS Act) was introduced into the House of Representatives shortly after Hurricane Katrina in 2005, when so many pets had to be abandoned because there were no emergency accommodations for them. This bill includes a mandate allowing pets to be included in disaster preparations and authorizes funding for the creation of emergency shelters that accommodate both people and their pets. As an extra incentive, the bill also proposes that emergency offices not offering accommodations for pets would not qualify for Federal Emergency Management Agency grants.[11]

It makes good sense to prepare in advance for emergencies, especially because survival in an emergency such as an earthquake, hurricane, tornado, fire, flood, power outage, or act of terror is directly related to planning done before the emergency. Each family should create an emergency plan and supply kit specifically for their animals. This kit should include items that people also need, such as food, water, and basic first aid supplies, as well as identification tags, collars, leashes, carriers, and a way to deal with pets' bathroom needs.

Depending on the circumstances and the type of emergency, you may need to determine whether it is safer to stay or to leave, so develop plans in advance for both options. An appropriately sized portable pet carrier or crate might mean the difference between being allowed to take your pets with you or leaving them behind. If you must evacuate, try to take your pets with you, if possible. However, circumstances might prohibit that, so plan in advance for shelter alternatives that will work for both you and your pets. Kennels or veterinary hospitals near an evacuation center might serve as alternative shelters for your pets. Your vet might have additional suggestions for you. Research and gather a list of facilities in other places where you might have to seek shelter if you must evacuate. Keep this list with your emergency supply kit so you will have it with you while you are in transit. Create a backup emergency plan with

Overcoming Health Problems, Pet Loss, and Other Adversities

PLANNING AHEAD

An emergency supply kit for your pet should include:

- Nonperishable food and water in sealed, waterproof containers, a manual can opener or other device, and a container to place the food in.
- A first aid kit with antiseptic ointment, isopropyl alcohol or peroxide, saline solution, cotton bandages, bandage tape and scissors, surgical gloves, first aid book, clean towels, copies of their medical records, and an extra supply of all medications taken on a regular basis—with all items stored in a portable waterproof container.
- Prepararation for possible primitive sanitation options. A litter box and clean litter or newspaper, garbage bags, a scoop, and a disinfectant are essential.
- Identification and a way to confine or restrain your pet. Make sure your pet wears a collar with rabies tags and identification. Include at least one leash and/or harness, plus a duplicate backup set of each.
- Registration, adoption, and/or vaccination records and a photo of you and your pet together. In case of separation, these items document your ownership and can help reunite you.
- Familiar items such as a favorite toy to help your pet cope with the stress of the situation and the close quarters you might need to share with other animals and people. Microchipping your pets and/or enrolling them in a recovery database can also help you find them if you become separated. Include the contact number in your kit.

neighbors, friends, or relatives to care for or help evacuate your pets in case you can't. Knowing ahead of time that you might have to think creatively and improvise during an emergency to use what you have on hand for several days will help you keep a level head and increase your and your pets' chances of survival.[12]

Chapter 8

SEASONAL DANGERS

Burns from hot sidewalks; insect bites or stings from ticks, wasps, fleas, spiders, and other insects; and dehydration and heat exhaustion are only some of the common dangers during summer months. So take your dog for walks and play outdoors, but exercise caution when the temperatures soar and avoid areas where insects harboring diseases such as West Nile virus, Lyme disease, or Rocky Mountain spotted fever may be lurking. Conversely, cold weather dangers include contact or ingestion of ice-melting chemicals or antifreeze, cuts from ice, frostbite, and hypothermia from extended unprotected exposure to frigid temperatures.

SAYING GOODBYE: BEYOND THE BONDS OF FRIENDSHIP

> "For the past 11 years, whenever I felt like crying, there was always a tongue ready to lick up the tears. Now that tongue is gone and my tears won't stop flowing."—Katie Green[13]

Most daily interaction with our pets is usually pleasant and uneventful. When we share our lives with companion animals, however, we inevitably face difficult moments where we must deal with unexpected accidents or illness and eventually say good-bye to these creatures we love so much. Unfortunately, one of the prices we pay for loving our companion animals so deeply is that we also suffer deeply at their loss.

While we hope our animal friends live to a ripe old age, healthy to the last minute before they die peacefully in their sleep, that isn't always the reality of what happens. We have been successful as a society in helping our companion animals live longer, just as we have done for ourselves. Along with that progress we have also unwittingly opened up the door to a new problem: Many diseases that kill humans now also kill our companion animals. None of us want our pets to suffer, so it becomes up to us to offer them the mercy and compassion they deserve, even if it breaks our heart. Instead of prolonging the life of a seriously ill or injured animal, euthanasia is considered a compassionate and humane way to end a companion animal's intense suffering or declining quality of life. While the suddenness of accidental death is extremely traumatic, making the decision to euthanize can be equally as painful.

People who experience such strong feelings about the death of a pet have those feelings because they are capable of emotional attachment and a deep, intimate bond. People often describe the moments leading up to and following a pet's death as feeling "surreal," as our minds try to cope with what seems impossible. It is in our attachment and bond, however, that we also find comfort as well as sorrow, as we move through the different stages of grief.

GRIEVING: LOSING A COMPANION ANIMAL

The loss of a pet is a difficult thing to face. Losing a companion animal can seem like an insurmountable void because our pets may be with us when we wake, when we sleep, and throughout the day. For many young people, their companion animal has been with them through important years of their childhood, as well as through numerous tough times. Unfortunately, many people fail to grasp the emotional impact death can have on teens who have formed intense bonds with companion animals. For many of us, our pets are more than "just pets"—they are our friends, our family, and our partners. And when they suffer, get sick, and/or die, the impact of their death or illness is *very* real, whether the animal is a dog, cat, bird, horse, gerbil, or goldfish.

Chapter 8

> **"POEM FOR PINKIE," BY KATIE GREEN**
>
> **Reminiscing reminds me of the love we once shared**
> **A bond so strong I was reminded of it everywhere.**
> **My pal, my friend, brings joy to me even when we are apart.**
> **My dog forever and always will be close to my heart.**[14]

Grief over the death of a pet can be as intense as grief for a human death or other loss, such as a job or a marriage. Not only do grieving humans lose the nonjudgmental source of love and friendship they had with a friend, they also may feel that they have no one to care for and nurture, and therefore aren't needed.

Critical steps in dealing with the death of a companion animal involve learning about the various stages of bereavement and allowing yourself to go through each of them. The amount of time it takes to grieve, and the ways each individual moves through the different stages, can vary. Some people move quickly through the stages, while others may stall in one or more stage for long periods of time. According to an article that appeared in the March 2000 issue of *Counseling Today*, people who have lost an animal with whom they felt especially close may have more difficulty feeling that their grief is accepted by those around them, which makes them feel even more alone. This can cause them to minimize or hide their feelings, which can prevent them from going through the grieving process necessary to heal from their loss.[15]

An important step in dealing with a pet's death is sharing your feelings with others who understand and validate your loss. Grief honors the love you had for an animal companion as well as recognizing their passing. Nonprofit organizations such as the Association of Pet Loss and Bereavement (APLB) and websites such as Veterinary Wisdom (http://veterinarywisdom.com/parentarticles.htm) can help people know they are not alone or wrong in their grieving over an animal by providing information and support to those suffering loss of an animal companion. Many colleges with veterinary programs offer hotlines staffed by specially trained veterinary students. APLB and other pet bereavement organizations also offer chatrooms where people can express their emotions without having to physically display them in front of others.

For teens, the death of a pet often represents the death of a type of sibling. If they knew the pet most of their lives, the loss is substantial. College graduate Penni Jess experienced that with her first dog, Auggie. "He was a part of my life since I was one year old, so basically he was *always* a part of my life! I couldn't imagine my life without him until he was gone."[16] Faye Nuddleman grew up with Doberman pinchers. In 2003, however, when her last remaining dog had to be put down, she accompanied her mom and was there when the dog was put to sleep. "That was the worst experience ever. Alexis had cancer. She developed a huge growth on the back side of her back leg that was so large she couldn't even sit down when we injected her. Before the shot was done, she fell to the ground and she was gone. All I saw was her eyes open and tongue hanging out. I cried for several days, and still have dreams about her at night even though she's been gone for a long time now. I was always alone when I was a child, so I saw her as my playmate. Alexis was my security blanket."[17]

A teen's pet has usually been present through many changes, from childhood issues to puberty. And the loss of a pet is often a teen's first encounter with death. How the pet died and how the family deals with the loss and subsequent grief can determine how teens deal with death for the rest of their lives. High school student Nichole Freeman adds: "[Companion animals] are very much your friend, and it's very sad when they die. I think that's one of the main reasons people have multiple pets because when one dies and is gone, there is still another one there for you."[18]

The *Counseling Today* article also notes that although children's reactions may manifest themselves in different ways than adults do, adolescents are the most likely age group to

Chapter 8

> **WAYS TO HELP GRIEVE THE LOSS OF A COMPANION ANIMAL**
>
> - Take photos of your companion animals when they are in good health. Create a scrapbook or memory box or make a special keepsake with your pet's paw prints.
> - Hold a funeral, candle-lighting ceremony, or memorial service where every family member recalls a special memory.
> - Arrange for burial in a pet cemetery and visit the grave as often as you feel the need. Or add a decorative item or plant in your yard or garden to memorialize your animal friend.
> - Find appropriate containers for preserving ashes of cremated pets that reflect their character. Or hold a special ceremony and sprinkle some of the ashes in a place that was meaningful to you both.
> - Write down your feelings and memories in a journal or write a poem or song that documents something special you experienced with your animal friend.
> - Speak about your pet with other people who knew it. Join a pet loss support group, such as those offered by different Humane Societies.
> - Spend extra time with existing pets and help them also deal with the loss.

withdraw or experience difficulty eating or sleeping. And many adolescents may exhibit various forms of denial, including a lack of any emotional display. These young people may be experiencing sincere grief without any outward expression.

Laurel Lagoni is the cofounder and former director of the Argus Institute for Families and Veterinary Medicine at Colorado State University's James L. Voss Veterinary Teaching Hospital. She developed and taught the first comprehensive end-of-life emotional support protocols and clinical communication skills curriculum at a major university veterinary school, and she feels there are many reasons for this reaction in young people. "Of course, each child is unique and different and will respond to loss in much the same way they respond to life, in general. Many teens are expressive and will talk, cry, etc. as needed. This is more likely if they have had parents or other role models who have shown them healthy ways to express their feelings. For many teens, though, a pet's death is their first experience with loss and the grief process. Since the feelings and behaviors are new to them and they probably haven't seen any adults grieving openly, they are often caught off guard and a bit scared of the intensity of the feelings. The teen years are a time of self-consciousness and conformity. The last thing they want is to be singled out or to become the target of ridicule. Since teens feel the emotions welling up each time they think of their pet or when someone else mentions the pet or suggests they talk about the death, they work very hard to avoid or dismiss those conversations and experiences since they absolutely do not want to cry in front of others. Another reason teens and young adults often don't get to have their own grief process is that they are often asked to take care of younger siblings, death-related details, or even other household tasks that still need to be done while other family members deal with the death. In other words, they are often treated as adults when their feelings and vulnerability are actually more on the level of a child."

One case example Laurel describes involved a female teenager who exemplified the classic conflicts teens feel. "She wanted her cat's cremated remains returned to her, but she thought her friends would think she was weird if she went so far as to keep them in a beautiful urn or container. Instead, she put them in an empty mayonnaise jar and kept the jar in her closet. She said this way she could keep her ongoing relationship with her cat a secret and see him and talk to him every morning while she got dressed without anyone else knowing. If a friend did see the jar, she could explain it away in a rather offhand manner, 'Oh, that's just our cat. I didn't know what to do with him, so he's in that jar. . . .' Her real feelings were much more tender and intense than that, but she instinctively knew her feelings would not be accepted by her peers."[19]

Chapter 8

IT HAPPENED TO ME: THE BOND IN ACTION

Although it is difficult to experience the illness or death of a pet perceived as a teen's close family member, if the animal died as a result of something the teen feels responsible for, the guilt can be unbearable. One morning in May 2004, Julie Kisman's dad let the dogs out, as he always did, at the same time her seventeen-year-old brother was ready to leave for school. "My brother was in the garage getting ready to back his car out of the garage. He saw both Bridget and Magic sitting by the boat in the driveway and told them both to move. Well, eleven-year-old Bridget must not have heard him. Instead she walked *behind* the car while my brother was backing out. My brother felt his tires roll over something. He jumped out of the car and saw he had run over Bridget. He totally freaked out and ran into the house screaming and yelling for my parents." Julie's mom and brother kept Bridget as calm as possible while her dad tried to lift the car off of her. All this commotion woke Julie up, but she was still half asleep. Then she saw Bridget under the car.

Once her dad got Bridget out from under the car, Julie and her mom wrapped the dog in blankets and rushed her to a twenty-four-hour emergency vet office. Although no bones were crushed or broken, Bridget was having trouble breathing. She was put on oxygen but unfortunately wasn't stable enough to pull through. Although Bridget had been a part of her entire family since she was a six-month-old puppy, Julie felt especially bonded with her. And because she was also the family's first dog, this tragedy was especially difficult for Julie to talk or write about. "My brother felt really horrible for what he had done. My parents were very worried about him for the first two weeks because he was really down. They made sure someone was home with him all the time just in case." Julie, as well as her parents and grandmother, kept reassuring her brother that anyone could have accidentally hit the dog, including a neighbor or friend. They emphasized that it was an accident and that they all forgave him. Now it was up to Julie's brother to forgive himself. Fortunately, with support of family, friends, and neighbors—and with the passage of time—he got over it and began to heal. "Now, because of that accident, every time anyone backs out of the garage, we make sure our two other collies are in their kennel, especially if we go out together as a family."[20]

Overcoming Health Problems, Pet Loss, and Other Adversities

One of the most difficult issues to deal with in grieving is guilt, which is often coupled with anger. This is especially experienced by people who have had to have their pets euthanized because of age or illness. People who feel responsible wholly or in part for an accidental death or for not recognizing an illness early enough to prevent death may also feel guilt and anger.

In some instances, the loss of a shared companion animal can actually provide an opportunity for family members to draw closer. Because everyone is grieving, a common bond is created when family members share their feelings about the loss along with memories of times spent with the deceased animal. Christina Aviza feels that her boyfriend may not have understood the magnitude of her loss when her dog died, but knowing he was sympathetic and willing to listen to her helped. And while Christina may have been grieving herself, she wanted to be there for her mom, too. "Spike was mainly her dog, so it was probably the hardest for her. His death brought my family closer, but not for long because my stepdad and I aren't very close. But it helped with my mom and me."[21] By coming together in grief and putting past problems aside, each family member also honors his or her own special relationship with that pet.

TURNING LOSS INTO SOMETHING POSITIVE

> "It would be upsetting any time you'd have a loss but it's definitely apparent when animals die. . . . Maybe knowing that these animals [reptiles] don't live as long helped me through that."—Kyle Fetters, suburban Illinois teen[22]

Chapter 8

Although losing a pet can be difficult, many families and teens find ways to turn it into something positive. Whether because of their basic individual outlook on life or because they discover it helps in the grieving process, people who take positive action as a result of loss not only give tribute to their individual pet, they also affirm their relationship to the animal.

Kyle Fetters has dealt with loss many times, since reptiles do not have the life spans many other animals do. But he also dealt with losing one of his dogs when he was about sixteen or seventeen years old. "He was the first warm-blooded animal I lost. I came home from work one day and he was really sick. You can see that and just know it's his time but it's still very upsetting. But he lived his life; he hopefully lived a great one and you try to keep it positive. You don't want to think things like, 'He's gone now, what am I going to do?' Instead, you need to remember all the good things you did together. I remember walking down by our creek and having him faithfully following right behind me. That's basically what we did; we'd take these

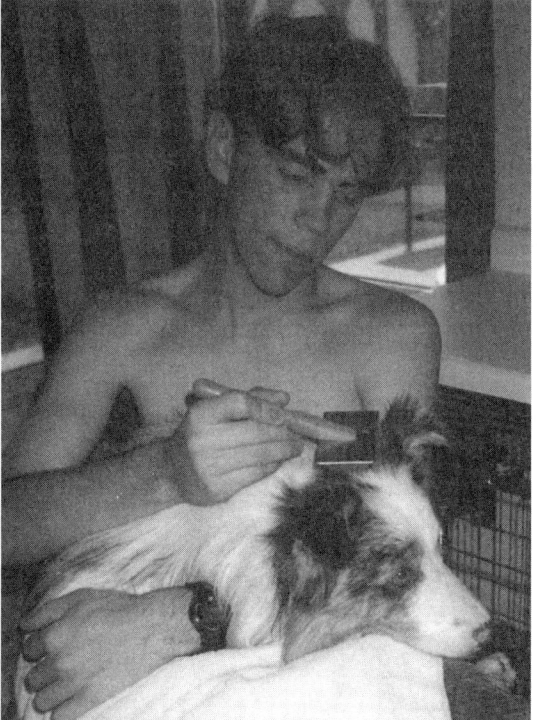

Sometimes just an ordinary moment, such as Jason Green grooming his buddy Tyler, becomes a treasured memory when an animal companion is gone. Photo used with permission, Jeffrey Green, Total Recall Dog Training.

little adventures together. He was always my companion growing up. So yes, it was very upsetting, but you just gotta keep it positive."[23]

Jason Green was out of town each time when two of his family's dogs died less than a year apart. Although he was already living in his own apartment, he still had a close bond with one of the dogs and was devastated when he heard the news, since the dog seemed fine just the week before he left. At first he felt guilty he wasn't there to say good-bye, and that he had not been able to spend much time with the dog after moving out the year before. But he also realized there was really nothing he could have done, since everything happened so quickly. Even if he had tried to fly home to say good-bye, he never could have arrived fast enough, since both of these deaths were from unexpected natural causes. Jason prefers to just remember his friend in a positive way to honor his life. "He had such a wonderful life with our family and was such a happy

IT HAPPENED TO ME: THE BOND IN ACTION

After her collie's accidental death, Julie found a way to express herself and honor her pet's memory by making a difference for animals that needed some love. Julie had already been involved in rescue and had previously fostered many dogs. "About four months after our loss, I got a call from a Bichon Frise rescue group, asking if I would be able to foster a dog that was recovering from surgery. She had had tumors removed from her tummy, back, and leg and looked funny because she was shaved in different areas. Of course I said yes!"

Julie and her dad drove an hour and a half to pick her up. At first, Sophie was very unsure and nervous in her new foster home. But as weeks passed, she opened up to her foster family and developed a special attachment to Julie. "She followed me every place I went. My parents finally gave in and let us adopt her after my sister and I begged and begged! Although no other dog will ever replace Bridget, Sophie came into our hearts and home when we least expected it and made us all happy once again. She still follows me everywhere and goes almost everyplace with us. We call her our little lost lamb."[24]

guy. We will all miss him and no other dog will ever take his place. I'm glad that he wasn't sick for a very long time, so he didn't have to suffer, and I take great consolation in the fact that he knew he was loved."[25]

Our animal companions are each different individuals with unique personalities that can't be replaced. It is important that people allow themselves enough time to grieve and feel emotionally ready before welcoming a new animal into their hearts and homes. Spending quality time with a new pet will help establish a new bond and prevent feelings of resentment that the new pet can't replace your deceased friend. Children's book illustrator Terri Murphy recalls when her son's girlfriend lost her dog. Right after it happened, his girlfriend said the memory was too painful to even talk about it. "The family ended up getting a puppy the very next day. Each person deals with [death] differently, I guess."[26] While some people may immediately rush out to get a "replacement" for their lost companion as an attempt to avoid feeling some of the grief, other people decide to never get another companion animal to avoid ever experiencing another painful loss.

UNDERSTANDING

People grieving for their pets often feel alone because of other people's reactions. Grief counselors specializing in pet loss can offer strategies for healing. Laurel Lagoni explains, "Many studies show grief for a pet to be as significant as that of another member of a person's immediate family. The participants in one survey ranked it the third most painful loss, just after the loss of a spouse or a child. Grief counselors tell people to take the loss seriously and allow yourself time to grieve. Take some days off work if you need them and spend time in the evenings letting yourself cry, reminisce, and pay tribute to your pet. Take extra care of yourself for the days and weeks following a loss. Grief is confusing and exhausting so people do not feel like themselves for a while. Try to get more rest and be sure to educate yourself about what to expect from a period of grieving. Many of the symptoms of grief can be alarming if you don't understand they happen to everyone. While this topic is still considered to be too morose and taboo for most social conversations, talk at least once with a qualified counselor just to reassure yourself that your grief is progressing as it should. Many people spend a lot of time and energy worrying about why they seem to be taking the death of their pet so much harder than anyone else has. A qualified counselor can help them understand the universal nature of grief and help them create a plan for caring for themselves as they experience it. Normal grief can last for many weeks, months and even years, but will lessen in intensity as time goes on."[27]

"MAN'S BEST FRIEND," BY REBECCA BRITZ

When they greet you with excitement and their faces become brighter
As you enter the door your heart becomes lighter.
One jumping on you, the other intently kisses
While you think to yourself how much you would miss this
Because a true companion is hard to come by.
Which is, in the end, why we try and try
To give our pets back what they've given to us
When they showed unconditional love without even a fuss.
From keeping us warm when a blanket we lack,
Not wanting to receive anything but your approval back
They give us love and so much more
Why would we give them less than what they strive for?
Playing Tug-of-War, a hug here, and bone there,
It is easy to do because nothing can compare
To the feeling you get everyday that you're with them,
Every moment captured is a priceless gem.[28]

Chapter 8

It also helps when friends and family members are sympathetic to your loss and validate the grief you feel. Forming an informal support group with other people who are grieving or have recently grieved over a pet can help you get through the loss. Julie's experience was that everyone on her block was very supportive and "lent a shoulder to cry on" because they all loved Bridget. She was also fortunate to have a caring, compassionate boyfriend and supportive, understanding friends from the various rescue organizations who understood what Julie was feeling.

Many people seek solace in prayer and spiritual beliefs or find comfort in an actual burial process, especially if they include something meaningful such as an informal graveside service where each family member says or does something meaningful. Other people choose cremation and either keep their pet's remains in an urn or sprinkle them in a memorable place that is especially meaningful to them. Writing poems or journal entries can help teens verbalize their emotions as well as record special memories of their pet.

Kyle's family kept everything very simple after his dog died. "It was kind of weird, because there he is right in front of you no longer alive. It's like he's there, but he's not really there. I just kind of wanted to get it over rather quickly. It was definitely upsetting."[29]

After Kelli's Pembroke Welsh corgi died during her sophomore year in high school, her family buried her down by the creek, because that's where she liked to be. "And that helped me. I mean, that actually helped me because anytime I'd feel sad or be having trouble over her, I'd go down there and just sit for a while alone and it would make me feel better. It calms me somehow."[30]

Julie's family also dealt with Bridget's death by burying her. "Once Bridget was peacefully resting in the hole we dug for her in our backyard, each of us placed a favorite thing she liked in with her. Then we covered it up. A week later we placed flowers on top of her burial place. We also made a heart-shaped paw print out of rocks by the site. I still walk down there every now and then and just sit there, remembering what Bridget meant to me and wishing she was still with us. Many friends, neighbors,

Overcoming Health Problems, Pet Loss, and Other Adversities

> **IT HAPPENED TO ME: THE BOND IN ACTION**
>
> Experiencing a companion animal's illness or debilitating physical condition can be as difficult as the actual loss suffered when that animal passes away. Nothing can really prepare someone for living with a dog that has seizures. But that's what Katie experienced with her dog, Madison, and the illness eventually led to his death. Katie remembers vividly, "Madison had one seizure-free year and we all thought the medications finally had his illness under control. However, one day he had a massive seizure around dawn and died. The vet assured us there was nothing we could have done but we were all totally devastated. I don't know how he did it but my dad wrapped Madison's body in a towel and carried him to the vet clinic while the rest of us cried. I wanted to be at school that day because I really needed a distraction, but I felt so sad. I actually wound up not taking my final drivers ed test that day—even though I was scheduled to take it—because I was so sad, and one of my teachers gave me a pass to stay out of one class because I couldn't stop sobbing. He bought me a soda and just let me vent about how I was feeling. I'll never forget Madison. He was the sweetest, most gentle dog and I will always have a hole in my heart from the loss."[31]

and other family members sent or brought over cards specifically for the loss of a pet. It was very nice of them to do that, and it actually helped us heal."[32]

Each cyclic or seasonal event your pet was once a part of will be difficult at first. But time itself heals, and with its passage, the pain becomes more tolerable. Depending on the bond you had or the circumstances of the animal's death, however, you may never completely lose the feeling that someone you cared for is gone.

Sometimes companion animals develop an illness or medical condition that severely compromises their quality of life. Some people believe we should "let nature takes its course" and allow our animals to die naturally, while others believe it is cruel to allow animals to suffer when they are obviously in pain or discomfort and have no chance of recovering. One of the most difficult decisions people have to make is if and when to euthanize their pet. Sometimes this is something you can plan or anticipate, such as in an elderly animal with decreased kidney function. It can also wind up being an immediate decision that has to be made when an animal is severely injured from an accident or when an aging animal goes in for simple routine surgery and the vet discovers it has advanced cancer. Deciding whether or not to euthanize can be especially difficult and painful for people who cannot afford expensive treatments such as chemotherapy or surgery.

Making your grief "active" by doing some of the things suggested here can help ease the pain and bring closure to your loss. Accepting that the pain is real and giving permission to feel it is the quickest way to get over the loss. Although it may take a while, time *does* heal, and most people become able to look back with smiles and happy tears. After all, your animal friend is still there in your memories.

HOW ANIMALS HELP: HUMAN ILLNESS OR DEATH

Although most young people do not have much experience with death by the time they reach college, many of them may have lost elderly relatives. When Natasha McDonald's boyfriend was hit by a car, she sought comfort through the horses she bonded with at the therapeutic riding stable where she volunteers. Natasha turned to the horses again for help when her aunt died. "I went to the barn and just spent time with my favorite horse, Trey. Because I was able to just talk to him and know he was listening, it was really helpful. I can't explain it, but while I was talking to him, I felt so peaceful and calm. I knew that he was listening to me. He also made me feel like he was always there for me so I could get through these tough times."[33]

Janet Carhuayano also remembers how difficult it was when her grandmother died. "I was really close to my grandmother. About two years after I got Lacey, she passed away and I was devastated. I was so depressed and so sad I wouldn't talk to anyone about it at all. But Lacey just stayed there with me and put her head on my lap. It was a great feeling knowing she was there with me because, you know, there was just nothing there that I had to say. She just knew I was depressed. And even though I was dealing with stuff I didn't want to talk about, I didn't want to be alone. I just didn't want to talk. I wanted to deal with it on my own and she was there, helping me so I wasn't alone. With Lacey, I had someone who wouldn't bother me, asking, 'How are you feeling?' or saying stuff like. 'You have to talk about it; you need to get over it and start dealing with it,' like all the people around me were doing. Instead I got to deal with it in my own way with my dog."[34]

Grief from the loss of a pet may also bring back memories and revisit old wounds from previous losses, both human and animal. While grieving for a pet you've just lost, you might also find yourself thinking about one you lost as a child. Or you might discover an additional layer of unresolved grief stemming from the loss of a significant person in your life, such as a grandparent or neighbor. When that happens, the death of your pet may become an avenue through which you can heal more than one loss.

HOW PETS GRIEVE

While humans express grief by speaking about it, writing tributes, or going through various burial rituals, animals have to bear their grief in their own unique ways, without the benefit of mutual mourning and ritual. But, like humans who feel depressed when a loved one dies, grieving animals often refuse to eat and lose interest in activities or objects they once enjoyed. It's up to us to show them the same compassion and understanding they give us.

Christina experienced one dog's grief when her older dog had to be put down. "We had to put Spike down two days before Thanksgiving in 2006. Our other dog, Maggie, has been grieving him ever since. Whenever Maggie went near the urn where we have his ashes, she puked. She wouldn't even go on the couch that was Spike's 'bed.' She also wouldn't go into our half-acre yard anymore; she limited herself to just a small area."[35]

Chapter 8

Katie also recalls how her dog Tyler acted after Madison died: "Tyler took Madison's death very hard. It took weeks for him to even come back into the kitchen again, since that is where he had to silently witness the death of his best friend just a few feet away and then wait until my dad woke, came down, and discovered what had happened. He was totally traumatized from the experience. I wound up hand feeding him every meal for weeks, kibble by kibble, because he refused to eat."[36]

We can help our grieving pets by keeping their routines as normal as possible and allowing the surviving animals in multiple-pet households to work out their new social hierarchy. Any changes in animals' behavior while grieving—such as being allowed to sleep in our bed, when they weren't allowed to do so before—should not be reinforced. It can be difficult dealing with a pet's grief while we are also grieving and need to heal. While it might increase our bond, we can also feel resentment toward the surviving animal, especially if the animal that died was our "favorite." On the other hand, just knowing that the remaining animal also carries memories of the deceased pet can make us feel closer to both.

Along with being surprised at the depth of her own grief, Jessica Katz experienced a glimpse of how other animals grieve during her internship at a bird refuge. "Peaches, a Malaccan cockatoo, arrived from a horse farm with her sister, PJ. The girls were always whinnying to each other, hopping back and forth between cages to preen and snuggle with one another." When Jessica received an e-mail saying Peaches had been found on the floor of her cage, she burst into tears. Although Peaches was only fourteen years old, she had the heart of a forty-year-old and died from a heart attack. "Her death struck everyone directly involved at the Refuge. PJ had even been trying to wake her sister up, but to no avail. It was quite incredible to see how PJ mourned. She sought comfort from everyone, and it was heart-wrenching to hear her horselike whinny receive no response. There was a male bird there that PJ was also close to. She tried going over to him for comfort, but he would have nothing of it. She was just so miserable; she wound up being taken upstairs for a few hours and comforted by humans. She was grieving so much it was awful. Slowly, however, with the eventual help of her 'boyfriend,' Sigh, PJ started to recover some of her sassy personality."[37]

Can the bond between human and animal be so incredibly strong it surprises even the most devoted pet owners with its intensity? Animals can motivate us to exercise when we're lazy and help us weather life's challenges. They also fill us with an incredible depth of emotion when they fall ill or die. Through it all, the emotional connection is well worth it. But even if we have to worry about their safety and grieve at their passing, that amazing human-animal bond can encourage and strengthen us, and give us the means to overcome adversity together.

NOTES

1. Katie Green, interview with the author, December 2006.
2. Katie Green, interview with the author, December 2006.
3. Kelli Herbel, interview with the author, October 2006.
4. Herbel, interview with the author, October 2006.
5. "Daily Dog Walks Work Off Weight for Owners, MU Researchers Find," University of Missouri–Columbia News Bureau, September 28, 2005, https://cf.iats.missouri.edu/news/newsbureau singlenews.cfm?newsid=6662 (accessed May 11, 2007).
6. Annalies Kocourek, interview with the author, August 2006.
7. Katie Green, interview with the author, December 2006.
8. Marty Becker, *The Healing Power of Pets: Harnessing the Amazing Ability of Pets to Make and Keep People Happy and Healthy* (New York: Hyperion, 2002), 90.
9. Katie Green, interview with the author, December 2006.
10. Brigitte Mason, interview with the author, August 23, 2006.
11. "Pet Evacuation Bill Passes," *Pet Age* (August 2006): 16.
12. www.ready.gov/america/getakit/pets.html (accessed April 17, 2007).
13. Katie Green, e-mail to the author, December 2006.
14. Katie Green, e-mail to the author, December 2006.
15. Regina Reitmeyer, "Dog Gone?" *Counseling Today* 42, no. 9 (March 2000).
16. Penni Jess, conversation with the author, January 2007.
17. Faye Nuddleman, interview with the author, April 2007.

Chapter 8

18. Nichole Freeman, interview with the author, December 2006.
19. Laurel Lagoni, e-mail to the author, April 17, 2007.
20. Julie Kisman, e-mail to the author, March 2006.
21. Christina Aviza, interview with the author, November 23, 2006.
22. Kyle Fetters, interview with the author, September 2006.
23. Fetters, interview with the author, September 2006.
24. Kisman, e-mail to the author, March 2006.
25. Jason Green, conversation with the author, April, 2007.
26. Terri Murphy, e-mail to the author, November 2006.
27. Lagoni, e-mail to the author, April 17, 2007.
28. Rebecca Britz, e-mail to the author, October 2006.
29. Fetters, interview with the author, September 2006.
30. Herbel, interview with the author, October 2006.
31. Katie Green, e-mail to the author, February 2007.
32. Kisman, e-mail to the author, April 2007.
33. Natasha McDonald, interview with the author, December 2006.
34. Janet Carhuayano, interview with the author, October 2006.
35. Aviza, interview with the author, November 23, 2006.
36. Katie Green, interview with the author, December 2006.
37. Katz, interview with the author, December 2006.

At Your Service: Assistance Animals and Therapies

We aren't born knowing right from wrong. The complexities of making correct moral decisions are a part of the learning process as we grow from childhood into adulthood and beyond. And if we fail to learn the difference between kindness and cruelty, all the decisions we make will be governed by a decision-making ability gone wrong. Law enforcement professionals, child-advocacy organizations, psychological associations, and FBI profilers agree that animal abuse can be a precursor and warning sign in people who eventually direct violence toward humans. In an article in the *Washington Times*, People for the Ethical Treatment of Animals educator Holly Quaglia notes that there have been consistent warning signs in recent decades of school shootings: Each of these young murderers had a history of abusing and/or killing animals before they turned on their classmates. If a child is taught to value the life of an animal or animals, however, that child will be more likely to value the lives of other children.[1]

LEARNING EMPATHY

The ability to empathize and the capacity for compassion are important human skills. Empathy connects us to another living creature's feelings, moods, or circumstances. And, like right and wrong, compassion is a learned behavior. One way to learn empathy for others is through compassionate interaction with companion animals in the home or neighborhood and through

"Babies don't understand they are handicapped. I guess babies are kind of like dogs in that way, because animals that lose a leg or become paralyzed don't know they are handicapped. And small children know, yeah, maybe they have a brace on their leg, but they don't understand they are disabled until they hear someone say they are."

—Jenn Papa, Illinois high school student[2]

> "Animals will love you back and be kind to you as long as you treat them with kindness. And when teens work with animals closely, especially ones who have been abused or neglected themselves, eventually these young people start to learn from them. It's as if the animals start to get inside their head and instill values. These teens eventually discover they don't need to change themselves to fit someone else's model. And when they do find themselves, everything else just kind of falls into line."—Rich Weiner, director, A Refuge for Saving the Wildlife[3]

volunteering at places where people or animals are in need, such as animal shelters, rescues, therapeutic facilities, and service-oriented organizations. Not only do we learn empathy for the animals that need our help, but those skills can also transcend into relationships we have with other people.

ANIMALS THAT SERVE

Most of us don't realize the numerous ways animals help people with physical or other disabilities. We might have heard about dogs helping the blind, seen a dog visiting a nursing home, or watched a service dog walking alongside someone, but we don't see the intensive training process behind the scenes. Dogs and other animals used as service or therapy animals need to have the correct temperament; be intelligent, predictable, and sound; and have the desire to serve. Service animals are specifically bred for these qualities. Puppies are placed in volunteer homes, with a set of people who work with the animals, socializing and familiarizing them with all types of environments and situations where the dog will be responsible for making correct decisions. Later, these dogs may also be trained by volunteers who teach them specific tasks and commands for the individual they will ultimately be placed with. It is a lengthy process, but one that is extremely rewarding to be a part of. While there is no shortage of need for these dogs, there are a limited number of volunteers to help in the process.

At Your Service: Assistance Animals and Therapies

When they think of service dogs, most people immediately think of Guide Dogs for the Blind, but there are many other types of service and assistant dog programs and organizations nationwide. People suffering from epilepsy, diabetes, or emotional disorders also benefit from service dogs. Various service categories include guide dogs and horses, service dogs, search-and-rescue dogs, military dogs, K-9 law enforcement dogs, and therapy dogs and other animals, including horses, marine mammals, rabbits, cats, and birds.

Kristen and Annalies Kocourek have a medical condition that requires each of them to have a service dog. Their family acquired both dogs from an organization called East Coast Assistance Dogs (ECAD). Kristen explains: "ECAD dogs are trained at residential schools where the students are wards of the state or in juvenile detention systems. For many of those kids, working with the dogs is the first time they have been loved unconditionally and the first time they are taking responsibility for another living being. It is a win-win situation. The students working with these dogs all have major challenges, just not disability-related ones. Plus, many graduate from the program and are then able to return to their homes and society after working with the dog training program."[4]

EMOTIONAL TRAUMA AND NEUROLOGICAL DISORDERS

Emotional trauma can affect brain chemistry in many negative ways, including suppressing the manufacture of neurochemicals that influence sleep stages, depression, and memory, or act as mood stabilizers and help regulate impulse control. Recovery is difficult because the trauma itself lodges in a part of the brain not immediately accessible to rational thought. When children or teens are severely traumatized, they lose the ability to soothe or reward themselves and may have difficulty sleeping, suffer from depression, lose their ability to learn, and experience other problems, which is why many victims of abuse act out in irrational and often unpredictable ways, and have difficulty in school and with positive interpersonal relationships. Many traumatized teens cannot find a way to connect or reconnect to

Chapter 9

the world on their own because emotional trauma leaves them feeling that nothing is safe or to be trusted anymore.

Animals tend to fascinate instead of threaten. They can also help provide the hugs and the physical sense of nurturing that many neglected or abused children and teens need, but do not know how to obtain from their unsafe environments. According to the website Edutopia, scientific studies have proven that blood pressure drops during positive physical contact with animals, such as petting or stroking their fur.[5] Victims of trauma or abuse often feel anxious, but the drop in blood pressure and regular relaxed breathing, coupled with the feeling of being able to "let go" and trust, allows many victims to finally release their feelings. While some teens may have difficulty with animals because of their inner anger, after months of work learning how to approach animals (and, by extension, humans) in a nonthreatening way, they receive the reward of having an animal accept their touch.

John S. Lyons, director of mental health services and policy programs at the Department of Psychiatry and Behavioral Sciences at Northwestern University, is one of the authors of a study that explored the benefits of animal-assisted therapy. In this study, eight adolescent girls undergoing substance abuse treatment were positively impacted in just a few visits with specially trained dogs. The report stated that participation in this program allowed the girls to gain more self-awareness and honesty with themselves and others, even though the girls and animals did not live together. According to a 2002 article in *Current Health 2*, a Weekly Reader publication, Lyons believed that the dogs in the study were valuable to the troubled teens for two reasons. First, handling the dogs with obedience commands, positive reinforcement techniques, and grooming helped them develop a sense of achievement and ability to master their environment. In addition, interaction with dogs that were always in good moods and happy to see them promoted a sense of mutual good feelings. The nonverbal interaction these girls experienced with the animals offered them a new way to communicate, as well as experiencing nonthreatening, loving interaction.[6]

At Your Service: Assistance Animals and Therapies

EQUINE THERAPY PROGRAMS

More than six hundred equine therapy centers in the United States provide a variety of therapeutic riding programs for children, teens, and adults with behavioral/emotional challenges, physical/cognitive disabilities, attention/sensory disorders (such as ADD or autism), and conditions like multiple sclerosis or depression. By making a "connection" with the riders, the horses help them improve muscle strength, flexibility, and posture; increase focus and concentration; improve sensory processing abilities; and gain self-confidence and self-esteem.

For people with difficult issues, therapy experiences can often give them a reason to wake up every day. Diana Schnell, executive director of Equestrian Connection in Libertyville, Illinois, is also the mother of twin teen sons with cerebral palsy. Working with equine therapy has been as much a therapy for her and her sons as it is for every person that walks into the stable. It is truly a place of hope, healing, and great peace. "My

Teen volunteers assisting a young rider during a therapeutic riding session at Equestrian Connection. Photo used with permission, Katie Green.

twins needed therapy because they were like rag dolls, because of poor muscle tone from a more unusual form of CP. But over the years, I have seen the full spectrum of kids here, from psychological issues to physical disabilities to kids not able to form relationships. Teenagers are so vulnerable. They're looking for buddies, looking for acceptance, and looking to build their self-esteem, without even realizing it. Working with children who didn't get the gifts they got really opens their eyes and helps with their own overall awareness of themselves and of their gifts, and a greater appreciation for what they have."[7]

These centers can offer group or individual therapy programs. Therapists (including physical, occupational, speech, and art therapists) and North American Riding for the Handicapped Association–certified riding instructors may work with the various children, teen, and adult riders. At Equestrian Connection, for example, approximately two hundred teens and adults volunteer throughout the week, performing various tasks like getting saddles and tack on the horses to "side walking," which involves walking next to riders in the riding arena to prevent them from losing balance and falling off the horse.

These therapeutic facilities do more than help build muscle tone and strength. For teens who go for the therapy, it also offers them a peer group. Diana explains, "The disabled teen population is not only looking to get stronger, they're also looking for friends, someone to identify with. They're also looking to not be judged, and, of course, the horses don't judge them. These young people are looking to be empowered, and that's what they are able to do here. You can have the disabled teen that starts by being a rider and then later turns into a helper, so they suddenly find themselves on the giving side instead of only getting all the time. And giving to others makes them feel good about themselves."

Diana recalls one teen with learning disabilities who came in as a rider. "Kids had made fun of her from an early age, so she was afraid to even try to be social. She said to me, 'If I could just learn to read people like I can read horses, like if their ears went back or something, then I would know what people are thinking and I could do something different!' And that just blew me away, because here's someone who can connect so strongly with the horses where she can't connect like that with anyone else." Learning to read the horse and to be able to connect with it on a deeper level is empowering. Diana continues, "And then there are kids that are not good in team sports because they don't have the skills, can't take direction, or have processing issues. But these kids can come here, get the individual guidance they need, and also develop a skill that makes them feel pretty good when they're five or six feet above the ground on a powerful sixteen-hundred-pound animal that they are controlling. That's part of what we offer; we provide them with putting some sort of control into their life, because they don't feel that they have that."[8]

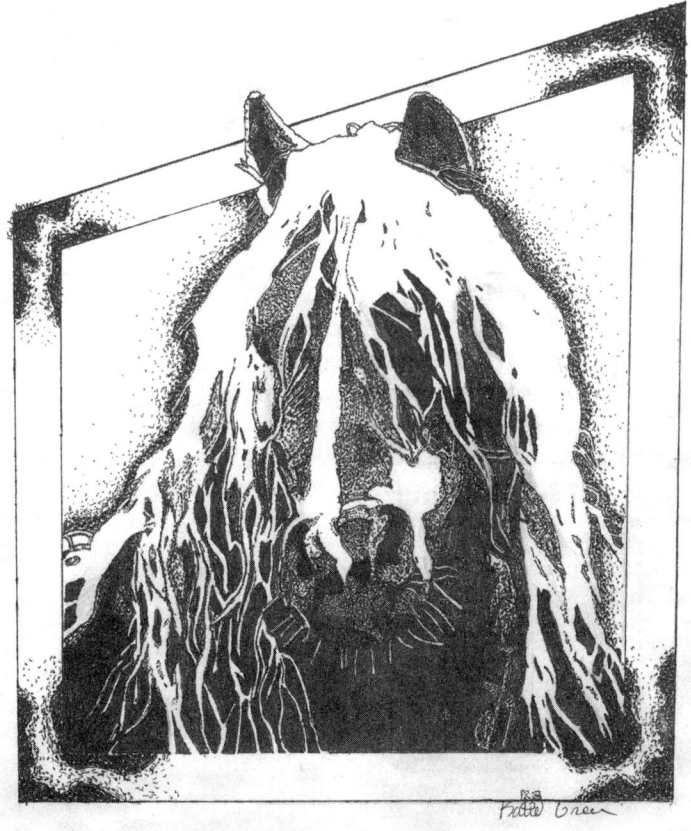

Many of the horses used in therapeutic riding seem to exhibit an intuitive sense about their often fragile riders. Drawing by Katie Green, used with permission.

Chapter 9

MAKING A DIFFERENCE

There are additional ways teens can benefit indirectly from therapeutic programs. Like Crossroads Foundation, therapeutic stables may also work with juveniles ordered by the county court system to perform community service. These teens may have committed only minor violations, like a traffic violation or underage drinking, but serving at a therapeutic facility can change their whole life.

Some of the horses at these facilities come from situations of neglect or abuse themselves. Is it possible that some teens connect better with animals that have also been abused or neglected? Diana feels it is all about trust. "They realize, 'Well, I just built trust with this horse; maybe I'll be able to build trust with people.' Horses that come in from abusive situations are angry. And when these teens see how the horses get turned around and learn to trust, they realize they can do the same thing in their own lives." Sometimes young people from abusive situations come to the facility. Diana feels that after being there for a while, these teens begin to perceive it as a place of safety, and after completing service there, they come back later to volunteer on their own. She has seen incredible things happen during psychotherapy sessions where these teens begin talking to and relating to the horses. "It often comes out later that they can then start talking to people about their issues, because in being involved with our program, that teen was suddenly not as vulnerable. That is because everyone here is vulnerable. We've been made that way because we've been humbled by our experiences and taught to appreciate what we do have. And we can reach these teens who feel they're not perfect or popular or anything, because here they *are* perfect and popular and everything."[9]

Like animal shelters, refuges, and other forms of animal therapy programs, therapeutic riding stables depend on volunteers. Equestrian Connection draws volunteers of many ages , including a very strong teen representation. Some teens volunteer through various school service programs, while others may discover the place through a friend. Either way, they usually wind up getting hooked. Diana spoke about one teen volunteer who had no friends but had a lot of experience riding.

"She has turned into one of our best volunteers, because she's kind of an expert with horses. So here she gets to feel accepted and appreciated by everyone and basically gets all the things she wasn't getting before with her peers or from her school situation. She's even been able to make friends with other teens that volunteer here."[10] Diana believes it is the horses that have enabled her, as well as other teens, to make those kinds of connections, get a sense of peace, and forget their own problems for a little while through helping others.

The horses also give young people who don't have physical power a sense of strength and power about themselves. If they have trouble coordinating movements, the horse empowers them with a sense of being able to make those movements effortlessly through space. And for many young people with physical impairments, riding may be their only time out of their wheelchair other than at bedtime—and the only time they get to experience the sensation of the freedom of movement.

Physical therapist Andrey Parvanov works with his patients both inside a clinical office setting and on-site at a therapeutic stable. Because he works with children and teens with various physical conditions, such as cerebral palsy, he focuses mainly on the physical rather than the behavioral and combines traditional treatment with equine therapy. And while these riders are developing their muscles and gaining strength and flexibility, their experience is also one of joy combined with a feeling of accomplishment. "I treat these kids in a clinic, doing all these exercises using harnesses and a treadmill. Usually they will cry or be scared. But put them on a horse and they're all smiles because they are so wrapped up in the pleasurable sensation of the horse and the rhythmic movement. So the child that tenses up with fear and anticipation of pain in a clinical setting will relax instead and let the horse help him. And once they stretch, they'll do it again. Emotion brings motion. You love it and you remember it. In the end, you don't train the body—you train the brain! They're doing the same work, exercising the same muscles. But because of the horse, nobody even realizes it is work. They come with a smile; they leave with a smile."[11]

Chapter 9

> **Sometimes great breakthroughs in medicine occur through a combination of personal experience and understanding similarities between human and animal behavior and response. In the book *Animals in Translation: Using the Mysteries of Autism to Decode Animal Behavior*, author, animal behaviorist, and scientist Temple Grandin, writes about her teen years and how animals played a huge part in them. An autistic child, Grandin was sent to a boarding school that had a riding stable. Although the horses there had behavior problems, she still fell in love with them and reaped the therapeutic benefits from her interaction with them. Once she hit adolescence, she experienced a wall of nonstop anxiety, but in the end she felt it was animals that wound up actually saving her. At a visit to a dude ranch one summer, Grandin observed that when cows are placed in a special metal cage (called a "squeeze chute") with walls that contract, they are less fearful of vaccination shots. They may be fearful at first, but they relax as the walls surround and touch them closely. Because of her unique perspective from being autistic, she immediately understood why: When the machine contracts, it creates a sensation around the animal similar to when they were in the womb, the same reason human professionals recommend swaddling a baby to calm and soothe them. Grandin decided to build a machine at home based on this metal cage to see if it would help her to calm down. It did. Grandin wrote that she felt she made it through her teen years mainly because of that squeeze machine and her horses. Today, every autism clinic in the world uses this device.[12]**

While some young people may already have shifted the focus from "all about me" to helping others, many have never been exposed to children with disabilities. Because the horse isn't judging, it can act as the conduit connecting the volunteers to the riders. While many of the volunteers are strictly there for the horses, amazing transformations often take place as these volunteers begin to connect with the disabled riders and witness the results of the therapy and the horses. Some of these teens have even made career decisions to go into physical therapy or related fields because of their experiences. Diana observes that her student volunteers evolve the longer they volunteer there. "They are not as self-absorbed; they become givers and doers, and many of them will go into fields of service. And if not, they'll serve some way in whatever field they go into."[13]

Some teens volunteer at these facilities because of their interest in the children. High school junior Tina Swinkels plans one day to work directly with children, possibly as a physical therapist. "My main focus is to work with children, but I think that animals are great for kids. Animals are trusting, loving, and don't see any difference between the kids with disabilities and those without. It's amazing when you see children who miss out on so many things in their life feeling special—and, most importantly, feeling like they are in control, which is something they very rarely get in their lives. When they get to the stage where they can control their horse, I can see how amazing it feels to them. For once in their life, these kids get to be completely 'normal' to someone." Tina remembers one specific child she worked with, a little girl who was blind. "She would touch the horse, hold her face close to it, smell it, and try to get to know it. She used every sense she had. And then she got on and rode beautifully without being able to see where she was going. That was probably one of the most amazing things I have ever seen."[14]

While most teens who volunteer regularly for community service do it through some type of high school program, the majority of these young people don't volunteer because they *have* to be there. The teen volunteers I spoke with all emphasized they *wanted* to be there! When offered the option of sleeping in late on the weekend and shopping at the mall, they unanimously insisted they'd rather be at the stable at 8:00 a.m. to volunteer with the horses and the kids and hang out with the friends they have there. And, as one young person mentioned, the more you give, the more you get back.

SWIMMING WITH DOLPHINS

A more unusual approach to animal-assisted therapy is using marine mammals to help people with various disabilities that originate in the brain or nervous system. While these facilities are only found in areas near oceans, there are many located throughout the world that incorporate swimming with dolphins and sea lions as part of their therapeutic programs. Most of

Chapter 9

> **IT HAPPENED TO ME: THE BOND IN ACTION**
>
> In addition to trail riding and competing with her horses, animal shelter founder Christy Anderson also did a lot of volunteering with equine therapy during her high school years, and she found it very rewarding. Christy remembers one incredible breakthrough vividly. "There was one time when there was this little six- or seven-year-old boy who refused to eat. And my job was to try and get him to eat something. We decided to take him on a barn tour so he could see how the horses eat. We showed him all the horses, brought him into the grain room, and said, 'This is what horses eat' and tried to get him to look at the grain, but he didn't want anything to do with us. Then we gave him a bucketful full of bran mash, showed him how to mix it together, and put his hands into the sloppy mixture. He got it all over his hands and was very upset about it at first. Then we brought him up to a stall. Well, the horse in that stall came right over to us and started licking the bran mash from his hands, and the kid just thought that was *the* most hilarious thing in the world! He wouldn't even look at anyone before, and here he was now looking straight dead-away at this horse licking the bran mash off his hands and out of the bucket. And then the kid started eating the bran mash, too. We eventually convinced the little boy that apples and carrots were suitable alternatives. The parents came back later, totally elated, saying that they couldn't get their child to stop eating carrots and apples! It was so good because he was literally starving to death. I don't know exactly what his problem was, but he was then able to survive on carrots and apples and bran mash." This experience and others taught Christy that animals can have a huge impact on the lives of people and that animals would always be a part of her life.[15]

these "swimming with dolphins" programs were developed primarily to help children and their families cope with various developmental, physical, and emotional disabilities that include autism, cerebral palsy, and Down syndrome. Through specially supervised programs and therapists, dolphin-human interaction offers families a unique opportunity to bond and connect with a special-needs family member in an enjoyable, safe environment and provides a therapeutic experience that focuses on the emotional and physical well-being of the participants.

IT HAPPENED TO ME: THE BOND IN ACTION

Vet tech student Rebecca Britz decided to do an internship with marine mammals during a summer between college semesters. "I went to the Florida Keys to do an internship at one marine mammal facility and ended up doing internships at two marine mammal places! I was able to work with a lot of different things that people only dream about doing. It was a wonderful experience for me and I appreciate the people who gave me that chance." Rebecca researched and located her first marine mammal opportunity, with Marine Mammal Conservancy (MMC), on the Internet. It was through MMC that she was subsequently placed at Dolphins Plus. "The two marine mammal places were very different from one another because they each had a different purpose—no pun intended! MMC was for rehabilitation of injured or beached animals; Dolphins Plus is a therapeutic facility where humans can swim with the dolphins and had a dolphin-child therapy [program] for kids with special needs. It was wonderful to see the changes in the children happen right before your eyes!"

Although Rebecca's interest was mainly with the animals, she felt every experience was beneficial. "The interns who actually worked and/or helped with the special-needs children were mainly students working toward a different type of degree than the one I was seeking. It was more related to working with special-needs kids. So those interns who were going into a profession of that nature would help the kids—and that included more than just kids who had autism—and they would then stay with that specific group of dolphins."[16]

Since the object of dolphin therapy is to increase sensory activities, programs are performed in pools with captive or semicaptive dolphins, and therapists assist the children, who can touch or swim with the animals. The therapists usually work on specific areas such as speech, behaviors, and motor skills, and the programs are customized to fit each individual's specific needs.

While dolphin therapy is not meant to be a cure, it has shown promise by enhancing the healing process and helping to alleviate some symptoms associated with various conditions. Results have shown hormone, endorphin, and enzyme changes in blood samples of participants taken prior to and following a therapy session. While it is not yet understood why or how this happens, there is ongoing research at universities and dolphin research centers to find the answer. Some researchers feel the encounters with the dolphins may evoke a deep emotional response that triggers the release of these chemicals and motivates these children while another theory suggests that the rhythm and vibration of the dolphin's natural sonar affects the human brain by modifying brain wave activity. And while this animal-assisted therapy does not promise dramatic results, it is yet another demonstration of the bond between humans and animals.

MAKE A DIFFERENCE

For teens and young adults looking for a way to combine careers in psychology, education, counseling, physical/occupational therapy, or other related areas with a love for animals, opportunities abound to experience what it would be like to actually work in these fields. Numerous facilities nationwide include animal-assisted therapy programs. Facilities and nonprofit organizations like Inner Harbour, Dolphins Plus, and Equestrian Connection depend on volunteers to help things run smoothly. Volunteers have various responsibilities, from training therapy dogs and horses or interacting with special-needs children to grooming and helping take care of the animals. Education majors can also assist with tutoring the residents.

At Your Service: Assistance Animals and Therapies

> **IT HAPPENED TO ME: THE BOND IN ACTION**
>
> High school student and volunteer Nichole Freeman has personally experienced the therapeutic effect animals can have on people firsthand: "I was really sick the summer before my freshman year of school. I think pets really help because they don't worry as much about you as the people around you are doing. And when you are really scared, that's very helpful! Like, it's very nice just to have someone that is not constantly asking, 'Are you okay?' Instead, they are like, 'Oh, you wanna come play with me!' And that is definitely a big thing for people who have health problems. Sometimes when you are sick, it isn't just affecting you physically, it also affects you mentally. The pet may sense something is wrong, but they don't treat you any differently; they still treat you as a friend."[17]

SERVICE DOGS

> "When I need quiet time, Brooklyn lays quietly by my side. I can share any secrets with her or discuss touchy things with her and she won't tell a soul. She's faithful, loving, forgiving and my best friend. I can cry into her fur and she understands. Or I can laugh and she joins in on the fun."—Kristen Kocourek, high school student from the Midwest[18]

Service dogs are trained with a specific set of skills that match the needs of the individuals they are placed with. The range of jobs these dogs can be trained to perform is truly remarkable, including tasks as simple as picking up a dropped pencil to ones as complicated as guiding a person to the correct airport terminal. Some dogs even have the innate ability to detect and warn their handlers about potentially dangerous medical conditions, like seizures, and make sure they are in a safe position before it begins. In other words, service dogs can be a lifeline as well as a companion.

One of the biggest challenges people owning service dogs experience is the general public's lack of awareness that service

---

A PERSONAL GLIMPSE

Because of their medical conditions, Kristen and Annalies Kocourek have learned not to take anything for granted. Their service dogs have given them new leases on life and taught them what is truly important. Kristen says, "Life-and-death situations are very common in our house, and often involve me. I'm a survivor. Because of all of the medical bills, things like going to a movie are special times. We definitely value life and live it to the fullest. Every day we survive there is hope we will be here tomorrow. If we are really lucky, maybe the doctors will find a cure while we are still living. If not, I know my parents have done everything in their power to help me succeed and grow up." Annalies agrees: "When you're sick, you can go two ways. You can either grow up real quick or never grow up at all, and you're always immature. But I think my sister and I chose the former and grew up the instant we found out we were sick. We realized there were more important things than parties, boyfriends, and shopping."[19]

Their dogs have given Annalies and Kristen the ability to get around and do things they wouldn't have been able to do otherwise, because wherever Annalies and Kristen go, their service dogs go, too. Because dog and owner must work flawlessly together and they often find themselves in public places where dogs are not usually allowed, the sisters and their dogs often attract a lot of attention. Annalies says, "Brooklyn and Kristen are one of the very best teams. Brooklyn is very devoted and Kristen makes sure Brooklyn is doing what she's supposed to do and not slack on commands. She has one of the softest voices I've ever heard, but she's all business."[20]

animals in public are working animals, not pets. Handlers and dogs walking through crowds of people are continually challenged by people distracting or exciting the dog because they do not understand that these service animals are doing a job. Just leading their human companions through a crowd requires concentration and decision-making skills, and intentional distractions only make the dogs' job more difficult. The federally mandated Americans with Disabilities Act specifies that service dogs can go almost everywhere their owners go, including classrooms, stores, theaters, museums, and airports. To help identify service dogs in public places, they wear special bandanas or vests. That way people won't think they're just pets and try to distract them while they're working or deny them service or access to restaurants or other public places.[21]

All teens go through tough times growing up, but teens with medical conditions or disabilities can go through some really rough spots. Annalies observes that dogs can let go of their emotions, while people can't. We hold on tightly to our emotions like they're something precious to us, but dogs just let them go. Not only do service dogs give their handlers the confidence to get around and feel safe, having a service animal can also boost self-esteem at the same time. Teens with physical disabilities don't want to be seen in public holding hands with their parents, siblings, or even friends. Service animals can give their owners a sense of independence without embarrassing them.

A difficult problem for teens with physical disabilities or other medical conditions is social isolation. Because others may not be sure what to say or how to approach someone who appears to be "different," these teens are often just left alone. But with a service dog, things change. Whereas otherwise classmates might avoid contact with them, the dog helps initiate conversation and friendships, since most conversations center around the dog and the cool things the dog does rather than focusing on the teen's physical problems. Kristen comments, "I'm really shy but when I'm with Brooklyn other teens come over to start a conversation. I met my best friend after she came

Chapter 9

to talk to me about Brooklyn. Plus, Brooklyn is a guy magnet! Most guys *love* dogs!"[22] Interestingly, similar benefits exist for the service dogs themselves. Most dogs love to be with their people or their family, and service dogs have the companionship of their special people all the time!

One hallmark of a terrific service dog is having a "second sense" when something is wrong, even if it is something the dog was not trained to handle. Annalies remembers one event where her service dog, Stitch, showed his true innate capabilities. "About a week after I got Stitch, I was standing in line for something and Stitch started jumping on me and walking in front of me. That was really annoying! Then he jumped up on me and put his paws on my shoulder and just wouldn't leave me alone and got me really upset with him. So I sat down, and about two minutes later, I had a seizure. It was like he knew I was going to have one and he was just trying to get me to sit down. We didn't know he could do that. He did that on his

---

IT HAPPENED TO ME: THE BOND IN ACTION

High school student Jenn Papa is interested in training service dogs one day. This interest is more than just curiosity, however; it comes from something very close to her heart, since her older brother was born with cerebral palsy and hydrocephalus. "I would love to help others be happy, help them put their problems aside and live how they want. I have always wanted to do something with special ed or special needs [people], either helping them live with service animals or doing physical therapy with animals. I think being able to bond with animals makes them better and happier. Our own dogs aren't service dogs, but we had one dog named Roscoe that was very bonded with my brother. Roscoe always knew when my brother was sad or felt bad; he always put his head right on his leg. I think that kind of made my brother feel happy when he did that, because he knew the animal understood him. We recently had to put Roscoe down at age fourteen. The day we did it, I could tell my brother didn't feel well that whole day. I knew he missed Roscoe terribly. But our new puppy is seven months old, and already he likes to sit right next to my brother's wheelchair."[23]

At Your Service: Assistance Animals and Therapies

own. He wasn't ever trained for it. I think it is very cool that dogs can help us in this way. It's like Stitch is my 'furry aura.'"[24]

And in many ways, dogs and other animals can be guardians here for us. When we think of all the different ways that dogs have assisted us and worked beside us in so many different capacities, it is mind-boggling. For centuries, dogs have been at our side: hunting, guarding our family and property, herding livestock, providing friendship and companionship, and much more. And with dogs being utilized in the modern era for anything from drug- and bomb-sniffing work to therapy and service, it clearly demonstrates how our relationship with animals can be so spectacular and so rewarding.

THERAPY DOGS AND OTHER ANIMALS

The human-animal bond can also be experienced through the use of dogs and other creatures as therapy animals. These animals work with their owners/handlers as a team, providing therapeutic interaction with people unable to travel to a facility or attend a special program. These therapy teams can work independently or with groups to visit children and adults in nursing homes, hospitals, schools, and other places where

Nursing home residents enjoying a visit from a therapy rabbit. Photo used with permission, Richelle and Teresa Hellpap.

positive contact with an animal benefits people facing a variety of conditions or situations.

Good candidates for therapy animal programs are dogs and other animals that are sociable and predictable, easily controlled in uncertain situations, and comfortable around people with canes and wheelchairs or who might look or move "differently." These abilities in dogs are easily tested by passing an AKC Canine Good Citizenship (CGC) test. It also helps if candidates have had at least basic obedience classes and will dependably obey commands. Most important, both the human handlers and the animals themselves must really enjoy being with people. Teens exploring career options in medical, therapy, or caregiver-related careers can get firsthand experience with patients through interaction with therapy animals. Young people can get involved by contacting national organizations such as the Delta Society, Therapy Dogs International, or Therapy Dogs, Inc. Although the majority of these programs use dogs, many other animals can qualify to serve, including miniature horses, cats, and rabbits. In addition to working as a service team, volunteers can also assist local chapters with fund-raising, paperwork, scheduling visits, testing animals, public relations, and a host of other needs.

A FINAL THOUGHT

Teens who have bonded with companion or other animals have been given incredible opportunities that can only be experienced through that connection. Whether you enjoy working around animals, need a friend that won't let you down, require the services of a service or therapy animal, or have a strong passion to help animals and make a difference, you are definitely not alone. Millions of young people worldwide share those very same interests, needs, and passions!

The human-animal bond can be one of the most important experiences we ever have, but it is also one that should not be taken lightly or casually dismissed. Through their own innocence, animals return us to a place most people never find once they leave the magical realm of childhood. When we allow animals to bring us into their world, we experience a place where everything is based on trust and unconditional love. We also take a positive step toward reaching our full potential as adult humans. And, like the many animal lovers that have filled these pages with their insight, inspiration, and compassion, when we embrace our responsibilities, we also become the animal advocates and guardians of tomorrow.

NOTES

1. Alexandra Rockey Fleming, "When It's Time for a Pet; Children Learn Compassion, Sensitivity—at Proper Age," *Washington Times*, July 27, 2003, D01.
2. Jenn Papa, interview with the author, October 2006.
3. Rich Weiner, interview with the author, November 11, 2006.
4. Kristen Kocourek, e-mail to the author, January 2007.
5. Burr Snider, "Gone to the Dogs," Edutopia, www.edutopia.org/gone-to-the-dogs (accessed June 8, 2007).
6. Ellen Blum Barish, "Pets: Unconditional Love: You Know That (Your Pet's Name Here) Is Great Fun to Come Home To. But Did You Know That Your Pet Can Be Good for Your—and Your Family's—Health?" *Current Health 2* 29, no.13 (November 2002): 16.
7. Diana Schnell, interview with the author, February 22, 2007.
8. Schnell, interview with the author, February 22, 2007.
9. Schnell, interview with the author, February 22, 2007.
10. Schnell, interview with the author, February 22, 2007.
11. Andrey Parvanov, interview with the author, February 22, 2007.
12. Temple Grandin and Catherine Johnson, *Animals in Translation: Using the Mysteries of Autism to Decode Animal Behavior* (New York: Harcourt, 2005).
13. Schnell, interview with the author, February 22, 2007.
14. Tina Swinkels, interview with the author, December 2006.
15. Christy Anderson, interview with the author, August 19, 2006.
16. Rebecca Britz, e-mail to the author, October 2006.
17. Nichole Freeman, interview with the author, December 2006.
18. Kristen Kocourek, e-mail to the author, January 2007.
19. Kristen Kocourek, e-mail to the author, January 2007.
20. Annalies Kocourek, interview with the author, August 2006.

21. U.S. Department of Justice, Civil Rights Division, Disability Rights Section, www.ada.gov/qasrvc.htm (accessed September 30, 2008).

22. Kristen Kocourek, e-mail to the author, January 2007.

23. Papa, interview with the author, October 2006.

24. Annalies Kocourek, interview with the author, August 2006.

Appendix: Online Resources for All Things Animal

VETERINARY AND SCIENTIFIC RESEARCH

American Veterinary Medical Association, www.avma.org
Association of American Veterinary Medical Colleges,
    www.aavmc.org
Colorado State University, College of Veterinary Medicine and
    Biomedical Sciences, www.cvmbs.colostate.edu
Cornell University, College of Veterinary Medicine,
    www.vet.cornell.edu
Morris Animal Foundation, www.morrisanimalfoundation.org
Purdue University, School of Veterinary Medicine,
    www.vet.purdue.edu
TOPS Veterinary Rehab, www.tops-vet-rehab.com
Tufts University, Cummings School of Veterinary Medicine,
    www.tufts.edu/vet
University of California/Davis School of Veterinary Medicine,
    www.vetmed.ucdavis.edu
University of Illinois/Champaign, College of Veterinary
    Medicine, www.cvm.uiuc.edu
University of Wisconsin/Madison, School of Veterinary
    Medicine, www.vetmed.wisc.edu

PROFESSIONAL ORGANIZATIONS

American Pet Products Association (APPA),
    www.americanpetproducts.org
Cat Writers Association (CWA), www.catwriters.org
Dog Writers Association of America (DWAA), www.dwaa.org

Appendix

Pet Industry Joint Advisory Council (PIJAC), www.pijac.org
Pet Industry Distributors Association (PIDA), www.pida.org
World Wide Pet Industry Association (WWPIA),
   www.wwpia.org

ANIMAL REGISTRIES

American Kennel Club (AKC), www.akc.org
American Quarter Horse Association (AQHA), www.aqha.com
Cat Fanciers Association (CFA), www.cfa.org
International Cat Association (TICA), www.tica.org
United Kennel Club (UKC), www.ukc.org

HUMANE ORGANIZATIONS

American Humane Association, www.americanhumane.org
American Society for the Prevention of Cruelty to Animals
   (ASPCA), www.aspca.org
Avian Welfare Coalition, www.avianwelfare.org
House Rabbit Society, www.rabbit.org
Humane America Animal Foundation, www.adoptapet.com
Humane Society of the United States (HSUS), www.hsus.org
The National Federation of Humane Societies,
   www.humanefederation.org
Petfinder, www.petfinder.com
A Refuge for Saving the Wildlife, www.rescuethebirds.org
Wright-Way Rescue, www.wrightwayrescue.rescuegroups.org

ASSISTANCE AND THERAPY ANIMALS

Assistance Dog Institute, www.assistancedog.org
Assistance Dogs for Living, www.marilynpona.com
Assistance Dogs International, www.adionline.org
Autism Society of America, www.autism-society.org
Bright and Beautiful Therapy Dogs, Inc., www.golden-dogs.org
Canine Companions for Independence (CCI),
   www.caninecompanions.org
Crossroads Foundation, www.crossroadsfoundation.net
Delta Society, www.deltasociety.org

Appendix

Dolphin Human Therapy (DHT),
 www.dolphinhumantherapy.com
Dolphins Plus, www.dolphinsplus.com
East Coast Assistance Dogs (ECAD), www.ecad1.org
Equestrian Connection, www.equestrianconnection.org
Green Chimneys Children's Services, www.greenchimneys.org
Guide Horses for the Blind, www.guidehorse.org
Inner Harbour, www.innerharbour.org
Island Dolphin Care, islanddolphincare.org
Marine Mammal Conservancy,
 www.marinemammalconservancy.org
North American Riding for the Handicapped Association,
 www.nahra.org
Paws With A Cause (PWAC), www.pawswithacause.org
Therapy Dogs, Inc., www.therapydogs.com
Therapy Dogs International, www.tdi-dog.org
U.S. Department of Justice, Civil Rights Division, Disability
 Rights Section, www.ada.gov

ENVIRONMENTAL ORGANIZATIONS

Greenpeace, www.greenpeace.org/usa
Sierra Club, www.sierraclub.org

PET LOSS/GRIEF COUNSELING RESOURCES

Argus Institute for Families and Veterinary Medicine at
 Colorado State University, www.argusinstitute.colostate.edu
Association of Pet Loss and Bereavement (APLB),
 www.aplb.org
Grief Healing, www.griefhealing.com
Hoofbeats in Heaven, www.hoofbeats-in-heaven.com
People, Animals, Nature, Inc. (PAN), www.pan-inc.org
Pet Caring, www.petcaring.com
World by the Tail, Inc.'s Veterinary Wisdom,
 http://veterinarywisdom.com/parentarticles.htm

Bibliography

NONFICTION

Becker, Marty. *The Healing Power of Pets: Harnessing the Amazing Ability of Pets to Make and Keep People Happy and Healthy.* New York: Hyperion, 2002.

Canfield, Jack, et al. *Chicken Soup for the Pet Lover's Soul: Stories about Pets as Teachers, Healers, Heroes, and Friends.* Deerfield Beach, FL: HCI, 1998.

Croke, Vicki. *Animal ER: Extraordinary Stories of Hope and Healing from One of the World's Leading Veterinary Hospitals.* New York: Dutton, 1999.

Grogan, John. *Marley & Me: Life and Love with the World's Worst Dog.* New York: Morrow, 2005.

Herriot, James. *All Creatures Great and Small.* New York: St. Martin's Press, 2004.

———. *All Things Bright and Beautiful.* New York: St. Martin's Press, 2004.

———. *Every Living Thing.* New York: St. Martin's Press, 2005.

Hess, Elizabeth. *Lost and Found: Dogs, Cats, and Everyday Heroes at a Country Animal Shelter.* New York: Harcourt, 2000.

Lee, Mary P., and Richard S. Lee. *Opportunities in Animal and Pet Care Career.* New York: McGraw-Hill, 2001.

Warshauer, Sherry B. *Everyday Heroes: Extraordinary Dogs among Us.* New York: Howell Book House, 1998.

Weisbord, Merrily, and Kim Kachanoff. *Dogs with Jobs: Working Dogs Around the World.* New York: Pocket Books, 2000.

Bibliography

FICTION

Evans, Nicholas. *The Horse Whisperer*. New York: Delacorte, 1995.

Fletcher, Christine. *Tallulah Falls*. New York: Bloomsbury Children's Books, 2006.

Gipson, Fred. *Old Yeller*. New York: Harper & Row, 1992.

Goldblatt, Stacey. *Stray: A Novel*. New York: Delacorte, 2007.

Gruen, Sara. *Riding Lessons*. New York: HarperTorch, 2004.

———. *Water for Elephants: A Novel*. Chapel Hill, NC: Algonquin Books, 2006.

Hartnett, Sonya. *Stripes of the Sidestep Wolf*. Cambridge, MA: Candlewick Press, 2005.

L'Engle, Madeleine. *A Ring of Endless Light*. New York: Random House Children's Books, 2001.

London, Jack. *Call of the Wild*. New York: Tom Doherty Associates, 1990.

———. *White Fang*. New York: Tom Doherty Associates, 1989.

Martel, Yann. *Life of Pi: A Novel*. New York: Harcourt, 2001.

Peck, Robert Newton. *Horse Thief*. New York: HarperCollins 2002.

Savage, Deborah. *Summer Hawk*. Boston: Houghton Mifflin, 1999.

Index

abuse. *See* animal abuse; troubled teens
academic achievement, 51
acceptance from animals, 22, 24–25, 47–49
accidents, 86, 213
aggressive behavior, 54–57, 160
allergies, 93–97
alpha status, 39
American Kennel Club (AKC), 21, 182, 187
American Pet Products Association (APPA), 3, 9
American Society for the Prevention of Cruelty to Animals (ASPCA), 120, 143
Americans with Disabilities Act, 241
ancient Rome, 1
animal abuse: anecdotes about, 111–16, 117; on Internet, 118–19; legislative issues, 134–37; reasons for, 116–17; stopping, 120; types, 113–14, 186; as warning sign, 225. *See also* rescue, animal
Animal Cops, 114
animal registries, 248
Animals Asia Foundation (AAF), 16

Animals in Translation, 234
anxiety. *See* stress
APLB (Association of Pet Loss and Bereavement), 209
APPA (American Pet Products Association), 3, 9
ASPCA (American Society for the Prevention of Cruelty to Animals), 120, 143
assistance animals, 243–44, 248–49
Association of Pet Loss and Bereavement (APLB), 209
autism, 234
avian rescue organizations, 112–13, 125

behaviors, animal: aggression, 54–57, 160, 179; of exotics, 129–32; modeling of, 50–52
birds: abuse of, 112–13; behavioral issues, 57, 130–31; body language/vocalization, 38, 39; bonding with, 106–7; compassion from, 149; flock behavior, 32; fostering, 166; grief of, 222–23; intuition of, 41; needs, 92; rescue groups for, 131–32; science fair projects, 187

Index

biting, 54–57, 160, 179
body language: of animals, 37–41, 57, 59; importance of interpreting, 41–46, 58–59. *See also* intuition of animals
breakups, teen, 146–47
breeders, 124

cancer, 93, 203
careers: choosing, 175–79; first jobs, 178; in philanthropy, 188–89; preparation for, 180–81, 191–92, 234–35; in service sector, 189–91
cats: abuse of, 112, 114; bonding with, 103–4; hierarchy of, 33; rescue groups for, 128; touching thresholds, 56–57
character judgments, 69, 85–86
childhood exposure to animals, 1–2
choices, pet: allergies and, 93–97; birds, 106–7; canine-human bond, 100–102; feline-human bond, 103–4; hamsters, 108–9; importance of evaluation, 91–93; lifestyle issues, 97–100; reptiles, 109
clothing sources, 17
cockatoos, 10
coexistence with animals, 14–17
college environments: adjustments to, 28–29, 167–69; anecdotes about, 169–72; choosing, 165–66, 169, 171; dangers, 81, 84, 85; geographic limits, 187; internships, 183; majors/career selection, 177–78; time constraints, 166–67; working in, 191–92

Collie Rescue, 128, 181
comfort from animals, 28–29
communication: animal forms of, 25–27, 36–42, 44–46, 54–55; human forms of, 35–36, 41–45, 54; instincts and, 54–57; sounds, 38, 47, 53; speech, 46–47
community service, 153–58, 232
companionship of animals, 5, 73
compassion, 77–79, 88, 112, 225–26
competition training/shows, 42–45, 57–58, 92, 185
confidence of teens, 57–58
Counseling Today, 209, 211
counselors, grief, 217
Crossroads Animal Rescue, 155–56

dangers to pets: at college, 81, 84, 85; in food, 203; seasonal, 206; trash, 24. *See also* animal abuse
dating issues, 145–48
death of a pet, 207–8. *See also* grieving process
delinquent teens, 158–62
dependability, 83–85, 86
depression (pet), 140
depression (teen), 143
diets for pets, 196–97
disabled teens, 230–31, 234–35
disasters, 132–33
divorce, 144–45
dog parks, 150
dogs: bonding with, 10, 100–102; in cities, 112, 117; at college, 169–71; Collie Rescue, 128, 181; communicating with, 36–37,

Index

39–41; as food, 16; foster care, 181; hypoallergenic breeds, 95; laughter of, 53; prohibitions against, 108; as service/therapy animals, 75, 187–88, 226–27, 239–44; troubled teens and, 228
dog walking, 102, 190–91
dolphins, 235–38
Dolphins Plus, 237
domestication of animals, 6–8, 14
dominance and body language, 39

East Coast Assistance Dogs, 227
economic projects, 186–87
emergency plans/kits, 204–5
emotional bonds. *See* human-animal bonds
emotional trauma. *See* animal abuse; troubled teens
emotional well-being, 13–14
empathy, 80, 157–58, 225–26
entertainment industry, 2–3, 73–74, 136
environmental issues/organizations, 132–37, 249
Equestrian Connection, 229–30, 232–33
Eurasian gray wolves, 7
euthanasia, 123, 208, 220
exercise for pets, 197–98, 199
exotic animals. *See specific animals*
exploitation of animals, 186
exposure to animals, 1–3
eye contact, 38–39

families of animals, 32–33
families of teens: activities, 67; conflicts, 140–43; divorce, 144–45; grieving together, 212–14, 218–20; lack of understanding in, 126; parental bonds, 161; supporting animal interests, 139–40, 167, 176–77
fear, 26–27, 52, 121
feral animals, 14
financial issues, 183–87
first impressions, 85–87
first jobs, 178
fish: advantages, 98; at college, 168, 171; stress reduction and, 153, 154
food dangers, 203
foster care, 128–29, 181, 216
4-H activities, 43, 74–75
free range feeding, 196–97
friendship: peer acceptance of pets, 70–71, 80–83; pets providing, 63–64, 145–48; teens connecting through pets, 67–71, 87, 241–42; time constraints, 81–83

gerbils, 111–12
Greenpeace, 137
grieving process: animal reactions to death, 221–23; honoring pets in, 215–17; Internet resources, 249; losing a pet, 207–13, 217–20; losing a relative, 220–21
growing up with animals, 30–31. *See also* families
guardians, animals as, 243
guardianship of pets, 3–6
guilt, 212, 213

hamsters, 108–9
handicapped animals, 225

Index

The Healing Power of Pets, 201, 202
healing touch, 201, 202, 228
health of pets, 29, 93, 129, 196–200, 203
herding instincts, 56
hierarchy of animals, 33
history of domestication, 6–8
horses: body language and, 37–38, 45–46; bonding with, 73, 105–6; at college, 171–72; family support for, 140; herds of, 32; showing, 185; therapeutic activities, 180–81, 229–35, 236; training, 58–59
human-animal bonds: benefits for pets, 21–22, 65; benefits for teens, 5, 8–14, 65, 153–58, 244–45; communication and, 59–60; in competition/training, 58–59; healing and, 148–49; history of, 6–8; play and, 149–50; social relationships compared to, 145–48; stress release from, 150–53; vulnerability in, 23–24
"humane" definition, 8
humane organizations, 248
Humane Society of the United States (HSUS), 120
human illness/death, 200–203, 220–21
hunting, 17
Hurricane Katrina, 132
hypoallergenic dogs, 95

icebreakers, pets as, 67–70
identification of pets, 189, 205
independence (pet), 99–100
independence (teen), 241

Inner Harbour, 161–62
interest indications, 54–55
international travel, 172–75
Internet, 118–19, 120, 209, 247–49
internships, 137, 182–83, 184
interspecies communication, 25–29
intimidation, 54
intuition of animals, 41, 59–60, 69
Irwin, Steve, 109

"Keep Britain Tidy" campaign, 24

laughter of dogs, 53
learning disabilities (LD), 48–49
learning through observation, 49–52
legislative issues, 134–37
lifestyle issues, 80–83, 97–100
life-threatening situations, 27–28
loyalty, 60

Marine Mammal Conservancy (MMC), 237
marine mammals, 38–39, 235–38
matches, pet-owner, 124–25
media, 2–3
microchips, 189, 205
misinterpretations of behaviors, 54–57
MMC (Marine Mammal Conservancy), 237
moves, international, 172–75
movies with animals, 2, 134
mutual needs, 65–66
MySpace, 118

Index

natural disasters, 132–33
neurological disorders of teens, 227–28
nonverbal cues. *See* body language
nursing home visits, 88
nurturance, 22, 77–79

obedience training, 55, 58–59
obedience watch, 55
obesity in pets, 195–98
ownership and guardianship of pets, 3–6, 9

pack leaders, 33
parental bonds, 161
parenting skills, 83–84
peers. *See* friendship
peer-to-peer networks, 118–19
personalities of animals, 73, 98–100
pet and teen similarities, 11
PETCO Foundation, 122–24
Pets Evacuation and Transportation Standards Act (PETS Act), 204
pet sitting, 190–91
philanthropists, 188–89
play and bonding, 149–50
play pant sounds, 53
prey drive, 56
products for pets, 3
professional organizations, 247–48
Project Second Chance, 157–58

rabbits, 43, 71
rabies, 29
reactive attachment disorder, 158
Reading Education Assistance Program, 187

A Refuge for Saving the Wildlife, 112–13, 125, 183
reptiles, 44–45, 96, 109
rescue, animal: birds, 112–13, 125, 131–32; euthanasia and, 123; foster care, 128–29; organizations for, 117, 121–27, 181; shelter dogs, 53, 157–58
rescues of humans, 27–28
research books, 191
responsibilities of pet ownership: benefits, 80–83, 88; challenges, 3–6, 102; impact on friendships, 81–83; learning about, 18–21
Responsible Dog Ownership Day, 21
risky behavior, 81
role models, 50–52
Roman pets, 1

science fairs, 186
seasonal dangers, 206
Sea World, 184
secondhand smoke, 93
seizures (pet), 200, 219
seizures (teen), 242
self-esteem, 47–49
sensory experiences, 148–49
service dogs, 75, 187–88, 226–27, 239–43
service sector careers, 189–91
shelter dogs, 53, 157–58
shelters. *See* rescue, animal
shows and competition, 42–45, 57–58, 92, 185
sincerity of animals, 8
sleep habits, 99
smell, sense of, 26–27, 41
smoke, secondhand, 93

Index

snakes, 41
social connections. *See* friendship
societal views on animals, 85–86, 108
sounds, 38, 47, 53
speech, 46–47
spending trends, 3
spontaneity, 13
stares, 39, 54
statistics on pet ownership, 3, 9
stress: human-animal bonds and, 150–53; pet responses to, 52–57; pets reducing, 13–14, 15, 29–30, 31, 153, 154
submissive body language, 39
suicides, 142
surrogate pets, 127, 143
survival and socialization of animals, 65
swimming with dolphins, 235–38

technology, 135, 189
teen and pet similarities, 11
television, 2–3
temperaments of pets and owners, 98–100
territorial instincts, 33
therapeutic activities: delinquency and, 158–62; with dogs, 187–88, 226–27, 228, 243–44; with dolphins, 235–38; with horses, 180–81, 229–35, 236; Internet resources, 248–49

time constraints, 81–83, 166–67
touch: cats' threshold for, 56–57; illness and, 201, 202; need for, 65–66, 148–49, 161, 228
transitions for teens, 30–31
trash dangers, 24
travel, 171, 172–75
troubled teens, 79, 113, 158–62, 227–28
trust, 21, 232
turtles, 136

vaccinations, 29
veterinary forensic specialists, 114–15
veterinary/scientific websites, 247
violence, cycles of, 113
vocalizations, 38, 46–47, 53
volunteers/volunteering: with birds, 131, 132; as career preparation, 180–81, 191–92, 234–35; in shelters, 127. *See also* internships
vulnerability, 23–24

websites, 118–19, 120, 209, 247–49
weight loss (teens), 199
wolves, 6–7
working animals, 15–17, 72–77
Wright-Way Rescue, 122–24

YouTube, 118

About the Author

Gail Green has been an animal lover her entire life and an advocate of responsible pet ownership and the rewarding power of the human-animal bond. Her licensed art appears on products nationwide and includes the trademarked brand *Sweet PETatoes®*. She is the author of *The Ultimate Rubber Stamping Technique Book* and *Cat & Dog Lovers Idea Book*, as well as numerous magazine articles and columns. She has trained and competed in breed and obedience competitions with her border collies and has been actively involved for years with volunteer work involving animal therapy. She has been a part of the craft and hobby industry for many years and has taught creative classes and presented programs on a variety of topics at trade shows, libraries, and other venues. To learn more about her and to view additional samples of her work, visit her websites at http://gailgreen.net and http://sweetpetatoes.com.